GOOD COP, DEAD COP
A Novel about
the AfterNet

Jennifer Petkus

A Mallard Mystery
Published by Mallard Press
Denver

To my husband, Jim Bates,
who against all reason puts up with me.

Good Cop, Dead Cop
A Novel about the AfterNet
Copyright © 2011 Jennifer Petkus
All rights reserved.
ISBN-10: 0615484042
ISBN-13: 978-0615484044

visit the website: theAfterNet.net

Mallard Mysteries

Acknowledgements

I wish to thank my particular friend Lee Thomas. If anything police related I have written rings true, you can give her credit. I take the blame for any blunders. Thanks also to Roger McPherson who spotted a crucial firearms blunder.

Apologies

I know next to nothing about the Denver Police Department, the Denver Fire Department, the Weld County Sheriff's Department, Thornton Police Department or Gilcrest, Colorado, which I am sure is a very nice town and no disembodied have ever been kidnapped there. I do not know if there is a spooky abandoned school there. To my knowledge, there are no religious groups in Colorado Springs bent on trapping the disembodied. I apologize if I have offended anyone's beliefs about the afterlife, but this is a work of fiction after all.

And in case you were wondering, none of the news stories at the start of the chapters are true. And the Tattered Cover Bookstore in Denver has never thrown a party for the dead on Christmas Eve, but I'd like to think they would. And the editor of The Denver Post portrayed in the book has no similarities to the actual editor of The Post, who is my husband's boss.

The flashing rave video and the fake fog that swirled in the dark room made it difficult to read the chat room transcript on the monitors, but Brian knew he'd been betrayed as a fool.

> **minerofLove:** where do you want to go
> **miranda:** we could go anywhere, outta here. U up 4 a little peeping
> **minerofLove:** i dont I never
> **miranda:** its the closest we can get to sex
> **mike:** is he never gonna get it
> **homealone:** dude shes a guy he tries this with evry1
> **peter:** put him out of my misery
> **miranda:** OK Im busted

He could almost feel the flush that colored his face when he had a body. It didn't matter what had happened to him, what changes he'd gone through, he was still the same hick kid he'd always been. The whole night was a mistake and these people weren't what he'd thought. He looked at the rave on the monitors and contemplated the fate of the young people dancing outside the room. *You're all going to die and end up like us. You can dance to all the Christian rock you want, it won't make any difference.*

Well screw them, he thought. *I don't have to put up with any of this. If I want to leave, I can.*

He started toward the open doorway when he saw a man outside close the door to the room.

What the hell, he thought. *Why'd they shut the damn door? Maybe one of these jerks knows who to call.* Which is when he noticed the last comments displayed on the monitors.

miranda: who closed the door
mike: hey the walls moving

None of the people dancing outside noticed anything.

CHAPTER 1

WASHINGTON, D.C. (AP) — Since the discovery of the afterlife, police departments across the country can't retain officers and are finding it increasingly difficult to hire new ones, according to a Department of Justice study released today.

"Even before the discovery, many departments were bracing for a wave of retirements as officers hired in the mid-1970s approach retirement. ... But since 2000, recruitment goals are down nationwide 25 percent," the study said. "At the same time, violent crime, which was on the decline in the mid-1990s, has risen sharply. And most of the violent crime increase is not related to drugs, theft or property crimes, but to civil disorder: riots and demonstrations."

Deputy Attorney General Rosalind Bresnahan, speaking at a press conference to announce the study, said, "The riots may have peaked at the end of the millennium, but the potential is always there. The level of violence is escalating and the risks the police face are forcing many officers to think, 'Is this job worth the risk?'"

Munroe peeked around the doorway and ducked back.

Shit! thought Munroe. *I don't have to do that. I'm dead, remember. Oh yeah, that's right,* he said to himself. *Bullets cannot harm me. I'm Superman!*

He moved back into the open doorway and looked at the dark void of the room. His sight slid into the infrared but he saw nothing. No electrical or water services seemed to enter this room in the sub-basement of the old train station. *I never knew this cow town had anything this old,* he thought, *or this big.*

He pulled back out of the empty room and continued down the brick-walled corridor, following the infrared glow of the water pipes above him. He almost imagined he could hear the drip of water. How long had he been down here? Five minutes at the most, he thought. *Damn! If I could only wear a watch. They might be getting worried back there. Worried about what?* he countered. *They know nothing can happen to me.*

Munroe continued down the corridor and peeked through a glass door that showed a confusing scene. Lit only by a desk lamp somewhere in the back, he saw the shapes of mountains, in fact the same Rocky Mountains he saw every day looking west.

He looked at the sign printed on the glass door — "Platte Valley Model Railroad Engineers." It was a vast model train layout. *Interesting, I got to check this out sometime.*

Suddenly to his left he saw a glow move in the corridor and disappear as the suspect he'd been following ducked into another one of the little rooms. *How many are down here? I must be out beyond the walls of the building. I think I'm underneath the train platforms.* He continued down the corridor and saw that the pipes overhead stopped. Sliding back into visual light, he saw that the wall he faced confirmed that the corridor ended here. Looking to his right, where the person had run, he saw a solid door that was partially open. Sliding back into infrared, he saw on the door the smudge of a handprint now fading into invisibility.

The door left an eight-inch gap against the frame. *A little tight, but some momentum should get me through.* He backed up and willed himself through the opening, feeling himself stretched thin and tensing himself for the sproing of his essence reforming.

4

Ugh, hate that. OK, let's see what's here.

Only a small amount of light spilled through the open door, but it was enough for Munroe to make out that the room held stacked boxes about four feet high. Moving down the aisle formed by the boxes, he could see a small man huddled behind a large semi-automatic, using the boxes for cover. The room was maybe 10 feet by 20 and contained only the boxes, darkened fluorescent overhead lights and the suspect.

Maybe 20 years old, a kid, thought Munroe, and definitely not matching the description of someone almost six feet tall and well built. He might be Hispanic and he probably was a gang member and he most definitely was scared.

This was not a good situation. Only one way into the room and the kid had the doorway covered. *If they can't talk him out, he's leaving here dead.* Yet again, Munroe wished he could do something, anything physical. *If only I could wail and clank chains like Marley's ghost.* He moved closer to the kid to see if he had any other weapons besides the semi, which he now recognized as a .45-caliber Colt M1911, a beautiful weapon. *Wow, big expensive gun for a small kid.* The kid seemed to think so too, as he took the gun out of his right hand to wipe his sweaty palm on his pants. As he did so, he exposed it to view.

Damn! There's no magazine! And the hammer's down!

Munroe had to act quickly. He flew through the door so fast this time he didn't even feel the stretching. He recited his turns, left, right, left, left and up two flights of stairs and past the SWAT officers flanking the stairwell. He looked wildly for his partner and found her talking to the lieutenant.

Yamaguchi turned instinctively to her right when Munroe's "voice" came through her ear buds.

"I found the suspect. He doesn't have a hostage. He's at the far end of the station in the sub-basement. He's got a

.45 semi but there's no magazine and the hammer's down."

She turned back to the lieutenant. "Munroe found him. No hostage. Says he's armed with a .45 automatic but that … there's no mag and the hammer's down."

"Tell him it's the M1911. Tell him I don't think this kid is the shooter. Maybe we have a chance we can get him out alive."

She relayed this and his description of the suspect. The lieutenant gave her a look that Munroe recognized — complete disbelief that she wasn't making it all up. "Yeah, and I bet he's a retired beekeeper and walks with a limp," the lieutenant muttered.

Munroe tried to ignore the terminal's translation, even though the beekeeper gag impressed him. "Tell him the suspect is in a storeroom with one door. He's got it covered. He's hiding behind boxes. Cardboard boxes."

"How does he know this isn't the shooter?" asked the lieutenant.

"Lieutenant," she said for herself, "the witnesses said there were two suspects — one large heavyset, one small and everyone agrees only one shot fired. The other suspect must be somewhere else."

The lieutenant nodded and used the microphone clipped to his lapel, probably to tell dispatch that the other suspect was still at large, although her terminal translated the lieutenant's words for Munroe as "unintelligible speech."

The lieutenant turned and looked where he imagined Munroe must be and made himself larger. *He's trying to intimidate me. How funny.* Yamaguchi shied away from the lieutenant's body language and Munroe temporarily lost the field of her terminal.

"… this kid who fired." Munroe only caught the tail end of the lieutenant's remarks as he reacquired the field, but he could guess the gist.

"Because a scared kid who's fired his gun isn't going to

eject the mag for some misguided attempt at gun safety." She relayed this without his sarcasm, he noticed. Which was probably wise because he saw the lieutenant's grimace relax.

"I'll go in ahead and confirm that he still doesn't have a magazine and the hammer is down." She relayed this and added her own comment, "I'll have to go with your guys and relay for Munroe."

The lieutenant nodded and asked, "What's the distance for a TASER?"

She relayed for Munroe: "It's too long. I make the room 10 by 20 and he's at the far end. We'd want him to leave."

"Hard to get a shot in there anyway," the lieutenant said to himself. "Tear gas?" The lieutenant was now beginning to ask questions as if Munroe was actually there.

She relayed: "There's a problem, the door opens the wrong way. Someone would have to get up close and you'd have to toss it in but you really wouldn't expose yourself and the room would fill up fast."

"OK, Munroe, you'll advance and lead us in. Gooch, you stay with …" — the lieutenant looked around — "… Jenkins. I'll brief them and then we go in."

The lieutenant left them and she wandered away from the knot of men surrounding him. "Sounds like he's actually starting to believe you exist," she said.

"Sounds like he's starting to trust you, too," Munroe replied.

"Can we get this kid out alive?" she asked.

"Don't know. He's pretty scared and he has an awfully big gun. It all depends on whether he still doesn't have a mag and the hammer's down."

"We should have a signal," she said.

"Right. Once I know it's OK, I'll say … OK, what should I say?"

"You say … you say safe! That means we can try a TASER shot."

"OK, safe means it's safe to go," Munroe confirmed.

"Talking to yourself again?" the lieutenant asked behind Yamaguchi's ear. She turned to face him.

"Yes … uh, I mean we have our signal arranged. Alex will tell me it's safe to proceed, and I'll tell you."

Munroe said to her, "Tell him I'm going back down to make sure he's still in the room and I'll backtrack to meet you at the stairs one floor down." She relayed this.

"Sounds good," the lieutenant said and turned back to the others.

"Good luck, Alex," she said. When she realized he'd already left, she said. "Stupid. It's me who needs luck."

Munroe quickly returned to the storeroom, happy he had remembered the way and found the suspect still crouched behind the boxes. The kid was now shaking. *I hope those aren't the shakes you get after you just shot someone,* Munroe thought.

The gun, however, was still missing a magazine and the hammer was still down.

He left the kid and returned to the stairs as the SWAT team was just reaching the floor above. He connected with Yamaguchi, who relayed in a whisper, "Munroe says the suspect hasn't moved and we can move down to the sub-basement."

Munroe had already gone back down to the sub-basement and was waiting for them after again checking the suspect's location. Through Yamaguchi, he directed them through the turns until they reached the corridor that led to the storeroom. From what he could tell, they moved silently and he hoped the kid would be unaware of their presence.

Once in position, the SWAT leader called out to the suspect several times and told him to throw out his weapon and come out unarmed. After not hearing any response, he ordered everyone to put on their gas masks. Then he detailed one of his men to deliver the tear gas through the door. Munroe kept up a back and forth, checking to make sure the kid was still behind the boxes — and happy to see he had shrunk even farther back into his hiding spot — and then telling Yamaguchi the kid probably couldn't see the lower half of the doorway. She told the SWAT leader who signaled to the man with the tear gas, who then rolled it into the room and ran back to the others.

Munroe remained by the door, not eager to squeeze through the opening again. After a few seconds, gas came billowing out the door and down the corridor to the waiting SWAT team.

Damn! thought Munroe, *why's he doing that?* as he saw the SWAT leader push Yamaguchi back behind his men, effectively blocking the corridor and his access to the terminal she wore on her arm.

Movement from the door caught his attention and he saw the opening widen at the same time he saw the SWAT team stiffen, their weight shifting into their upper bodies.

The gun poked through the doorway and he saw that the magazine was missing and the hammer down. Munroe ran back to the others just as Yamaguchi shouldered her way through the officers who stood before her, exposing her right arm and the terminal she wore.

Munroe moved so fast he hit the wall of cops and bounced back but he had acquired the field long enough to say "Safe!" He saw her lips open and say the words, and then the team leader yelled his command. As the suspect came through the door amid the billows of tear gas, the beams from the laser sights of two TASERs and several assault rifles met the suspect in the chest. In a clearly defined moment, Munroe could see the darts and trailing wires of the TASERs leave the muzzles, which is when he realized that the darts would pass through him to the suspect.

There was no time for him to do anything and he knew the current was already passing through the wires when he felt something faint, like the memory of the limbs he'd once had when they were beginning to fall asleep. But the wires quickly shifted position as the suspect dropped and the cops rushed forward to secure him. Yet again Munroe bounced off a wall of cops and found himself squeezed between the end of the corridor and their bodies. He forced himself over them and came back down the other side and saw her standing, left behind when the others rushed the suspect.

He came up beside her and caught the field of the terminal.

"… roe!" she said and he knew she was calling out his name from the shape her lips made.

"I'm here, Linda."

"Alex, you OK? I lost contact …"

"I bounced off 600 pounds of cop. Then I found out what a TASER feels like to a dead person."

"And?"

"Kind of tingly."

After an hour of the endless waiting, debriefing and milling around that always resulted after a SWAT incident, Yamaguchi and Munroe were told to go home.

"I'll want supplemental reports from you and Munroe," the lieutenant told her. "And tell Munroe he did a good job."

"I'm sure he heard, lieutenant."

"He might have said something about you," Munroe told Yamaguchi after the SWAT lieutenant left. "If you hadn't moved forward when you did, I wouldn't have been able to reach your terminal."

"No big," she said. "I know you can't pass through solid matter. They don't."

Munroe said nothing. He knew the other cops were quite well aware of his limitations intellectually, but she knew Munroe as a person, as her partner. Most of the other cops only regarded him as a piece of high-tech equipment, represented by the terminal on her armband, or at best as their pet ghost.

"Come on, Alex, let's get out of here."

As they passed through the train station lobby, they passed the SWAT officer who threw the tear gas into the room. "Hey, good night, Gooch," he called out to her. She raised her hand and gave him a small wave, but didn't look back.

"I thought you hated being called that," said Munroe, as he tried to keep up with her stride and the rise and fall of her terminal's interface field. "Aren't you going to tear into him?"

"I'm too tired to tell him off. Besides, he's one of the cute ones." She opened one of the doors to leave the station and kept it open the extra beat required to make sure he made it through. Outside it was after 1 a.m. and Munroe was surprised to see how busy the street was until he remembered it was the weekend before Christmas and downtown Denver did have a nightlife, even when the temperature was in the teens.

"Oh, yeah, what was his name?" he asked.

"Bimmelman, Schmimmelman, something like that?"

"It's Zimmerman. Officer Arliss Zimmerman, as you well know."

"Yow. OK, maybe not cute enough to make up for that name." Munroe decided not to throw back at his partner her full name, Laurelinda Yamaguchi.

They reached their parked cruiser and Munroe waited for her to open the door. Again, she waited the extra beat that allowed Munroe to get in before her. He instantly found the large field of the police cruiser's terminal and felt comforted by the luxury of full Internet access. He immediately began checking his email and Facebook page and blog. Yamaguchi meanwhile pulled out her ear buds and took the portable terminal off her armband and inserted it into the charging dock.

Munroe found little other than spam emails that offered to reconnect him with his loved ones or dubious methods of engaging in disembodied sex. He did, however, see the latest email from Apple that promoted their new, home AfterNet terminal. *Nice,* he thought, *if only I had a home.*

He deleted everything and looked back at Yamaguchi, who as usual was already listening to the local public radio station. At this hour, it would be the BBC World Service. If he let this go on, she would start talking about how evil U.S. foreign policy was, and he'd remind her there was a Democrat in the White House, and she'd counter how he and his fellow Republicans had controlled Congress for too long. He had to do something quick.

"So, how's your mom?"

"Oh, don't get me started." She turned down the radio because she clearly would start. "Do you know she actually called the watch commander the other night because I missed a chat with her last week … " Munroe knew he had some peace and quiet while she recounted her tales of horror about her wacky Japanese mother who made such a looming presence in her life. Munroe logged in to the AfterNet to see the latest news, then entered the Lost Love forum, his favorite guilty pleasure.

"Looking for Mr. Wright" was the most recent post and Munroe read about Mrs. Nora Wright. Her husband died five years ago and would he please get in touch with her because her new husband just couldn't give her the satisfaction that he had and would he be kind enough to share his secrets with husband number two.

Although the post was only an hour old, there already were 60 replies, mostly from women wondering what secret Mr. Wright possessed and that they'd be happy if he'd share his secret with them or their partners as well. Munroe realized that as a purely intellectual exercise — and that's all he had left now — he was kind of curious himself. He was just about to start his reply when he realized that she had just said that they'd returned to the department.

He quickly replayed her rant and was pleased to see it contained little new and that the entire conversation had been one sided. *That's just one of the things I like about her,* he thought. *She knows I'm interested in her life but doesn't require me to keep telling her "uh huh" and "is that so."*

She parked the car in the garage and said, "OK, that's enough for me tonight. I'll do my report in the morning."

"If you want, I'll write yours and you can just sign it," he offered.

"Oh, would you? Maybe after that we can plant some evidence." She was a stickler for following the book.

"Hey, it's not like we shot anyone. You didn't see anything I didn't see."

"Thank you but no, I'll write it myself."

She pulled the portable terminal out of the charger and slipped it into its armband and replaced her ear buds. She opened her door and for once was a little too quick for Munroe, who was slammed back into the car by the door. Yamaguchi instantly knew what she had done and quickly opened the door. "I'm sorry, I'm sorry," she said.

"Wow, when you get pissed off … " he said, after getting out of the car. She laughed and said, "I said I'm sorry."

They walked inside the department and entered the secure area. She signed herself out and set her radio into the charging rack. She said goodnight to the front desk officer and walked to the door and waited for him.

"Goodnight, Alex."

"Goodnight, Linda. Hey, I forgot to ask, did you find something for tomorrow night?"

"I'll say I did, and it's a killer, and no, I'm telling you

nothing about it, you'll just have to wait." She paused with her hand on the door handle and said, "I still feel bad about you having to hang around the department all night."

"Oh, it's not so bad. I have the whole Internet to wander around and I can get out if I want to."

"You know, the offer still stands."

"Thanks, maybe I'll take you up on it someday."

"I am serious. Think about it," Yamaguchi tried to look where she imagined Munroe to be and was a few inches high. She eventually put on a lopsided grin, shrugged her shoulders, waved bye and left.

The field disappeared as she walked away. Munroe observed how the swing of her hips translated to her thick, black ponytail and to the various items of cop equipment she wore on her belt. He felt like a lecherous old man and then remembered that's what he was. Sixty-two when he died, crapping through a tube, two ex-wives who hated him and thank God no kids. *What a shitty way to die,* he thought. *And Linda thinks of me as a cute puppy, or maybe a gay friend.* That's probably what kept him from taking up her offer of letting him stay in her apartment. He was a harmless, sexless creature to her, and although he could still remember what the tightening of his groin felt like, he knew he was a harmless, sexless creature.

Heavy sigh, he said to himself and moved toward CID.

The Criminal Investigations Division was a large open room with a sea of desks where the detectives worked. Although Yamaguchi and Munroe weren't detectives, they were assigned a desk in the room. At this time of night, the whole floor was empty except for a handful of cops in the adjacent break room. They were watching TV in the corner of the room. *Barney Miller*, he noted. He'd always liked *Barney Miller*. He wished they'd turn on the captions.

Munroe settled in before the terminal at his desk. Unusually his chair was there, which made it easier for him. He saw that Yamaguchi had put his picture back on his desk and so once again he confronted his physical self. It was the picture taken when he hit the 15-year mark with the Seattle PD. He'd been a homicide detective for five years then and had cleared a high-profile murder investigation that year, so his career was flying high. He was accepting a plaque from the chief, but Linda had blown it up and cropped it so that only he was in the picture. There he was, still feeling young at 50, with thick, dark hair only hinting of gray, big boned and clumsy looking even in this pose. He was smiling and he thought he looked good. Hard to reconcile with the last memory he had of his face. It was in the hospice and it was the last time he was still able to wash his own hair and comb it in the mirror afterward. He had lost fifty pounds, his face was pale and he'd given up shaving. He'd recognized a dead man's eyes when he'd seen them and the whole farce of getting better and leaving the hospice was finally over. He knew he'd be dead in a week, and he was right.

Damn! I went through this the last time I saw this. I got to tell Linda to get rid of it.

But Linda needed it, he realized. *Maybe if she sees me as a real person, sees me as the man I once was, I won't just be Casper the Friendly Ghost to her. And maybe if I stop playing hide and seek with it, maybe I can come to deal with it, too.*

Munroe forced himself to ignore the picture and captured the field of the terminal. The display instantly came alive and the terminal recognized him. He opened a report form and entered the details of the arrest and submitted it. Then he made another one for Yamaguchi. Picking his words carefully, he tried to make it obvious that her action to get the terminal field in the open might have saved the suspect's life. He forwarded the form to her and would let her decide whether she'd use it.

He again checked his email and found nothing new, other than a reminder from Yamaguchi that she'd pick him up at 6 p.m. outside the station. She was almost as big a slave to email as he was, and probably sent it from her phone just minutes ago.

He wrote back to her. "Get to sleep, Yamaguchi. Big day tomorrow and you don't want to be seen with bags under your eyes. Oh, and I forwarded the sup to you. Review and sign. Or not. Good night."

Chores done, Munroe wandered back to the AfterNet. *I should either update my blog, process some reports, or just what was that secret Mr. Wright possessed?*

Yamaguchi tossed her belt onto the couch, missed and winced at the sound of a nightstick, two handcuffs, pepper spray, flashlight, two extra magazines, a knife, phone and gun hit the hardwood floor. She picked it up and reflected for the umpteenth time how heavy it was. She pulled the terminal out of her armband and stuck it in the charger.

Looking around quickly to make sure all the blinds were down, she started peeling off her uniform. First the leather jacket, then the down vest, then the heavy wool shirt, then the bulletproof vest and finally the T-shirt that protected her skin from the bulletproof vest and finally her bra. She felt 20 pounds lighter, which was in fact, correct.

By this time, she was in the bedroom and now she pulled off the ugly shoes, the ugly wool pants, the long johns and the hose she wore to keep the long johns from chafing. She flopped onto her bed, a woman again.

I really don't need to dress that warm anymore, I'm not on patrol. I don't have to stand around in the cold writing traffic tickets. But she knew the minute she dropped the warm clothing, she'd be stuck somewhere cold, nasty and wet.

I wonder what he's doing now, she thought, not for the

first time. *Poor guy, stuck in the department all night long until I pick him up the next day.* It really made no sense because she knew Munroe didn't need the sleep. He could easily take another shift with a different partner and work around the clock, if the city would ever foot the bill for more disembodied liaison officers like her.

She frowned at the thought of Munroe working with another partner. *I'm sure he wouldn't like it. Besides, he always tells me he has plenty to do in the off hours.*

Oh crap, I better remind him I'll pick him up at six. She slipped on a nightshirt, went back to the living room and used her phone to send him a reminder. His reply to her came back before she could put it to sleep.

She looked at the supplemental report he'd forwarded and decided Munroe had done a good job making sure her quick thinking was mentioned without making it look too much like bragging. *Maybe I can borrow a few words here and there and it'd be OK.* She went back to the bedroom and decided to crawl into bed without even brushing her teeth.

So he's already surfing the web. Damn he's addicted. But then, what else does an old, dead cop do? She yawned. *Goodnight, Munroe.*

CHAPTER 2

... and Linda Wertheimer reports that non-profits are feeling the pinch.

LINDA WERTHEIMER, correspondent: The assembled musicians are actually happy when they're told the Dallas symphony will be performing a shortened season this year.

(SOUNDS OF MANY PEOPLE TALKING) I guess it's better than killing the entire season. This means all I have to do is find a third job.

WERTHEIMER: That's Audrey Ames, second violinist with the symphony. Like many, she thought she'd be out of a job after the symphony announced that falling donations might make it impossible to continue the 2004-2005 season. Rudy Clarkfield, chairman of the symphony board:

CLARKFIELD: We felt the drop most in estate planning. Since the discovery we ...

WERTHEIMER: The discovery of the afterlife?

CLARKFIELD: Yes, since then, people have reconsidered their estate plans.

WERTHEIMER: Estate plans. That's where people have made wills and have promised to turn over their estate — stocks, bonds, property — upon their death?

CLARKFIELD: Yes, I'm not going to say it's a major source of income, but we rely on it. And it may sound ghoulish, but we plan on it. But since 2001, we've had many people write the symphony out of their estate plans. And we certainly haven't had anyone new say they want to include us.

WERTHEIMER: The symphony's financial problems worsened after a disembodied man decided he wanted his estate, estimated to be worth $15 million, to revert to him instead of the symphony. A court has agreed to halt any disbursement from the estate until the case can be heard.

Of course, many other organizations rely on funds derived from estate plans, including this public radio station. That's why we need your help …

Munroe looked at the clock in the CID room. It was 8:15 a.m. He figured he'd been around the world twice since he'd started. He'd read newspaper stories about serial murders in Japan, Sweden and France; read the results of the test match between South Africa and England (not that he knew anything about cricket); looked up the M1911 .45-caliber ACP; found out that the Platte Valley Model Railroad Engineers met the first Friday of the month at Denver's Union Station (open to the public the last Friday of the month); failed to find anything about the effects of a TASER on a disembodied person; checked the progress of the two Mars rovers; left some helpful (he hoped) comments at a support group for the recently dead; updated his blog with his two cents about the stalled bill to grant voting rights to the dead; registered with two news services so he'd get alerts about serial murders; checked his bank account; confirmed that his Amazon purchases were on track; and downloaded and watched *Seven Samurai* again.

It definitely wasn't like the early days of the AfterNet, when the only places he could go online were the public kiosks. He'd wait, sometimes for hours, until he could get online on those early terminals, which were abysmally slow, and then struggle to visualize a simple query in his mind.

And now he was simultaneously juggling six open browser connections and was maintaining two chats. He could have handled more, but the department had lousy Internet access.

And I'm the old fart who wouldn't use a computer, he thought contritely. *Now, I'm a surfing fool.*

He turned his attention back to one of the local Denver rooms, chatting mindlessly with a guy who claimed to be Ben Franklin. He was not doing a very good job of it while spouting endless Poor Richard sayings. He was also ignorant of Silence Dogood, which Munroe thought a nice irony. There was also a woman who said she died in 1971 of cervical cancer (*thank you, too much information*), another man who claimed to be Voltaire but who couldn't understand Munroe's high school French (*which is actually in his favor*) and a living woman who said she was bored in Capitol Hill and was sitting naked in her kitchen and would leave the door open for any disembodied men.

Why do I bother with this? he thought. He was about to exit the chat when another person — beccathompson43 — joined.

beccathompson43: How yall doing?

Everyone answered her back with a hello but Munroe apologized that he was just leaving.

beccathompson43: Please dont go. Im checking all the denver chat rooms. Have any of yuo talked to minerofLove recently? he said he sometimes visited this room
voltaire11: Loose ur boyfriend?
beccathompson43: Hes my son
voltaire11: Apologies, Madame. I spoke without thinking.
beccathompson43: its OK. I was supposed to meet him in Golden and haven't found him.
jollycopper: Is your son disembodied?
beccathompson43: yes, he died two years ago and he decided to go on the europe vacation we promised him after graduation.
jollycopper: How much is he overdue?

beccathompson43: 4 days. Im worried.

jollycopper: Probably nothing to worry about. I'm a Denver cop. I can keep an eye out for him if you like.

beccathompson43: would u? Id appreciate it. Can I send you info about him?

jollycopper: Sure. Send it to jollycopper@denverpd.org

gettingsleepy: Way to go, jollycopper. I never nu u were a real cop.

jollycopper: You know kids. And we disembodied get trapped by the silliest things, especially when traveling.

poorrichard: I was trapped in an outhouse for four days.

jollycopper: Listen, becca, let's take this private.

Munroe sent beccathompson43 a private chat message. She told him her son died of an embolism when he was 21. He'd been attending the Colorado School of Mines and after his death departed on what grew into a year and half long trip around the world. She'd gotten constant emails from her son and chatted with him through the AfterNet.

Rebecca and her husband lived in Brush, Colorado, and they received a message a month ago that Brian was back in Denver. However, a friend of the family was ill and she was taking care of the friend's children, so they told Brian they'd have to delay meeting him until Dec. 14. They had planned to meet him at the school where Brian was contemplating finishing his degree.

But Rebecca had camped out at the school for four days without success.

beccathompson43: i don't know what Im going to do. I lost him hwen he died how can I lose him again?

jollycopper: Like I said, kids have no sense of time, and I can tell you, when you're dead, time becomes even more meaningless. You should alert AfterNet security, but keep doing what you're doing. Leave a message in the Denver forums, keep visiting the chat rooms. I'm sure he'll show up. Nothing can happen to us, remember that.

beccathompson43: Thank you very much jollycroper I will try to remember that. and Ill send a message to security right now.

jollycopper: The name's Alex Munroe, and I'll email you if I find him.

After Rebecca left the private chat, Munroe finished his surfing for the night, although by now, it was 8:30 a.m.

Wish there were something more I could do, thought Munroe, *but realistically I can't put out a missing person's report on a dead kid. And I'm sure he simply got distracted. Maybe I'll check with AfterNet security tonight, make sure they got her report.*

Munroe rose from the terminal. While he'd been talking with Rebecca Thompson, the handful of detectives who worked Saturday had arrived and in the break room, the TV had been turned to CNN.

May as well take advantage of the shift change and go for a walk, Munroe thought.

Munroe waited for someone to exit the building and snuck in behind him. Outside, downtown Denver was still sleepy. *The Denver Post* website said it was clear and cold at 10 degrees. Why he still checked the weather, he didn't know. From the department, Munroe drifted toward the 16th Street Mall, his path occasionally shrouded by the fog that spewed from manhole covers and sewer grates. He saw the huddled forms of the homeless who still remained asleep in window wells or near building exhaust vents that also belched clouds of steam.

A lot of homeless, but still not as bad as Seattle, Munroe thought, as he passed a knot of homeless men begging in front of a Starbucks.

As usual, the Starbucks made him think of home, Seattle. He ducked inside the store, on the heels of a young woman as she passed through the door held open by an older man, who did the gesture automatically while still holding his morning paper before him.

The line of people ordering coffee was five deep and the store was packed. Three men were holding an impromptu meeting and were watching a PowerPoint presentation on a laptop. A young man in need of a shave, wearing a Greek sailor hat and pea coat (the Old Spice theme went through Munroe's mind) was talking to a pretty girl wearing an impossibly short skirt for such a cold morning. Four women were hunched together at a table giggling. They all had security badges that showed they worked at the AfterNet.

Munroe drank in the scene, almost smelling the coffee and hearing the sounds of life on a cold, December morning. The depression hit what would have been the pit of his stomach if he'd still had one, until he noticed the AfterNet terminal in the back of the store.

Moving toward it, he recognized it as a simple public terminal, the display meant only for the occasional living person who might want to use it for Internet access. The display indicated the number of disembodied users currently online — 32.

Wow, I wonder when Starbucks installed these. I bet they're in all the Starbucks by now. The thought cheered him, the thought of all those terminals in all those Starbucks. The thought that disembodied people like him still needed the warmth of a meeting place warmed him as well.

As much of a junkie as he was, he didn't need to go online, but he did anyway and watched the number of users currently online change to 33.

Yamaguchi spent the day primping. There wasn't another word that would correctly describe her actions: she gave herself a manicure and pedicure (slightly grossed out by how long she'd allowed her toenails to get), removed the calluses from her feet (otherwise her dry skin would shred her hose), exercised on her stair stepper (while watching her TiVoed soaps) and then went to her hairdresser at 1 p.m.

Afterward, she stopped at the dry cleaners and thanked God the alterations were done and the dress was ready and that she wouldn't have to rely on her backup. She shouldn't have waited until the last minute to take it in.

Back home, she inspected herself in the mirror, holding the dress in front of her. *Oh God,* she thought, *those hours at the gym were worth it.*

At 4 p.m., she took a quick shower and spent an hour fussing with her hair, once rewetting it because the flip on the left-hand side of her head went the wrong way. Finally, with the help of a hot brush and hair spray, she got the desired symmetrical effect and was pleased.

Of course, now she was getting hot after the hot shower, the hair dryer and the hot brush. So hot, in fact, that despite the season she opened a window. *Oh crap, this is why I don't go through this too often.* After a few minutes, she sneezed a few times and closed the window.

By 5:30 p.m., she was starting to get worried, her eyes flicking back and forth between her watch and her face in the mirror as she applied her makeup. *OK, don't get rushed, plenty of time, Munroe won't mind if I'm a couple of minutes late.*

Despite her worries and a sneeze that made her jab her eye with a mascara brush, her makeup was perfect by 5:40 p.m. She grabbed her bag, her coat (*I'm going to freeze in this thing*) and went out to her car, when she realized she'd forgotten her gun. She went back into her apartment, grabbed the fanny pack with her off-duty weapon and went back to the car. *Fashionably late, that's all I am, fashionably late.*

Munroe kept wandering back to the corner so he could see the clock on the City and County Building. 6:15 p.m. *Come on Linda, where are you? You're past fashionably late.* He wandered back to the parking garage. Finally he saw her little car enter the garage. She pulled into her usual parking spot and reached across to open the door. Munroe got in quickly.

"I'm in," he told her.

She reached across and essentially through him to close the door, a breach of etiquette she'd normally never commit.

"You're late."

"… and my gun so I had to go back and get it." He'd lost part of what she said because the terminal on her armband kept changing positions as she closed the door and quickly backed up the car. The car came to an abrupt stop so he knew she was slamming the brakes.

"But that's no reason for you to drive like a maniac."

"I'm sorry, Alex. Just had a lot to do."

"I thought you said you had the whole day free?"

"I had the whole day free to get ready. My beauty regimen is a little more involved than yours."

"Well, I did shave," he joked. "And I picked a tie that brings out the color of my eyes."

"I'm sure you look quite dapper. So, what did you do today? Spend most of it online?"

"No," he lied. "I spent most of the day exploring beautiful downtown Denver." In reality, he only spent four hours in the Starbucks online, and then another three at the downtown Tattered Cover bookstore, and then another hour watching a college football game at a sports bar. Essentially about the same sort of day he might have spent while alive, minus the cigarettes, caffeine and alcohol. He reflected that he had to die before taking his doctor's advice.

"Hey, are you going to wear your terminal on your arm

like that the whole night? Won't that clash with this killer outfit you promised?"

"Don't worry, I'm going to put it in my bag, and I'm going to use the wireless ear buds."

"Aren't those the same ear buds you said pick up weird voices?" asked Munroe.

"Oh, let's not talk about the voices I keep hearing, Munroe. They keep telling me to ditch you and find a real partner."

Munroe chose to ignore her. He often wished for a way to do a *sotto voce* comic grumble via the terminal interface.

Yamaguchi's driving quickly brought them to the performing arts center and they began their usual argument about parking. She wanted to park in the center's parking garage.

"It's up to $10, Linda. Besides, there's always parking on 20th Street."

"Yes, if I want to walk six blocks in a dress and heels when it's 20 degrees outside and I'm already late. And it's windy, too," she added, slyly.

"Is it? Oh yeah, well then we wouldn't want you to walk that far."

She smiled and hoped Munroe wouldn't notice. Like many disembodied, Munroe hated wind. He said that moving through a strong wind for him was like walking through molasses. Of course, it was windy and the wind chill probably brought the temperature down to minus something, so she definitely wanted to park in the garage.

She found a spot in one of the lower levels that suited her small Honda del Sol and quickly parked, almost cutting off the SUV behind her. "Stupid monster car," she muttered, *sotto voce*.

"See, only 6:30. Plenty of time." Munroe ignored her and waited until she got out, then he exited while she waited.

"I'm out," he told her.

They left the parking garage and went down a level to the main gallery of the center. Luckily the air was calm and they made their way through the crowd heading for any one of four events that night at the center. Munroe had to dodge the people and several times lost her, but he found her waiting for him by the main entrance to the concert hall.

"OK?" she asked.

"OK," he answered. "You go in and I'll try to sneak in."

"We can try the handicapped entrance."

"No, I'll try to rise above it, if you'll excuse the pun."

"You're excused. Meet by the coat check."

She went inside while Munroe waited by the doors for a small lull, which never happened. So he rose above the crowd and squeezed in above the heads of the people. Luckily, he made it without being crushed. He remained above the crowd after he entered until he caught a glimpse of her at the coat check. He lowered himself back into the crowd, feeling slightly winded.

It was still 20 feet to the coat check and it took Munroe a minute to arrive, just in time to see her being handed the ticket for her coat. She turned back and looked into the crowd. Munroe saw the dress, a dark wine-red number with tiny straps that almost revealed an indecent amount of cleavage but still managed to leave her looking elegant. The fabric formed an enticing fold or band around her breasts and when she turned around because someone bumped into her he saw the dress exposed a lot of her back. She had a wrap the same color as the dress but it hung low behind her. She turned back to look for Munroe again and now he noticed that it was her hair that kept her looking elegant. Instead of her usual ponytail, her long, black thick hair fell straight down and then curved inward at the ends, adding a touch of modesty as it concealed her breasts.

Munroe always knew Yamaguchi was pretty but he'd

only ever seen her as a cop and had always assumed she was kind of hippy, but now he realized that was a false impression caused by her equipment belt, her vest and the unflattering police uniform. *My partner is a fox,* thought Munroe.

He also never realized how short she was. She was only five foot two, but as a cop, she carried herself with authority. Standing in heels, her new height slightly unnerved him. He searched for the terminal's field but couldn't find it, then remembered she'd put the terminal in her handbag, which she was holding in her left hand.

"That's some dress, Linda."

She smiled when Munroe's words came to her through the ear buds.

"Thanks, Alex."

"Something different with your hair, too."

"Got rid of the highlights."

"Your mother?" he asked, knowing her mother disapproved of anything that took away from her Oriental features.

"Well, partially. Well, OK, yes, it gives her one less thing to complain about."

A few of the people around her started looking at her, and an older woman said in a stage whisper, "Some people have no sense of the appropriate." Yamaguchi's eyes lowered and she backed away.

"The old broad say something?" asked Munroe, guessing from the sourpuss expression on the woman's face that she said something disparaging. The woman must not have been talking loud enough for the terminal to translate her words. Yamaguchi nodded and said, without moving her lips, "she thinks Im on cell." She was using the terminal's field to talk directly to Munroe.

"What a tight ass. You want I should rough her up?"

"Yamaguchi, glad you made it," someone said behind her, before she could answer Munroe.

She turned around quickly and Munroe lost the field of the terminal. He saw her talking to someone, a very tall, good-looking guy with a politician's smile whom he recognized as their boss, deputy administrative chief Paul Clemens. Her terminal and purse were still in her left hand and she was standing near another group of people so Munroe couldn't capture the field and get the translation of their conversation.

He saw her shake Clemens' hand and exchange pleasantries. *He's got to be saying something about the dress.* He saw Clemens laugh at something she said and he used the opportunity to put his hand on her shoulder, for just a second. Then she looked around and transferred her purse into her right hand and Munroe was able to talk to her again.

Finally remembered me, did you?

"… here somewhere." He caught the tail end of Yamaguchi's introduction.

"Alex, glad you could come," Clemens said, with the usual unfocused stare.

"Tell him that was a clear case of sexual harassment."

"Munroe says hi," she said.

"I was just telling your partner what a lovely dress she's wearing."

"Tell him I agree."

Suddenly the crowd seemed to be moving and groups of people were starting to wander off. It must have been the warning bell that the concert would be starting soon.

"The reception will be in the Aspen ballroom," Clemens said. "We'll want you and Alex there, of course." He realized he must have missed something while he was checking out the crowd.

"We'll be there," she said. Clemens turned away and Munroe realized another woman had been with the deputy chief the whole time — his wife, he assumed. *Left her standing there and didn't even introduce her, the creep,* he

29

thought, although he saw Yamaguchi nod to the woman as they left so maybe she was introduced while Munroe was incommunicado.

"I always hated deputy chiefs," said Munroe.

"Will you shut up?" she asked, while marching away from him. He hurried to catch up with her. "Come on, we're in the nose bleed seats." Their tickets were complimentary and were on the highest ring level, so she and Munroe climbed two big flights of stairs and then several more little flights to get to their seats.

At this height, most of the concertgoers were dressed casually and her dress stood out, which made her self-conscious. She showed her two tickets to an elderly usher and he peered with the aid of a small flashlight at the tickets. He handed her two programs and without a word led them to their seats at the end of an aisle. There was, however, a large man sitting in one of their seats.

"I'm sorry, these are our seats," Yamaguchi said. The man looked at her, then at the usher, then at the empty seat. "Sir, I have tickets for both these seats," she said, with the same voice she used to tell gawkers at an accident scene to keep moving. The man immediately got up and started showing his ticket to the person next to him, who got up and showed her ticket to the person next to her and so on until the whole row shifted over one seat. "Thank you," she told the large man, and sat in the aisle seat.

She shifted her purse to her right hand and Munroe sat.

"You do cause a lot of trouble," he told her. She shrugged without saying anything.

The house lights dimmed and after a minute, the audience applauded and Munroe saw the first violinist come out. After her bow and the last minute tuning, the conductor came out. It was her last ever performance before she left Denver for a job at another city and the concert hall was packed. It took a while before the applause died down and she could begin.

And for the next forty-five minutes, Munroe was unbelievably bored. Unable to hear anything, he could only amuse himself by watching the movements of the orchestra and the conductor, which was interesting for about two minutes. He vaguely recalled that he liked Handel's *Messiah* the one time wife number two dragged him to a performance, but he couldn't recall the tune. This time of year all he really wanted were Christmas carols and even that was denied him. So he started talking to Yamaguchi.

"The fat guy on your right is already snoring. You should shove him in the ribs to wake him." And, "Whoa, really bad toupee on the black guy two rows down. You can see the seam." And, "My those are perky breasts on the blonde with the bassoon. You can see them bounce from here."

Finally, she turned to where Munroe was sitting and with unerring accuracy looked at him. She mouthed the words, "Shut up" and with a deliberate motion, removed her ear buds and put them in her purse, then returned her attention to the music.

Munroe was reminded of being in church when he was a kid: a lot of adults acting very pious and he feeling very bored and mischievous.

If we had a portable terminal with Internet access, I could be doing something, he thought. *Maybe there's a terminal downstairs in the lobby.* Munroe's mind wandered randomly while he scanned the faces of the audience. He moved closer to observe the bad toupee. He thought of going down to the stage and observing the perky breasts first hand but wasn't sure how long he had until intermission. He moved up to the edge of their platform and tried to peer over, but despite being dead he still kept his low-level fear of heights. *If I fall, I'll just bounce. Still, it'll be unpleasant. Yes, but better than sitting through this. She'll never even know I left. I wonder how far I could fall. Well, they say we're invulnerable to just about anything. Yes, but it's that just about bit. Not like I'm exactly enjoying being this kind of dead, maybe there's another kind of dead. Yeah, but you like Linda, don't you. Well, yes. And being a cop, that's what you said was the only thing you were good for, isn't it? You got that going for you. And your health? That's right, your health is ...*

The house lights came up and the audience applauded.

Thank God, intermission.

"I'm sorry, I was just bored. Really, do you have any idea how boring a concert is when you can't hear anything?" Munroe was essentially talking to himself, although his remarks were addressed to Yamaguchi, who could ignore him because she had not replaced her ear buds.

They had returned to the lobby during intermission and she was standing in the ridiculously long line to buy a glass of wine at the bar. There were six people ahead of her.

"At this rate you're only going to have three minutes to drink it, you know." She continued staring straight ahead.

"All right, this is getting ridiculous. If you can't take a joke, then that's just your fault, Yamaguchi. If your anal little mind can't find the humor in a situation then you can just stick it up your ..."

That's when Munroe noticed the smile that had been creeping onto her face, and at the same time she lifted her right hand to push back her hair and reveal the ear buds.

"Oh, you little bitch. How long have you been listening to me?"

"Since left seat," she told him. She was again accessing the field directly and not speaking aloud. "Amuse yuorself until concert ends 30 mins. Meet u back by coat check, OK?"

So she's still mad, but I'm forgiven. "OK, enjoy yourself."

The line moved forward. "I plan to," she said.

Munroe left the bar and lobby and headed toward the exits. He hadn't found a terminal. *There's a Starbucks a block away. Let's see if they have a terminal.* As he left the auditorium he saw the clock in the main gallery of the performing arts center. *OK, I have forty-five minutes, enough time to check my email.*

Munroe was back in thirty minutes. He had checked his email in that time and also sent a message to AfterNet security, to make sure that Rebecca Thompson had notified them that her son was missing. It also gave him time to check the scores at ESPN and read yet another analysis of why the Seahawks would almost certainly lose against the mighty Denver Broncos offense and why he would almost certainly lose his bet with the stiff in Detroit who had egged him into putting his money where his mouth was.

Time to check out the perky blonde, he thought to himself, and waited until he saw someone sneak out of the men's room. He followed the man and re-entered the concert hall behind him. He worked his way down the orchestra level and then up onto the stage.

His view of the orchestra and the entire auditorium was impressive. *I should have been down here the whole time.* Although he couldn't hear the music, he could sense the rhythms of it by the motions of the musicians and the baton of the conductor. It pleased him to see the feet of the musicians as they kept time when he bent down low and saw their perfect synchrony.

He allowed himself to see everything at once, not concentrating on anything in particular, for once enjoying the 360-degree vision that terrified him when he first realized that he was dead. He looked up at the overhead lights and allowed himself to see the full spectrum, playing the wavelengths from infrared to ultraviolet almost as if they were musical notes.

He realized the orchestra had stopped, and then he saw that the audience was standing, first in clumps and then standing as a wave of people. The conductor turned to face the audience and he saw her beaming, red face and he noticed the sweat that plastered her short brown hair.

She turned to her orchestra and in turns motioned for individual musicians or sections to take a bow. Finally, she had the orchestra take a bow together and again Munroe marveled at their simultaneous bow, as if they were all still keeping time with the music.

Suddenly he felt like an intruder, sharing the accolades that were meant for the orchestra and he backed away from the stage, up the aisle of the orchestra level and toward the exit. He never even saw the perky blonde.

Yamaguchi eventually showed up at the coat check, although he almost didn't see her because the crush of people had forced him into a corner with limited view.

"Hi," he said.

"Hi," she said. "Did you amuse yourself?" She began walking away from the coat check.

"Yes I did. And how was the music?"

"Sublime."

"And is that good?" She ignored his remark. She knew that he knew the meaning of the word. *Well, I'm pretty sure I know the meaning of sublime: from the ridiculous to the sublime, right?*

"Are you ready for the reception?" she asked.

"Yes, looking forward to it."

"And no smart remarks in my ear." A man they were passing looked at her oddly. She smiled at him and walked a little faster.

Munroe had to dodge a very fat woman who blocked

his way and couldn't immediately respond. "R U listening?" she asked silently.

"Yes, sorry. No smart remarks. I'll behave."

"You know you can be very childish sometimes," she said out loud.

Munroe bit back a smart remark. "I said I'd behave. Uh, where are we going?" he asked, when he noticed they were leaving the building.

"The reception."

"I know that. I mean, isn't it in the concert hall?"

"Don't you read the email you're addicted to? I sent you the information. It's in the theatre complex, the next building over."

"Oh, yeah. I remember now," he lied. He decided he'd better keep quiet until they got there.

She led them to the theatre complex. It must have been even colder because Munroe saw the crowd hunched even tighter than before. He saw that she was trying to show a brave face even though she must be freezing, despite her heavy wool coat.

She entered the building's outer door. Inside, a doorman checked her invitation and he held the door open as she went through the inner door. Munroe followed as she headed for the coat check. As she was taking her ticket, she silently told Munroe, "Wait here Ill be back."

"What, why?" he asked.

"Because Im going to the bathroom."

Munroe waited for her. The novelty of touring women's restrooms had long since passed.

She returned and Munroe asked, "Ready?"

"Yup, let's do this," she said out loud.

She led them up a flight of stairs to the ballroom. Munroe marveled at her knowledge of the performing arts center. *I guess she's a culture vulture,* he thought. *Guess I don't know as much about my partner as I thought.*

Another doorman opened the door and she stepped

through. As Munroe entered, he noticed the field effect of an AfterNet terminal.

"Hi, name please," a disembodied voice asked.

"Uh, Alex Munroe," he told the voice. "Hey, hold on Linda, looks like I got to register."

She raised an eyebrow but waited while Munroe talked to someone he supposed was dead like him, but for all he knew was just a living person somewhere else.

"Please enjoy yourself, Officer Munroe, and feel free to use the terminals while you're here. There are several hot-spots throughout the ballroom."

Munroe was surprised. Since he'd died, he'd never had anyone extend that kind of hospitality to him except his partner.

"Wow, this is something, Linda. Wish I could have dressed up for the occasion."

Munroe saw a sea of women in evening dresses and men in expensive (although not always tasteful) suits. A string quartet was playing and a knot of people were being served food at a buffet table while a much larger group was at the bar.

"Ooh, open bar," she said, before getting in line for an-other glass of wine.

A few minutes later, she was balancing her wine and a plate of food and not doing a very good job of it.

"It's always so hard to juggle these," she said, while trying to devour an egg roll.

"You know, Linda, I wondered when I first met you whether you were cop material, but when I see you scarf-ing down food and wine at taxpayer expense, it puts my mind at rest."

"Giffit a wesht, Alesh," she said, turning her attention to smoked salmon on a cracker.

"Ah, Officer Yamaguchi," a man said while walking toward her, his hand extended. It was the Manager of Safety Marvin Montoya, the man to whom the chief of police reported, who incidentally was standing next to Montoya. The chief, Harold Moncrief, took the plate from Yamaguchi, who didn't know what to say.

"Swallow, then shake his hand," Munroe said.

She did what he suggested.

"I'm sorry I caught you mid munch," Montoya said, "but Harry pointed you out and I had to come over and say hello."

Yamaguchi had finally recovered her poise. "Yes, sir, thank you."

"Is your partner here?"

"Yes he is."

"May I speak to him?" he asked.

"Anything you say, sir, is translated for him, so you're already talking to him."

"Say hi for me. Tell him I like his police department," Munroe said.

"Munroe says hello, and he wants me to say he likes your police department."

By now, two other people Yamaguchi and Munroe didn't recognize had joined the group and a round of laughter greeted Munroe's remark.

"Does he? Well, good. Look, would you mind accompanying me as I introduce the two of you to some people."

She nodded, and said, "Alex says he'd be happy to … uh … "

Montoya looked at her with a grin. "I think the expression is a dog and pony show. Yes, I want to show you off to some people, with your permission."

She nodded again and Montoya led them to another group of people clustered around the conductor, Marie Alton, the star of the evening.

Montoya made introductions to the group and the conductor was intrigued. "I understand that the disembodied can't hear, so I certainly appreciate your spending an evening at a concert that might have been boring for you."

Yamaguchi could hardly believe what Munroe was asking her to relay.

"On the contrary, I had a very good time and I was actually on stage toward the end of the performance. Although I can't hear, I can still recognize the harmony of your orchestra."

The conductor nodded her head graciously at this and lifted her glass. Yamaguchi shot Munroe a silent "you went to see the blonde, right?"

"Quiet. They're eating this up," Munroe told her. He gave her more poetic observations of his time on the stage to relate.

Yamaguchi was soon fielding questions for Munroe left and right. "No, I can't see other disembodied people." "No, I can't pass through walls." "Yes, I don't need to sleep."

After ten minutes, many of the standard questions had been asked and answered. Again she marveled that people always asked Munroe questions to which they already knew the answers. Nobody ever asked him questions like, "How do you spend all that time?" to which she'd enjoy really knowing the answer.

Chief Moncrief pulled her aside after the questions had died down. "Good job, Yamaguchi. I appreciate you keeping Munroe in line."

"Actually, he was good as gold, sir," she answered. "And you know, he is listening."

"Yes, I know. But remember, I hired you, Munroe, and I know the Seattle chief of detectives pretty well, so I also know your reputation. So, thanks to both of you. It will be remembered." The chief returned to the group that had begun reforming around the conductor.

"Sounds like you made major kiss up points, Linda," Munroe said.

"You didn't do so bad yourself," she muttered.

"Talking to your partner?" a man asked her. He'd

joined the group after the introductions so she didn't know who he was, but he looked familiar. He was handsome, tall with short blond hair and blue eyes and around 40 to 45. Then she saw the "AV" pin on his lapel.

"Sorry, just curious," he apologized.

Munroe sensed another field and he knew the man was carrying a portable terminal, but like his partner's, it wasn't set for anonymous access.

"Yes, I was," she said. "Talking to my partner, that is."

The man stuck out his hand. "Bill Rybold," he said. She reached out to shake his hand but quickly moved it to cover her mouth when she sneezed.

"Um, Linda Yamaguchi," she said, and took a tissue out of her bag. He took back his hand.

"And your partner is … Alex Munroe, correct?"

"Yes, I'm sorry, I should have said. I know you, don't I?" she asked while dabbing her nose.

The man grinned. "I don't think we've met. I would have remembered. You might have seen me on television or in the newspaper."

"Oh sure," she said. "You own the cable company. But I thought … I mean, I didn't realize that …" Yamaguchi wasn't sure how to proceed. Despite her acceptance and familiarity with the disembodied, she had never met an avatar before. "Help me out here," she said silently to Munroe. Avatars were mostly a luxury for show biz types or the ultra rich.

"Why do you think I know what to do?"

"bcause ur dead."

"Go ahead, play the dead card. I don't know. I think you're supposed to just play along and pretend this guy really is Rybold."

The man decided to help her out by ignoring her difficulty. "I don't own the cable company. I am — or was — the CEO. When I died, I lost the job. But with a few others, I still have a controlling interest in the company."

"Oh, that's right," she said aloud, now remembering all she'd read about Rybold, who'd died a year or two ago. He was one of a growing number of people who'd prepared for his afterlife by creating a trust that would oversee his interests after his death, with the proceeds going to a bank account that only he could access. "Uh, why were you curious if I was talking to my partner?"

"I was wondering why you weren't speaking to him directly. Wouldn't that be more convenient, Officer Munroe?"

"I'm afraid I'm still a lot more comfortable, and more accurate, allowing the terminal to translate what I say out loud. If I try to use the field, I get a headache after a while. Uh, Munroe says I'm getting a lot better at it, but that he still has to figure out my shorthand sometimes. I tend to think in chat shorthand when I use the field myself. It's just a little bit easier but he hates it."

"You don't use shorthand yourself, Officer Munroe?"

"He says, 'You can skip the officer. Just Munroe. Or Alex.' And he never uses shorthand or emoticons or abbreviations. Says it dilutes the beauty of the language. I think he just likes to show off."

"Interesting. And, if I may ask, how did you get this job, Officer Yamaguchi?"

"Oh, please, just call me Linda. I … uh … well, my mom's dead … I mean disembodied. So I had some familiarity with the disembodied and when I went through the AfterNet orientation … because my mom insisted … that's when I found out that I could access the field pretty easily. And just about that time the department was looking for someone to work with Munroe. He says I lost and I ended up with him," she said, smiling.

"It sounds like you two have a good partnership. I was talking to your chief and he was saying, Alex, that you've been a great help to the department."

"LOL," said Yamaguchi.

"Excuse me?"

"He just proved me wrong."

"Oh, I get it," Rybold said, with a quick grin. "Let me ask a possibly rude question. Although you're undoubtedly a great asset for the police department, aren't you feeling a little … under utilized."

She was surprised that Munroe hadn't groaned when he heard "under utilized."

"Go on," she prompted. "Uh, that's Alex who said that."

"As I understand it, you were a detective, a homicide detective, and you had a very good reputation in Seattle. In fact, there was a book about a serial murderer in which you were prominently featured."

Yamaguchi said, "I never knew that. Sorry, please continue." She said silently to Munroe, "the only reputation I thought u had was pain in the ass."

"It just seemed to me that your skills are being wasted, Alex. Frankly, I think the department just thinks of you as a piece of equipment."

"Ouch, that hit home," she thought to herself. "You're not kidding," Munroe replied, and she realized that she'd let her thoughts leak into the field.

"Are you trying to steal my officers, Bill?" asked the police chief, who appeared from behind and clapped his arms around her shoulders. "I wondered how long it would be before you started chumming the waters. Great party by the way." The chief was putting his body between her and Rybold, Munroe noted.

"Thank you, Harry. And yes, I'm always on the lookout for people. Now, if you'll excuse me, I have other guests I should meet." He nodded to her. "Officers," he said, with a nod.

After Rybold left, the chief asked, "What's he been asking you?"

"Uh, sorry sir, he was, well mostly he was interested in how Munroe and I talk. You know, how I use the field."

"That's it?"

"Well, other than that last remark, which I guess you heard."

"OK, well, stay away from him."

"Did he pay for this reception?"

"What? Well, yes. Anyway, he gave the money to the CSO and that money went directly into this party. Look, I got more people to meet and greet. You two enjoy yourselves." The chief nodded brusquely and left.

"So, what the hell was all that about?" asked Munroe.

"Wheels within wheels, Alex. It is not for us the little people to question," she said quietly. "Hey, I want to get more food."

"You go ahead, I'm going to find a terminal hotspot. I'm kind of curious."

"OK, I'm going to sit after I get the food. These heels are getting painful."

She left and Munroe moved around the crowd and found three hotspots. He found a locally hosted chat room and discovered that there were about 50 disembodied people attending the party. Actually, there were probably many more, but only about 50 invited guests were able to login.

He found a conversation in progress.

brian.sullivan: got lousy advice from my broker
poodletoy: you still think this is a bubble
jollycopper has entered the room
paulieg: well, isnit?
sweetMary: I think someone new has joined us
jollycopper: Hello, didn't know there was a chat going on here.
brian.sullivan: what else we going to do for fun?
poodletoy: Youre the cop, right?
jollycopper: Yes, Alex Munroe. How did you know?
poodletoy: Rybold's been talking about you.

jollycopper: Really, when?

ribaldhumor: Just now, actually. Nice to speak to you directly, Alex.

jollycopper: Mr. Rybold? Oh, yes, there you are in the list.

ribaldhumor: Please, if I can call you Alex, call me Bill. I'm sorry if I got you in trouble with the chief.

jollycopper: Hey, I think my stock went up with the chief.

sweetMary: Bill dear trying to cause trouble? Headhunting again?

ribaldhumor: That's how I got to know some of you. By the way, I feel I've been neglecting you.

Munroe had located Rybold's avatar in the crowd, who seemed to be holding a spirited conversation with the conductor. He wondered if the avatar was cruising on autopilot or if Rybold was holding two conversations at once.

paulieg: thats right neglecting ur dead friends. how rude ;)

ribaldhumor: And I'm afraid I'll be neglecting you again. Even for me it's hard to hold five conversations at once. Alex, if you don't mind, once tonight is over, I'll send you an email. There are some things I'd like to discuss.

jollycopper: OK, I'll look for it.

ribaldhumor has left the room

sweetMary: so, lets get to know you better alex.

Yamaguchi ate with all the enthusiasm a healthy, hungry woman with the metabolism of a hummingbird can muster. She knew she'd never have to pay the price of overeating. Her mother remained thin all her life, and her father was still rail thin. She figured she had years to go before she had to worry about her weight. And for once she was eating without Munroe around who loved to remind her of the dangers of cholesterol, fat and colon cancer.

As she licked her fingers of the tiramisu fragments she

became aware that someone else was sitting down at her table.

"I've never seen anyone eat like that, except me," said a rich, low voice. She saw a handsome, solidly built black man looking at her as she was removing her thumb from her mouth.

"Hmm?"

"I said I've never seen anyone else eat like that," he said again.

"Sorry," she said.

"Hey, don't apologize. Just don't let my wife see you. She'd kill you in a minute," he laughed. He reached his big right hand across the table, "Ron Elbert."

She took a quick look at her hand before she took his. "Like the mountain? — Linda Yamaguchi."

Elbert, looked puzzled, then said, "Oh, I get it. I'm not a native, you know. Yes, I saw you talking to Bill Rybold. You're the cop with the dead partner. Excuse me, disembodied partner."

"And you are …"

"I work at *The Denver Post*."

"No you don't. You're the editor of *The Denver Post*." She recognized him now. She gave him a ticket two years ago, before she teamed with Munroe. She didn't think he'd recognized her from that, however.

"That's right. Some people don't consider what I do work." He laughed loud and deep. She recalled that he was an intimidating but friendly man, a weird combination that impressed her, even while he was sitting in his car calmly accepting his ticket.

"So, Linda, what did Rybold want?" Apparently he was also a man who used first names unasked.

"I'm not really sure. Maybe he was trying to hire me. My partner for sure."

"Interesting. Mr. Rybold's a busy man."

"What makes you say that?"

"Because he's been hiring a lot of disembodied people lately, or anyway, he's been said to be hiring them. He's been hiring almost as many people as the AfterNet, but it's hard to confirm." Elbert stood up and Yamaguchi realized he was at least six feet five. "Nice to meet you again, Linda, under better circumstances, at least for me. See you again sometime." He nodded and left.

"Who was he?" Munroe asked in her ear.

"Hey you're back."

"I leave you alone a minute and you've already got a boyfriend."

"Cool it, dad. A, you were gone at least 20 minutes, and B, he's the editor of *The Denver Post*, and I think he was pumping me for info about your admirer, Mr. Rybold."

"And I just had another contact with him in a chat room they set up here. There're about 50 disembodied people invited to the party here."

"Really, and Elbert, that's the *Post* editor, said Rybold's been hiring a lot of disembodied people."

"Seems like I'm a hot commodity," he said. "And I'm sure you are too, of course."

"Don't go getting a swelled head, Alex," she said and stifled a yawn.

"Getting tired?"

"Yeah, I think I am. I'm not used to these intrigues and I'm freezing."

"You do have goose bumps that go all over," he said, after looking at her in infrared. "I think we've done our job. Let's head out."

She took one last long gulp from what he was pleased to see was a glass of water and got up. The reception was still going strong and in one corner of the room, people were being photographed with the departing conductor.

"Leaving already, Officer Munroe?" the disembodied something asked him through the terminal field at the door. By now, he was starting to view the terminal and hotspots throughout the ballroom as more intrusive than courteous and didn't answer back. He and Yamaguchi made their exit after she collected her coat and returned to her car with little conversation except for the occasional assurances he gave her that he was in tow.

Back in the car, she put her portable terminal back in the armband and wore it clumsily around the sleeve of her coat. But she also turned on the car radio to listen to NPR. Munroe tried to remember what she'd be listening to at this time on a Saturday night and guessed it would be some sort of new age ambient crap — or at least that was his interpretation of her description of it. He remembered that his estimation of her fell considerably the first time she mentioned that she liked that kind of thing. And he remembered her disparaging remark when he mentioned that he liked improvisational jazz. They were reduced to one-word conversations that week. Then he saw her eyelids droop.

"Hey, Gooch, wake up!"

"What … what did you call me?"

"You were falling asleep listening to that stuff. Put on something loud or open a window."

"Are you kidding? It's freezing outside." But she did reach forward to turn off the radio. "Just talk to me, keep me awake."

He realized that they were nearing the department. "Listen, Linda, don't drop me off at the department. Drive yourself home and I'll keep you company on the way."

She reached up to pinch herself on the cheek. "OK, but what are you going to do?"

"We'll figure it out once we get there," he said.

She drove to her apartment while Munroe kept up an inane commentary on the upcoming Broncos-Seahawks game, which normally wouldn't have interested her, but he prodded her to say something in the affirmative to each remark. Before too long she was getting irritable, but at least she was awake.

They finally reached her Congress Park apartment and she parked on the street. She rented the lower floor of a converted Denver square. It was relatively expensive for the area but she enjoyed the charm of the building. At the door, she yawned and asked him, "OK, what's the plan? Do you stay here tonight? Do I call you a taxi?"

"Well, first go in, because you're freezing."

She opened the door and they went inside.

"If you don't mind, I'll stay here to … wait a minute, you can log me onto the AfterNet, right?"

"Huh? Sure."

"Just tether your terminal to your computer and I'll be happy, that is if you don't mind me spending the night. And maybe in the morning you can drive me to the station."

She yawned and nodded. "I'd be happy if you spend the night. Let me … make up the computer for you." She laughed and walked toward her bedroom. "Come on, it's this way."

He followed her and realized he hadn't known that's where she kept her computer. Her bedroom was large and oddly L-shaped. She had turned the stubby arm of the L into an office nook where her laptop sat on a roll top desk. She sat down before it and turned on the computer, then plugged her terminal into a recharging dock connected to the computer.

"Crap," she said, when she realized that she hadn't acted quickly enough to force her Macintosh laptop into the AfterNet OS during startup. She restarted it and this time clicked quickly enough to launch the proper OS.

He didn't catch any of this because he was too busy looking around her bedroom. Like her it was tasteful but definitely not feminine. It was decorated in the Arts and Crafts style of heavy dark furniture, with a Mission-style bed, a mock Morris chair and the yellowish-greenish wallpaper he remembered from his own Arts and Crafts house in Seattle.

Just because Nadine liked Arts and Crafts doesn't mean it's bad, he thought to himself, remembering his second wife, the dragon lady and queen of the damned. *And I'm sure it doesn't mean Linda's a bad person.*

He noticed that she had shrugged off her coat and suddenly he sensed the AfterNet field again, temporarily off while the computer was rebooting.

"OK, it's up, Alex. Yo, Alex?"

He only caught his name, but he guessed she was telling him the computer was ready.

"I'm here. Uh, I didn't know your computer was in your bedroom."

"Oh, I could move it into the living room but I'd have to move the terminal's dock and get behind the desk to get to the adapter and ..." Her comments trailed off.

"No, no, that's OK. I don't want to make trouble. It's just that, you know, you in bed and me here ..."

She rolled her eyes and he knew the discussion was over. "Oh, yes, well I'll just have to sleep with my gun under the pillow."

She got up from the chair, repositioned it before the desk and then put a throw pillow on the seat. Munroe settled on the chair, feeling more like a dog than a man but appreciating that the pillow brought him up to "eye" level of the computer.

She started undressing, but stopped and walked into her bathroom, closing the door behind her.

Well, at least I rate that much, he thought.

She came back out a few minutes later, wearing a Denver police academy T-shirt and flannel pajama bottoms. She crawled into her bed and then looked toward him. "Good night, Alex."

"Good night, Linda." She turned off the lights and went to sleep.

CHAPTER 3

From *The Atlantic Monthly*

The trees in the Aokigahara forest can cast dismal shadows even in summer, but in the winter, the funereal gloom looks especially inviting to those who brave the maze-like trails of this haunted forest.

It's suicide season.

"It really increases as we get closer to the New Year," said Tetsuo Harada, an official with the Yamanashi Prefecture parks department. "Since the afterlife, it's only gotten worse."

The Aokigahara Jukai, literally "Aokigahara tree ocean," has a long history in Japanese folklore and urban legend. Magnetic compasses reportedly don't work in the forest and steep paths have sent many to injury or death, despite the stone statues of Jizo Bodhisattva that are supposed to guard the traveler.

The forest was infamous as a place to end one's life long before the discovery of the afterlife in 1997. Ken Takamura, a professor of behavioral science at the Medical College Research Institute of Tokyo and author of "Aokigahara-jukai: Forest of Death in the shadow of Mt. Fuji," has said, "The problem in Japan is that there are more sites where people are exchanging suicide methods, looking for partners, than there are sites devoted to prevention.

"Now the suicide parties are organized. They pack in computers, terminals, satellite uplinks and they go online and synchronize their deaths with others around the country. And the forest, unfortunately, lures them."

In Japan, the national government has declared the suicide problem an "epidemic that can't be cured by medicine or relieved by public awareness."

"Everyone knows that people are killing themselves left and right," said Randall Levinson, a visiting scholar at Keio University's International Center. "But they can't do a thing about it. The problem's gotten so bad there have been schools that have had to cancel classes — too many students killed themselves. It's the siren call of the afterlife."

It wasn't a good night for Yamaguchi. Munroe counted five trips to the bathroom. She apparently never even remembered that he was there, or at least he so assumed from the fact that she never even glanced at the desk.

OK, well, I guess I never need to worry about that again, he thought to himself on maybe the second or third trip when he peeked into the bathroom and saw her perched over the toilet.

He went back to the computer and continued planning his trip for next month when she would be leaving town for a wedding and he thought he could take the trip to Egypt he'd always wanted. The website promised a living tour guide and a portable terminal with full Internet wireless access. Start in Cairo and the pyramids, then Karnak at Luxor, Valley of the Kings and finally Abu Simbel, all by riverboat and all for $500 per person. *The living would die to get these kinds of prices,* he thought to himself. *Not that many of them are brave enough to go.* With the instability of the Middle East since the discovery of the afterlife, Western tourism, at least among the living, had all but dried up.

He looked at the pictures again and thought of wife number one, Marlene, who turned him onto all things Egyptian, and also turned him off college professors who cheated on their husbands.

Next he checked his email again and found a response from AfterNet security.

From: security@theAfterNet.net
To: jollycopper@denverpd.org
Subject: Re: Missing persons inquiry
Date: December 19, 2004 2:32 a.m. MST

This is an automated response to notify you that we have received your inquiry. Please do not reply to …

So, nothing so far, but what else did he expect on a weekend.

He did, however, get an email from Bill Rybold.

From: (Bill Rybold) Bill.Rybold@theAfterNet.net
To: jollycopper@denverpd.org
Subject: Good to meet you
Date: December 19, 2004 1:10 a.m. MST

Dear Alex,

Enjoyed meeting you at the reception. Hope I didn't get you in hot water with your chief, but I think I probably raised your standing in the department.

By now, you suspect that I know your situation with the department. I know that your salary is actually coming out of an equipment budget because of the police union and I think that's emblematic of not only the department's view of you, but also the attitude of many government agencies and businesses. We disembodied — and yes, between you and me and others like us, I don't hide my status — have to stand up for our rights, otherwise we run the danger of being marginalized. (Did you see The New Yorker article: "Dispossessed and disembodied"?)

Sorry, didn't mean to get up on the soap box.

Now, I'm also sure that you know that I want to hire you, but you don't know for what. Why do I require the services of a homicide detective? Well, I don't require a detective, but I do need your brain (rubs hands and chortles maniacally). I need people who match a certain profile and have certain abilities to work for a start-up company, but I don't want to go into the details now.

Also, your next step is to do some research on me, and I'd like you to be informed before our next meeting.

If you're amenable, contact my secretary, Phyllis (see below), and let's set up a meeting.

Again, nice to meet you.

Bill

So Munroe researched Bill Rybold. He found several pictures from before Rybold's death and saw that his avatar did not at all resemble him. In life, Rybold was short, dumpy and plain. *Well, who wouldn't want to look better after their death?* He was 54 when he died.

Although not much to look at, he was apparently a very good businessman, rising up the corporate ladder in the very competitive Denver telecommunications world, and then surprising everyone by taking the top job in a relatively minor player in the field. But Rybold took ClearView Cable (now ClearView Broadband) into the Fortune 500 quickly.

His business expertise wasn't his only achievement, however. He was a bona fide geek, with several patents to his name in the telecom field. And Munroe found news profiles of Rybold that applauded his business *and* his management skills. When he took over ClearView, he didn't fire everyone and install his own team, but worked with what he had. There were several quotes from employees, from upper management to cable installers, which praised Rybold.

Unfortunately, he was saddled with a board of directors

who wanted to take a buyout offer from a competitor, which Rybold successfully fought until his death from some kind of freak pancreatic cancer, after which Rybold was removed as CEO and chairman.

After his death, Rybold didn't fight the removal and seemed to vanish until a few months ago when a columnist in the *Rocky Mountain News* spotted his avatar at a fund-raising dinner. Since then, Rybold came back with his new persona in a big way by sponsoring the reception. Munroe couldn't find any information on the man Rybold had hired to be his avatar.

All in all, Rybold seemed like a decent, if possibly vain man. *Of course, if I looked like that, I think I'd want to find someone better looking.*

He thought about Rybold's assessment of his situation within the department.

God knows he's right. What am I to the department besides their latest crime-fighting tool? What do I owe them? But the chief did give me a break when he hired me. And maybe I made some progress tonight and they'll think of me as a person.

Munroe found the secretary's email address and phone number. He added the information to his address list. Then he saw Yamaguchi turn over and get out of bed for the sixth trip to the bathroom.

About 7 a.m., Yamaguchi woke briefly.

"Alex, you there?"

"How you doing, partner?"

"I feel like dog poo."

"Yes, I gathered that."

"What time is it?" she asked.

"It's about seven. Go back to sleep."

"Need to take you back to the station," she said as she slowly tugged the covers away from her.

"Forget it. Look, I'll call a cab later — Metro's pretty good at picking up the disembodied. Is the front door locked?"

"Uh huh."

"OK, when you feel better, unlock the door and I'll tell them to knock and open it for me. For now, go back to sleep." He got no reply and realized she'd already gone back to sleep with her ear buds clutched in her hand.

He realized that he'd been online seven hours straight, but the time had gone pleasantly after he'd found Melissa in one of the chat rooms. She was in New York City and she'd been dead 20 years, dying when she was 21. She died a long time before the discovery of the afterlife in 1997 and the start of the AfterNet in 2001, but remarkably she was a warm, funny, sane person, which Munroe doubted he'd have been in the same situation.

She had found his unabbreviated sentence structure in the chat room "quaint," while she used every contraction in the book, which he found maddening. He found it funny that at 41 years old, she was still a 21-year-old who seemed clued in to every fad of the last 20 years and apparently knew the plot of every episode of *Friends* and *Seinfeld*.

jollycopper: When did you start watching them?
messym: when they startd
jollycopper: They started before the AfterNet, didn't they?
messym: ? Duh.
jollycopper: You watched them without sound?
messym: :) watchd em at def cupls house whre i lived most of the 90s. they wre gr8, cute baby 2, and they wer young, in there 20s & they watchd alotta tv. a real barbie and ken but nice. i still keep in touch, but they wre freakd when they found out id been livng with em. funny there almost 50 now

Munroe had difficulty deciphering what she wrote at

times. He bet it took more effort for her to come up with her abbreviations than to type out a complete sentence. He was wrong, of course, she was forever 21 and knew when something was hip or *passé*, further surprising him by using *passé*. She eventually gave in to his requests and began using fewer abbreviations and he had a long conversation with her. He was fascinated by how she'd spent all those years alone without going mad, and he realized that her frozen state of maturity was her defense.

He added Melissa's name to his buddy list and she said she'd do the same, but he had few hopes. *I feel even more like a dirty old man than I do with Linda,* he thought.

Linda finally woke up again about eight and unlocked the door. She stumbled through the house like a zombie and other than a few incoherent ramblings didn't speak except to say, "Good night, Alex," after which she went back to bed.

The taxi arrived fifteen minutes later, the driver relocking the door behind him, and took Munroe to the Cherry Creek Mall. A lot of disembodied gathered at the mall Sunday mornings, using the public terminals throughout as ad hoc chat rooms. The elderly mall walkers, who enjoyed the peace and quiet of the mall before it opened for regular business, often joined them. The living were understandably curious about what awaited them and the disembodied, many of whom had no living relatives and were unable to contact their relatives on the AfterNet, viewed the elderly as an extended family waiting to happen. Most of the disembodied who attended the coffee klatch were themselves older when they died. Munroe perversely enjoyed being one of the younger ones.

The rest of the day he spent at the Denver Public Library, then the Tattered Cover bookstore and finally back to the station. He did get an email from Yamaguchi earlier in the day saying that she was alive. Back at the station, he also got an email from Yamaguchi's mother (addressed to him through his AfterNet address), asking him whether he knew why she hadn't returned her messages.

How the hell did she get my email address? he wondered, then realized she probably just looked it up from his postings. *I really shouldn't post my address everywhere. I hope I don't have to change it.* He sent her back a message saying that Linda was sick and that he was sure she'd return her email messages once she felt better.

And he got back a real response from AfterNet security.

From: (Steve Howland) Steve.Howland2@theAfterNet.net
To: jollycopper@denverpd.org
Subject: Re: Missing persons inquiry 20041219-0324
Date: December 19, 2004 5:34 p.m. MST

Dear Officer Munroe,

I'm sorry about the delay in getting back to you regarding your inquiry about Brian Thompson (minerofLove). We always want to work with the police, but your situation made it difficult because we can't normally initiate a trace based on an email request, but my supervisor said to go ahead because it's you.

Mr. Thompson last logged in to denver.theAfterNet.net at 3:35 p.m. MST December 11 from the downtown branch of the Denver Public Library. He used a public terminal, stayed on 23 minutes and went to the entertainment forum. He didn't leave any messages. He doesn't use the AfterNet as his email server, so we don't know when he last checked his mail, but his address is brianthompson4@hotmail.com, so I'm afraid you'll need to get any other email information from Microsoft.

If you have any other questions, feel free to contact me again,

or if I'm off duty, just tell anyone at security@theAfterNet.net
that your case number is 20041219-0324 and they can look
up this incident.

Thanks,
Steve Howland
AfterNet security

Munroe sent a quick email to Brian's mother, quoting
the message from AfterNet security and also asking
whether she'd heard from Brian. Then he opened a
browser and went to the Denver subdomain of the After-
Net and the entertainment forum. He did a search and
looked for all the messages that were posted in the forum
from Dec. 5 through Dec. 11. Most of the messages were
mundane: some Christmas party invitations (including a
Christmas Eve get together at the downtown Tattered
Cover sponsored by the AfterNet — *I should remember
that*), a poetry reading by a disembodied author (*I won't
remember that*) and a plug for the Christmas lights at the
Denver Botanic Garden.

So far, Munroe didn't see anything that would be of interest to a disembodied 23-year-old out-of-towner. Of
course, it was possible that a message that referred to an
event during that timeframe had already been removed. So
Munroe left a message in the forum asking any visitors
whether they knew of such an event. He wasn't optimistic
— many of the visitors to the forum were one-time or in-
frequent visitors, but he couldn't think what else to do. He
also sent another message to AfterNet security to see if
they could retrieve deleted messages, but he wasn't hope-
ful about that, either.

Munroe spent the rest of the night and the early morning reading. He had discovered Project Gutenberg and
right now was devouring Edgar Rice Burroughs. He'd
remembered reading *A Princess of Mars* as a kid and now

the idea of the ageless John Carter, fighting man of Virginia, delighted him.

About 9 a.m. Monday morning one of the detectives in missing persons came by and taped something on the side of Munroe's terminal, with the note "Thought you'd find this funny." It was a cartoon and was adapted from the old *New Yorker* cartoon showing two dogs at a computer and the caption, "On the Internet, nobody knows you're a dog." This one showed the Grim Reaper, with the trademark sickle, sitting at a terminal and the caption, "On the Internet, nobody knows you're not dead."

Munroe stared at it awhile and just couldn't find the humor. He knew what they were going for, but it just didn't have the right — something. He also couldn't figure out the detective's motive for leaving the cartoon. Was it really just "thought you'd find this funny" or "we know you don't really exist" or "we don't think you should be taking a job from someone living"?

Whatever the motive, Munroe was now stuck with it until Yamaguchi was back. And should he even ask her to remove it? Would it brand him as someone without a sense of humor? — a death sentence, so to speak, among cops. At least they'd finally stopped stealing his chair. Maybe this was a form of acceptance from them. He'd never had any problems with Rollins, the detective who'd left the cartoon. Rollins *was* black after all; he should be sympathetic with the plight of another minority. *Hmm, was that a bigoted assumption of mine?*

Of course, the disembodied weren't a minority. With hundreds of billions more dead than alive, some living viewed them as a real threat.

And Rollins might know that Munroe was there from the activity on the terminal's screen, so should he respond now? Send an email to him? What should he say?

While living, this was a situation that Munroe had rarely encountered. He prided himself on being able to handle almost any situation — apart from ex-wives. He had been, after all, a white, male cop — lord of all he surveyed — although he liked to think he never let *that* sort of thinking affect his attitude or behavior. But now he found himself questioning his ability to act like a cop.

Well screw that, he thought. He opened up a new email window and sent a one-line message to Rollins: "Very droll."

Let him figure that one out. Sometimes the ambiguity of email had its uses.

Munroe got out of the station before he had to deal with the consequences of his reply. He spent the morning at the same Starbucks and even got a few hellos from the crowd. This morning the table the terminal sat on also housed a few empty coffee cups — he didn't know if this was an attempt by the baristas to make the table seem more homey or more likely just the attractive force between an open surface and an empty cup.

Munroe got into a chat with the others and found that two of them had been customers of this particular Starbucks while alive. And another person was still working as a consultant for the company she worked at while alive, just a block away, and she often used the store as her office.

Munroe had wondered at Starbucks' financial incentive for installing the terminal, but the others online pointed out that aside from the initial investment for the terminal, it cost them almost nothing. And the consultant also mentioned that she had a meeting in an hour in the Starbucks, and her living coworkers certainly drank coffee.

The word "office" prompted Munroe to check his email and he saw that he had a reply from Rollins.

From: (Joshua Rollins) Joshua.Rollins@denverpd.org
To: jollycopper@denverpd.org
Subject: Missing disembodied report

Date: December 20 2004 9:15 a.m. MST

Munroe,

Glad you liked it. Hey, I was hoping you could do me a favor. I have a missing persons report filed by a Cheryl Miller on a disembodied woman, a dead Fort Carson woman, Staff Sgt. Tralawna Johnson. She was supposed to meet with Johnson in Denver last week and they never hooked up. She hasn't heard from Johnson since then.
You know we don't really have a policy on this. I don't even know where I'd begin. Would you mind taking a look?

Thanks

Josh

The email had an attachment containing the missing persons' report.

Munroe replied to Rollins, saying he'd contact Cheryl Miller, and then he emailed the woman, who was living, and asked if they could meet to chat.

While writing up the emails, he also saw that he'd got an email from Brian's mother saying that she still hadn't heard from him. She also said that she'd learned that Brian had a blog and gave him the address.

OK, two missing dead people reports a few days apart. He looked more closely at the report Rollins had sent and saw the date that Sgt. Johnson was supposed to meet Miller. *Correction, possibly the same day if I take Brian's disappearance from the AfterNet as the date he went missing. Two disappearances don't make a pattern,* Munroe thought to himself. *Still, it gives me something to do.*

Well, let's see when Sgt. Johnson dropped off the AfterNet, he thought to himself. He sent another message to Steve Howland asking for that information.

Munroe decided he needed to go back to the department and made his farewells to the group. Someone asked, "Same time tomorrow?"

Yamaguchi woke up to her ringing phone about 10 a.m.

"Hello," she said, after smacking her lips a few times to break up the gunk in her mouth. She was a little confused and was unsure what day it was. *Is today Monday?*

"Why didn't you reply to my email?"

"Mom?"

"I talked to your partner. He said you're sick."

Yamaguchi hated it when her mother used the phone. Her mother had paid someone to digitize her voice from recordings she had saved on her computer so she could use her own voice when calling people. Yamaguchi hated it. Although she'd gotten used to the idea of having a disembodied mother, the sound of her mother's voice on the phone was too eerie — especially with the slight Scandinavian-like accent that the speech synthesizer introduced.

"Yes, mom, I'm sick. I think I have the flu."

"Go to the doctor. You're sick."

"The doctor can't do anything. Mom, just send me an email. Or I can chat later. I just don't feel up to talking."

"Did your partner stay last night?"

"What?" *How the hell would she know that?* "Sorry, Mom, I … think I'm getting another call. It may be important, bye."

She hung up and didn't answer the phone when it rang a few minutes later. *Mom, don't do this, not today.*

The phone didn't ring again and Yamaguchi relaxed, hoping that her mother had given up. *This isn't fair,* she thought. *I shouldn't have to put up with her after she's dead. I hope to God she doesn't call the watch commander.* She still shuddered at the thought of the time an officer had come to her door on a "check the welfare." She was a rookie cop then. There were still cops two years later who could bring that up.

The fear her mother's call had induced made it impossible for her to go back to sleep. She got out of bed and went into the kitchen. She cleaned rice and put it in the rice maker and then made green tea the way her mother had taught her. She couldn't help but think of the last year of her mother's life. She had stopped taking her medication and had slid further into depression.

Her mother had loomed so large in her life then. Her father had left her mother a few years earlier. She couldn't really blame him, but after he moved back to Japan, she was the one responsible for her mother. Her father paid generous alimony, but it still left her with the day-to-day care of her mother, making sure she took her pills, paid her bills and remembered to eat.

She hated to admit it, but her mother's death came as a relief, a relief that lasted only a few months when her mother contacted her through the AfterNet.

She sat down at the kitchen table and poured her strong green tea from the small ceramic pot her mother insisted made the best tea. She could almost feel her mother's presence.

Oh, my God, she isn't here, is she? She ran back into the bedroom and saw that Munroe had shut down her notebook. OK, she couldn't have been calling from here. And the last time I checked, she was still in Japan, making life miserable for Dad.

She went back to the kitchen after taking the computer with her. While the rice cooker rattled, she checked her email. She saw a message from Munroe, telling her that her mother had emailed him.

Oh great, now I've dragged him into my circle of hell. She also looked at the last email her mother sent her and saw that it originated from the same Japanese mail server as before.

Suddenly she felt weak and she realized she was sweating, probably from her illness but she knew part of it was her fear.

I do love her, but she's quite insane.

The rice maker pinged and she got up and transferred the cooked rice to a pot and added water. She set that to boil. The rice quickly became a thick glop while she absentmindedly stirred it.

I suppose I could bounce back her emails. Oh right, remember the time you changed your phone number? she asked herself.

After a few more minutes, she got shoyu from the cupboard. Then she took an egg and the Ziplock of sour plums from the refrigerator. She added the egg to the pot, stirring it in. After the egg had cooked in the hot rice, she removed the pot from the heat and transferred the rice to a small Japanese bowl, her mother's favorite. She poured the shoyu, sprinkled dried fish shavings from a small plastic package and added the plums. It was the same food her mother always made for her when she was a little girl and was sick, and it was also the last meal she had made for her mother before she died. It would make most Westerners gag but was good for little Japanese girls and sick dogs, too, her mother would always tell her.

As usual, the food did the trick. The rice settled her stomach and the green tea quieted the caffeine withdrawal she was suffering. She put the dishes in the sink and went back to the bedroom and watched TV. That evening, she chatted with her mother.

He didn't know how long he had been waiting for something to happen. Unable to feel a pulse or hear his own breathing, he didn't have the cues to tell him how long he existed in the empty, dark void. He couldn't even tell if he was restrained. He'd have to be able to detect his motion relative to something in order to tell, so he couldn't tell if he was in a vast empty space or still in the box they used to trap him.

He had tried to see something in the darkness, but his environment was as empty of visual light as it was of the larger spectrum of which he was capable of detecting.

Maybe I finally am really, truly dead, he thought to himself. *Maybe I transitioned from being disembodied to this. Oh, that's stupid. Somebody forced me into this, and I don't mean God.*

He thought again about the other people in the room when the walls started closing. *Are they in here with me?* If they were, he had no way of knowing.

Suddenly light — visible bright daylight — hit him from every direction. He was suddenly outside in a park on a gorgeous summer day, which made no sense. It was December. And he was moving. Or more correctly, he was somehow being moved, against his will. He couldn't fight against it. He couldn't even feel that he could fight against it. He seemed to simply be flowing, like a leaf drifting in a stream.

He watched as children played in the park and he moved toward them. A young woman, his age, with long brown hair, threw a Frisbee back to one of the children and then walked toward him. She had a smile on her face and she reached out a hand toward him, and he saw a hand clasp her hand. And he followed her and he realized she was holding his hand. He couldn't feel her flesh, or his either, but he longed to feel it, to feel her warmth in his hand.

And then the scene faded and he was back in the dark again. The sunlight, the woman, his hand, were gone, and he wanted them back.

CHAPTER 4

Defero per Mortuus
August 11, 2004
Encyclical of Pope John Paul II on developments involving communication with the dead.
To our Venerable Brethren
Health and the Apostolic Blessing!
The Holy Church has long taught that there is a place or condition of temporal punishment for those who depart this life in God's grace but are not entirely free of venial faults or have not fully paid for their transgressions. This has been clearly stated by the decree of the Council of Trent (Sess. XXV) and restated in the Lumen Gentium of the Second Vatican Council.

"Some of the disciples are pilgrims on earth, others have died and are being purified, while still others are in glory," (*Lumen Gentium*, N. 49, cf. Eugene IV, Bull *Laetentur coel.*)

There is no need to remind you, Venerable Brethren, of the recent discovery of means of communicating with what could well be the souls of those in such a place or condition, The news, alas, was marred by ill-fated riots, which involved much disorder and bloodshed.

Although the belief that the purification process involves actual fire has been common in Catholic tradition (Augustine in Ps. 37, n., St. Thomas in IV, dist., xxi, q., i., a1) the Church has never issued any dogmatic decree on the subject. The main distress, rather, is the separation of the soul from God. But that there is also the certitude that once the time of purification is over, the soul will go to meet the One it desires.

There is nothing in recent developments that contradicts the teachings of the church. Prayers still avail to help the dead in their place of purification, as they have since the earliest Christian tradition and all Christians still have a duty to use our prayers and sacrifices to aid those in purgatorial expiation.

The difficulties this situation engenders have most serious implications for the moral life of the faithful, but they do not in any way change our teachings.

Back at the station Monday afternoon, Munroe found an email from a detective, Theresa Sunderland, with whom he'd worked at the Seattle PD.

Alex, hope you remember me from your time here. I was just starting in investigations when you got sick. You were pretty nice to me and I appreciated your helping out a newbie.
I hope I can ask for your help again. We've got a case here that's awfully similar to ones you may remember -- the rapes in the Denny Regrade area. At that time, a couple aspects of the case were held back from public consumption. We've now got a spate of rapes with a similar MO and those same aspects have resurfaced. But this time around, the last victim was killed and the one before remains on life support.
I know that back then, the UW security guard was the best suspect we had, based on the psych profile, but he had an alibi. Then the rapes stopped. But I talked to Bob Baker, who says that you had named another suspect, but can't remember his name. (Baker's not doing so well and is in assisted living, btw.) I guess you weren't actually working the case so nothing came of it and I can't find anything in the case file.
I hoped you might give me a clue who you suspected. I'd appreciate the help. They still talk about you here like you were Sherlock Holmes.
Hope everything is good for you in Denver.

Munroe felt a little numb after reading the email. He realized he hadn't read a Seattle paper in weeks. *When did it stop being my city?* he thought. *I should have known about those rapes.* He was also a little shaken to see Bob Baker's name. Baker had been his partner back on patrol and they'd shared a lot. Including Munroe's wife, which he discovered after he'd died.

The email also dredged up the sad story of how he left the department. Although as a homicide detective, the rapes weren't in his purview, he'd offered his opinions. Several of his superiors, including the chief of detectives, however, were still fuming over the fallout from the stupid book in which he'd been mentioned. Munroe had found himself on the outside. He wasn't surprised his suspect wasn't named in the case file.

He felt old and sad as he replied to Sunderland's email and gave her the name of the man he suspected and his reasoning. He promised he'd give her any help she needed.

He was about to go to the *Seattle Times* website, when he saw he had a response from Cheryl Miller, the woman who reported her friend missing. Miller said she would be in the AfterNet's religion and faith chat room from 1 p.m. to at least 2:30 p.m. today and it was already 1:50.

remainsoftheday: jesus died for our sins so living or dead it really doesn't matter
jollycopper has entered the room
jesus31: its true I did
remainsoftheday: shut up freak, I mean the real jesus
godBpraised: hey, chill. we don't go questioning identies.
jesus31 has as much right to be here as anyone

Munroe recognized Miller's username: godBpraised. He clicked on it and saw that she was one of the moderators. He sent her a message, hoping they could chat privately.

godBpraised: thank god you finally showed up. I was getting bored.

jollycopper: Seems to me like you were being mom back there.

godBpraised: the recently dead can be so immature

jollycopper: Jesus claims to be recently dead?

godBpraised: Not him, the other one.

jollycopper: OK, whatever. I looked over your report. Detective Rollins already explained the police department can't actually investigate a missing disembodied person, right?

godBpraised: yes, but he said he knew someone who might help

jollycopper: That would be me. Can I ask why you're so concerned about Ms. Johnson? His notes say you only recently met online.

godBpraised: yes, she died just a month ago in a stupid traffic accident. she's a Ft Carson army soldier and she got sent to India as part of the "peacekeeping mission". She seemed to really need someone to talk to.

jollycopper: Did she have problems with her religious beliefs?

godBpraised: Yes, I'm afraid its a familiar story. A very religious person and I think a vrey good person. When she died, she felt abandoned by God. we met in this chat room. We talked a lot. I think talking to a living person comforted her.

jollycopper: Why's that, do you think?

godBpraised: Ive been alive a long time. Im 82 and thank God still haelthy, but I had a scare last year, had a stroke. I was prepared to move on and meet my friends online, but I got better. still cant type worth a damn. And I told her God gave us a gift when we discovered the atferlife. We chant question the timing of that gift, anymore than I can question why I had a stroke or why I got better.

jollycopper: I guess that's the only attitude that makes sense.

godBpraised: That's right, young … how old where you when you died.

jollycopper: 62

godBpraised: I guess your young compared to me then.

jollycopper: So, you arranged to meet at a church?

godBpraised: her idea. I took a bus down from Cheyenne to meet her.

jollycopper: What church?

godBpraised: Daniels AME, on 33rd Street. I guess she knew the minister there.

jollycopper: What do you think happened to her?

godBpraised: She said she was going somewhere Saturday night. meet some people, mix with the living. I said that might be a good idea. so I think shes stuck somewhere in a room or a closet or something stupid. shes doesn't have the instincts yet to check ehr exits

jollycopper: She'll probably get out eventually. We all do.

godBpraised: its not a good time for her to be trappd Think you can do something?

jollycopper: The best I can do is see when and where she was last logged in and backtrack from there. I assume you've been looking for her?

godBpraised: I have messages everywhere and I keep checking all teh chat areas.

jollycopper: Tell me if you find her. I'll also check out the church, ask around.

godBpraised: thank you. I should go. I think jesus jus insulted john the Baptist

Munroe left the chat room. The old woman had impressed him and he added her name to his address book. Then he tackled his next task, Brian Thompson's blog.

Brian used blogger, the same as Munroe. Brian's last entry was Dec. 9. His mother had posted messages asking him to contact her, the most recent posted yesterday. *I wonder if I can ask Google if Brian's accessed his account since Dec. 11.*

The page was a standard template. It was the usual

young person's blog, started when he was alive, a two-month gap around the time he died, then a lot of entries from around the world when he started his trip. There were a lot of photos of Brian with his friends — a nice if slightly dense-looking kid who enjoyed outdoor activities and school athletics. One girl appeared in several early photos and in some of them, she and Brian were either hugging or kissing. Reading some of his early posts, Munroe guessed she was Brian's girlfriend, Karen. About three months before he died, however, he said they broke up. But reading between the lines, he guessed that she left him.

After his death, there were understandably fewer pictures. Some of the pictures were probably lifted from tourism websites: Piccadilly Circus, the Eiffel Tower and the Cologne cathedral. And there were some pictures probably taken by phones, of people at restaurants and bars and in homes. They were probably people Brian had met online while traveling who had forwarded the pictures to him.

But to make up for the lack of pictures, Brian started writing a lot. He looked at the first entry posted after Brian's death.

"Well, I'm dead now. I guess I'm lucky because I don't remember dying, but they say few people do. My mom said I had a pulmonary embolism, which I looked up. Basically it's a big ole blood clot and I guess it had something to do with a bicycle accident when I broke my leg.

"I never knew I had this problem. I've been healthy my whole life. I guess I even kind of looked down on people who were sick because I never was. If I really come clean, I guess I thought it was their punishment for the life they lead. I always thought, you live a good life and believe in God, you'll be okay.

"But being dead is not what I deserve. I worked hard at school. I don't have anything to be ashamed of. I never hurt

anyone. I tried to live my life the way I was taught. You know.
Do unto others.

"So why am I here? I mean, I knew about the afterlife. I even
went on the Afternet and talked to some dead people. But I
just didn't think it would happen to me.

"Mom says young people never think their going to die. But I
knew I would die someday. But I thought heaven still existed
for some people who were good enough. Now I know that's
not true."

Munroe recognized Brian's feelings. He shared them
with Brian and apparently Sgt. Johnson. At least Brian
didn't go through the hell of thinking that it was only happening to him. But he also appreciated what it must be like
for someone so young and seemingly healthy to die so
suddenly, and then have your whole belief in God and
heaven turn upside down. For Munroe, God had always
been someone of whom to be suspicious, so it didn't surprise him when God let him down.

He looked at the more recent entries and saw that Brian
was sliding into depression, which wasn't unusual, and
that he was trying to find his belief in God again, which
was unusual.

"There has to be a reason for this. How can there be a soul
but no God?

"The Explorers say God's design is not easy to read and that
the path is not easy to follow, but that I must have faith that
the destination is worth the effort. I want to believe that but I
don't think I have that kind of faith anymore. And I'm tired of
being laughed at for even asking if there is a God."

Munroe looked at the last entry.

"Mom says Mrs. Wallace is sick and she's going to stay in

Brush until her surgery. I told her I'd stick around the school
and she'll try to meet me at the latest by the 14th. Theres
going to be a party tomorrow night and I think I'll go to that."

A clue, Watson, Munroe said to himself. Now he knew
what Brian had planned for Saturday night. And then he
remembered what Cheryl Miller had told him. He went
back through his user log and found the chat transcript:
She said she was going somewhere Saturday night, meet
some people, mix with the living.

Are we getting beyond coincidence? Munroe thought.
*Two people, both worried about their religious beliefs,
who disappear around the same time?*

Munroe sent a message to detective Rollins to let him
know he'd talked to Miller, but not about his suspicions,
which seemed pretty tenuous. Just as he was hitting send,
the floor dropped out from under him, or more correctly,
someone had pulled out the chair he was on and he
bounced to the floor. *360-degree field of view and I still
can't tell when one of those bastards is going to do that,* he
thought from his vantage point on the floor. Normally
Yamaguchi looked out for his chair, although she was also
the cause of some of the trouble when she put up a sign
asking people not to steal his chair. For a week, a chair
didn't last at his desk for 15 minutes before someone stole
it.

He decided to leave the CID room and hang out at one
of the bars along the 16th Street Mall. He'd send an email
to the secretary for the detectives' room and maybe she'd
put the chair back at the end of the day.

He ended up at one of the brewpubs on the mall, one of
the quiet ones that had large screen TVs left on all day.
Before the discovery of the afterlife, Munroe always found
that bars were the best places to watch TV, and they still
were. Bar owners usually turned on the subtitles to keep
the noise down or so that you could follow the game even

if it was noisy. So Munroe camped out at the bar and watched ESPN Classic. Unfortunately it was an old Broncos game: the stupid "The Drive" AFC championship game against Cleveland that Denver fans worshipped. Then again, he hated the Browns even more than the Broncos. *I mean what kind of a name is "the Browns?"*

Of course, being disembodied means you're at the whim of whoever wants to change the channel. About an hour into the game the TV switched to CNN, and he watched one of the more intriguing things he'd seen since dying. Apparently Honda, the car manufacturer, had created a robot that could act as an avatar for a disembodied person. From what he could tell, you stuffed a disembodied person into the helmet of the robot and then you control the robot. *Great, I can be RoboCop,* Munroe thought, until he realized the robot was about four feet high and school bus yellow. *Perhaps not the image I want to project.*

After the brewpub, Munroe went back to the department. His chair had been returned and he checked his email. Nothing from AfterNet security yet, but he was notified that there was a response to his query in the Denver entertainment forum.

From: (Marco Peloske) marcothemagnificent@hotmail.com
To: jollycopper@denverpd.org
Date: December 20, 2004 9:11 p.m. MST
Subject: Re: Deleted December event

> On Dec. 19th, 2004, 4:14pm, Alex Munroe wrote: Does anyone know if an event, scheduled between Dec. 5 and 11, has since been removed from this forum…

Hey, jollycopper, I think I know what you're looking for. There was some kind of Christian rave next to the Wazee Supper Club that was advertised. I can't remember if it was for the

11th or the 4th, however. The only reason I remember is that I read the announcement and I had pizza that night at the Wazee. I believe the message said the disembodied were invited as well.

HTH, Marco

OK, this sounds like something young, disembodied and spiritually confused people might attend, Munroe decided. Munroe checked and noticed that Marco Peloske was on-line, so he requested a private chat. Unfortunately, Peloske couldn't remember who had posted the message, or whether the poster was living or dead.

He thought of checking the place out, but he thought it would make more sense to catch up on the disembodied witness reports. Besides, without Yamaguchi, he couldn't accomplish much on his own. He sent an email asking whether she'd be well enough to come in Tuesday, then he tackled the first report: A disembodied woman saw a man peeing on the street at 10th and Grant. *Time to bust some crime.*

After reading and routing two hundred reports, Munroe had potentially solved two cases, including the annoying tool shed burglar who had been plaguing district three for six months. He'd noticed that one of the disembodied witnesses had used the word "schlemiel" to describe a suspicious person. For no particular reason, it reminded him of the story that had gone around the station of the man who had been held for menacing and had managed to run into the same door twice while being chased by officers. He remembered from his smattering of Yiddish that a "schlemiel" was basically a clumsy oaf. The suspect had a history of burglary, and the disembodied witness picked him out of some mug shots Munroe had sent. So now Munroe was rewarding himself by watching the online play-by-play of the Denver Nuggets-Phoenix Suns game and reading another Edgar Rice Burroughs book when he realized a man was standing behind him. It was 9:15 and the CID room was empty.

The man reached forward and through Munroe to tap on the screen. He made a sock puppet gesture with his hand.

"Go ahead," Munroe said through the terminal's speakers. The young man, who apparently was a Denver firefighter, jumped. The man's uniform nametag said "Morris."

"Munroe? Glad I found you. FD needs to borrow you. Dispatch says it's your day off but …"

"No, it's OK, but my partner's off."

"I know. Look, I have the FD's portable terminal and I was trained how to use it. We've got a HazMat spill and we'd like your help." Munroe noticed that the man didn't know where to look, his eyes kept darting back and forth. Morris was still young enough to be unsure of himself in new situations, and talking to a dead man through a terminal was high on the list of new situations.

"OK, let's go."

"Great, OK, let me switch on the terminal. I have it … it's right … no, here it is," he said triumphantly after finding the terminal and ear buds stuffed into his trouser pocket.

"Do you have an armband?"

"What? What armband?"

"So you can wear it on your arm."

"Oh, I didn't see one. Can't I just keep it in my pocket?"

"Only if you want me speaking to your crotch. I have to keep pretty close to it."

"Oh, right. Uh, duct tape?"

"Now you're thinking. Just keep it in your shirt pocket for now. All right. Lay on, McDuff. And try not to lose me."

Munroe spent four hours with Morris at the HazMat spill near Interstate 70 and Colorado Boulevard. Chlorine had mixed with some other chemical and made a dense, deadly fog and the FD was worried that not all the workers had been evacuated at the manufacturing plant. Luckily the spill was inside the building and was mostly contained. So Munroe wandered around inside the plant, looking for the injured, although he knew that if anyone was still in the building, they were probably dead.

He had the advantage, of course, of infrared vision and unlike the firefighters, wasn't limited by the capacity of an air pack. Luckily he found no one. A better headcount showed everyone had gotten out of the plant.

Thank God no one was in there because our response time sucked, thought Munroe. Munroe had lost contact with Morris as they were leaving the station and heading to the firefighter's car. Morris drove half a block away before he realized Munroe wasn't in the car with him. Luckily the firefighter was smart enough to simply pull to the side, open the car doors and wait for him.

Once they got to the scene, more comic routines ensued. Another firefighter had to tape the terminal to Morris' arm before he got into his gear, but he managed to tape the terminal with it turned off. So they had to remove it, turn it on and re-tape it, but while they were testing the terminal, Morris said he heard many voices. Munroe also was aware of others sharing the field and he quickly realized the problem.

"Morris, you've got this on anonymous access. We're picking up all the disembodied in the area. We've got to go back inside your car and set the terminal to single-user mode."

Luckily they were able to get inside the car without unwanted guests and Morris was able to tune the terminal to Munroe's signature.

"Sorry, Morris, I forgot about setting the terminal.

Linda usually takes care of that." The young man looked a little pale. "Hey Morris, you with me?"

"There are that many dead people around all the time?" he asked, staring straight ahead.

Oh, he's got the heebie-jeebies. "Don't let it scare you. Right now, I'm the only disembodied person you've got to deal with. Got it?" Morris nodded and they got out of the car.

But their problems continued while Morris suited up in HazMat gear. After he put on his breathing mask, his voice was so distorted that the terminal's speech translation became ludicrous.

"Eustachian bike be file I go slide, OK?" Morris asked.

"I couldn't understand a word of that."

"You stake by meat while I gum in slide, OK?" he repeated.

"OK, I think you said, 'You stay by me while you go inside.'"

Morris nodded.

The cross-talk act continued, although Morris found if he pushed up just a little on the breathing mask his speech was recognizable, but Munroe worried that Morris might be breaking the seal around his face and told him not to do it. In the end, Munroe just went into the building, looked around, came back outside to report to Morris, and went back for another look, again and again.

After they concluded no one was inside, Munroe and Morris held an informal debriefing, or bitch session, with the HazMat chief.

"So that went well," Morris said.

"Sure, if we were a volunteer fire department somewhere in the third world," the chief said. "What the hell took you so long getting here?"

"I had to track him down. It was his day off. And I lost him once."

"You lost him?"

"It's hard to see … I mean. I lost him outside the PD. But mainly it was a matter of finding him."

"I see," the chief said. "Well, it looks like we better have a little better training once our unit arrives. We'll work it out in the morning. Come by my office." He left and Morris stood there looking at the ground.

"Your unit?" Munroe said, wishing he could make his digitized voice convey dripping sarcasm.

"What?" Morris asked, startled at the voice in his ear he'd forgotten. "Oh, yeah, we've got a dead … disembodied person coming at the end of the month." He suddenly seemed to recognize Munroe's unvoiced sarcasm. "Sorry about the unit remark. The chief … you know the brass … they don't think of us as people anymore than they do … someone like you. We're just manpower … sorry, staffing." Morris did say the last word with sarcasm but it couldn't be conveyed to Munroe.

"Damn, what a fucked up operation this was," Morris said.

"At least no one was inside," Munroe offered.

"This time."

"Are you going to be the partner of the person you got coming?"

"Well, yeah. I hadn't really thought of it that way." Another firefighter walked up to Morris. "Get out of the way, Morris," he said. He grabbed Morris by the shoulders and moved him aside so he could load a large ventilation fan into the back of the HazMat truck. "Were you talking to yourself?"

Morris walked away without answering him. "Let's get back in my car before …" he said to Munroe. Back in the vehicle, Munroe said, "You better start thinking of yourself as … what's this person's name?"

"Who, oh, Sarah … uh … Richardson."

"Well, you're Sarah's partner. You're not on the line, are you? You're not at a station?"

"No, they pulled me to do this, and for the training ... you know, how to use the terminal. I still don't know if I'm being punished. I've got a reputation as a fuck up."

This kid needs some morale boosting, Munroe thought. "Did you work with a disembodied person during the training?"

"No."

"Is Sarah ... was she a firefighter?"

"Yeah, but she died a year ago, in the line. I think it was ... it was in a flashover, in Boston."

"OK, you'll have to train together as a team. When we first started, Linda and I, that's my partner, we did all the stupid stuff you and I did today. It took her a while to learn how fast I could move and that she needs to hold the door open for me and stuff like that. She even needed to learn how to walk so that she could keep the terminal field steady for me. Look, if you like, I can work with you and your ... who was that we were talking to?"

"Oh, that was the HazMat captain. He just wants to chew me out. The Operations Division Chief is really my boss. They haven't quite figured out where I ... and my partner fit."

"Well that sounds familiar. Look, I'll talk to my deputy chief and tell him about tonight's adventure and see if I can work with you."

"You might want to rethink that. The two departments guard their turf."

"Yes, but at the moment, I'm their fair-haired boy ... or whatever. Well, if we're done here, how about you take me back to the station?"

On the drive back, Munroe gave Morris hints on how to work with his future partner.

Yamaguchi was in bed watching TV, idly wondering if it was time to pee yet. At least 15 minutes had gone by without a trip to the bathroom and she'd like to stretch it to 30 if she could. Peeing was her body's response to any kind of illness or discomfort. If she had a cold, she had to pee. If she was cold, she had to pee. Fever: pee. Sinus attack: pee. *I'm sure if I ever get shot the first thing I'll need to do is pee,* she thought.

The need to pee almost drove her to the point of quitting in her rookie days. She hated the whole process of going to the bathroom in full cop regalia, including the stares of the public and the hurried way they would finish their business whenever she entered a restroom.

Once in the stall, she would have to remove her equipment belt. Then what do you do with it? She remembered the time she used the coat hook on the back of the door, only to see the soft metal snap off and the belt plummet to the floor. Luckily that time her reflexes let her catch it before it hit the floor. It didn't help that there was a sign on the door: "Use hook for coats only. No purses or heavy objects."

Far worse, though, was the time she wasn't paying enough attention and she dropped her equipment belt on the floor. Her pepper spray went flying across the floor of the restroom and her collapsible nightstick fell in the toilet. Of course, her shoulder mike, which was attached to her radio, which was on the belt, fell on the floor and keyed the emergency button. So for the next few minutes dispatch heard her radio transmitting the sounds of her fumbling around the floor of the bathroom with the occasional expletive.

Of course, she eventually trained herself: only use single occupant restrooms when possible, look for toilets with a tank where you can rest the belt, or stalls equipped with those fold-down shelves.

And now Munroe wants me to come in tomorrow when I have nasty cold, a perfectly legitimate excuse for calling in sick. Of all the inconsiderate partners ...

CHAPTER 5

By John Lester
National Geographic

"Let's move on to the next grid," says the man with the hang dog face, the three-days growth of beard and the red stocking cap that looks like it was chewed by the previously mentioned canine. "We'll find him eventually. Just a matter of time."

Bob Bodigger is referring to his friend, trapped in a submersible under 5,000 feet of water in the Indian Ocean. Even if it takes him a month or more, Bodigger swears they'll find Ronnie "Fitz" Fitzgerald. Even if they have to return next season, he swears they'll find Fitzgerald. Actually, they have all the time in the world, because Fitzgerald is already dead. As a matter of fact, he died ten years ago in remarkably similar circumstances.

Bodigger recalls, "Fitz was working for Shell in the North Sea, one of the lucky bastards that has to descend to the sea floor inside a hardsuit (an articulated diving suit that maintains sea level atmosphere). He had to clear some wreckage that had fallen off the rig above but he got stuck in it instead. He died in that suit.

"Most normal people would swear off repeating that experience. But no, once I had designed the AutoShark, Fitz wants to know if I can find a way for him to pilot it."

The AutoShark is Bodigger's pride and joy: an autonomous robotic shark that can effortlessly prowl the deep ocean for up to a month. It's not designed to carry passengers and it's not supposed to need a pilot. But Fitzgerald convinced Bodigger to put a transparent plastic sphere and an AfterNet field interface inside the AutoShark. This would allow Fitzgerald to field test the AutoShark for Bodigger and let Bodigger pay a debt he owes Fitzgerald. You see, Bodigger designed the suit in which Fitzgerald died.

Yamaguchi quickly covered her mouth with a tissue to conceal her cough when she entered the station. She didn't want to be branded another Typhoid Mary, like the poor cop two years ago whom everyone blamed for spreading a stomach flu that kept the swing shift understaffed for two days. She did her best not to be noticed, but some people nodded to her as she passed by and one cop jumped back two feet when she sneezed directly in his face after they met at a corner.

She clocked in for the day and went to the CID room. Munroe's terminal was on. She woke up the computer at her desk, sat down and then switched on the portable terminal in its armband. She immediately heard Munroe's voice.

"Hey Linda, how you doing?"

"Oh, God, I feel like crap, Alex. I'm draining in the back of my throat. I feel like my head weighs five pounds more than it should. I'm achy. I can't breathe. I cough."

"Yeah, and you're ugly too."

"What!?"

"Sorry, just a joke."

"What's this?" she asked, pointing to the cartoon taped to the side of his terminal. She looked at it, frowned, then removed it and threw it in the trash.

"Thanks for coming in."

"You're welcome. What's so damn important that I'm here and not in bed?"

"It's a missing person's report."

"We don't do missing persons, Alex, and even if we did, they're rarely urgent."

"It's a favor for Detective Rollins."

"OK, better explain."

Munroe explained to her about the two disappearances and his lead on the Christian rave.

"I don't know, seems like coincidence," she said.

"Humor me for the day. And it beats going through dis-embodied witness reports," ignoring the fact that he had cleared their backlog last night.

"Got that right, although I think you were just going stir crazy. Where are we going?"

Munroe gave her the address in LoDo. They went down to the squad room and she picked up some dirty looks as she sniffled while picking up a radio. "Use some Lysol when you bring it back," the desk sergeant told her.

They went to their cruiser and Yamaguchi barely gave Munroe enough time or space to get in. *Grouchy,* he thought.

"How's your mom?" he asked.

"Not going to work this time, Alex. Mom and I had a long talk. Oh, and she seems very interested in you."

"Thanks. How'd she get my email address, by the way?"

"Are you kidding? You spread that thing around like most guys …"

"You need to turn right here, Linda."

"Oh, right. So, hear anything from that guy who's hot for you?" she asked, laughing. "No, seriously, hear any-thing?"

"Hah, hah. Yes, he said he wants me to make an ap-pointment. He wants to hire me."

Yamaguchi glanced at him in the passenger seat. "You're not going to, are you?"

"No, I'm not. I am a happy member of the Denver PD team. Uh, parking space at 3 o'clock."

"Got it." Yamaguchi parked the cruiser on 15th Street near the corner with Wazee. LoDo was Denver's trendy lower downtown, although Munroe still didn't think Denver had a big enough downtown to justify the term. Many parts of LoDo had been turned into lofts, restaurants or office buildings, but there were still a few warehouses.

"Which one is it?" she asked after they got out of the car.

"The one next to the Wazee Supper Club," he told her.

She crossed the street carefully as the cars sped along 15th. She looked up at the two-story building. It had probably been built around 1900, 1910. Munroe stayed beside her, but decided not to say anything until her first impressions.

"They've used this building for raves before. Owned by a man who owns a couple of the buildings on Wynkoop. Met him at one of the Japanese-American society meetings. My mom hated him." She walked around the corner and looked down the alley. "You couldn't get in last night, huh?"

"Nope, didn't even try without my trusty sidekick." She muttered something that the terminal didn't translate and walked back out to the sidewalk and the main entrance. She looked through the glass door and saw a flight of stairs leading up. There were two doors at the base of the stairs and two more at the top landing. She tried opening the door but it was locked. She knocked on the door with her knuckles.

"No answer," she said, but not really to Munroe. She took out her nightstick and rapped on the door harder. Still no answer.

He peered up the stairway. "Can you make out the sign on the door?"

"Where?"

"Top floor." Munroe looked carefully but he could only make out a smudge.

"It's a bad angle. Looks like ... looks like ..." she sneezed on the door and had to wipe the glass clean with her sleeve. "Barf ... Barf? No, Barfly. Barfly Tentmaker? No. Barfly Entertainment."

She took out her phone and made a call. "Hi, dispatch? John, that you? Yeah, it's Linda. How you doing? Yes, I got a cold. Oh you did, did you? Hey, can you make a call for me? See if you can reach anyone at Barfly Entertainment ... I kid you not. On 15th Street. Yeah, tell them to meet me on the street. OK, I'll hold." Munroe could see Yamaguchi's lips move but the terminal provided no translation. She was humming. *At least her mood's improving,* he thought.

"OK, thanks, you're a prince among men," she said and hung up.

She looked back to the top of the stairs and the door opened. A man came walking down the stairs, looking surprised to see her. She could see he had an iPod hung around his neck and earphones pushed back on his head.

He unlocked the door and opened it.

"Yes, officer, may I help you?" Munroe thought he looked the part of the late 20s slacker — baggy pants, a bowling shirt, several piercings and spiky red hair. But he was polite.

"May we come in?" she asked.

"We?" he asked. She nodded.

"Sure, come on up."

Yamaguchi motioned for him to go first, and he walked up the stairs. She followed him through the door and into an office that was the dream of any hip, young entrepreneur. The office had high ceilings and large, north facing windows. Five desks held Apple computers, their monitors seemingly hanging in mid-air and looking like flowers seeking the sun. People were working at two of the computers. Large and small posters advertising concerts and raves were plastered all over the walls, which were brightly painted except where they were trendy bare brick.

The young man who'd invited them in led them to curved, modern-retro plywood chairs arranged around a wire spool table. He motioned for them to sit.

"Nice office, what do you do here?"

"We make the posters and stuff advertising impromptu musical entertainments."

"Nicely put," Yamaguchi said. "We'd like to know if you might remember an impromptu event that took place in this building Dec. 11."

"What's the 'we' mean? Like the imperial Denver police we?"

"Sorry, I forgot to introduce us. I'm Linda Yamaguchi and my partner, who is disembodied, is Alex Munroe. He's right next to me. You are right next to me, aren't you?"

"Standing by," Munroe said.

"Wow, a dead cop. I mean, you know, disembodied. I've got a couple of disembodied friends, but a ... disembodied cop. Wow. So he's talking to you right now?" She nodded and tapped the ear buds she wore.

"If I got some speakers, could I hear too?"

"Oh let him," Munroe said. She nodded again. The young man got up and took a small pair of speakers that were attached to one of the Macs and brought it to the table. Yamaguchi took her terminal from the armband and showed him where to plug in the speakers. She also removed her ear buds.

"So he can hear me now?"

"I can hear you," Munroe's digitized voice said. Even Yamaguchi felt a little surprised. She was used to Munroe being a little voice in her ear.

"Awesome. Now, what was it you wanted?"

"Whether you remember an event in this building on the 11th. And your name, if you don't mind."

"Oh, sure, Sean McCracken, but everyone just calls me 'Crackers.'"

"Sounds appropriate," Munroe said. "Oh crap, you just heard that, didn't you?"

The man smiled very widely and nodded enthusiastically. "That's OK. That's what everyone thinks. Now the 11th. Yeah, right, that was the 'Stiffs for Jesus' party. Sorry, that's what we called it," he said, shrugging. "But we didn't do any work for them. Just opened the door for 'em."

She asked, "You opened the door?"

"Uh huh, the owner of the building gave us a key to the space downstairs. We often let people in to see the place, to see whether they want to rent it. And sometimes we open up the place before a rave."

"So who did you see?" Munroe asked.

"A really hot girl."

"Any better description?" Yamaguchi prompted. She had taken out her notepad and was poised to write.

"My age, late 20s, long, straight, blonde hair, parted in the middle, green eyes, left handed, maybe 5 feet 7."

"A retired beekeeper who walks with a limp," Munroe said.

"What?" McCracken said.

"Ignore him. How do you know all this?" Yamaguchi said.

"Because she's the girl of my dreams, except for the left handed thing; I never knew she'd be left handed."

"And you know this because?"

"Because she touched me once on my right shoulder while she was talking to me."

"And her name?" Munroe asked.

"One of the guys with her called her Peggy. I forgot to ask her last name because I was too busy looking at her."

"Why did you call them 'Stiffs for Jesus'?" Yamaguchi asked.

"Because we checked them out when we left for the day. We told them how to lock up when they were ready to leave."

"Tell 'em 'bout the crucifix!" one of the young men working at a desk told them. Yamaguchi couldn't tell which one because they both still had their backs to them.

"Just getting to that, Randy," McCracken said. "There was a big crucifix in the room. We've seen crucifixes before, but they're usually upside down and drip blood. Joke. Naw, this was your standard white Jesus on the cross, with some Bible verses printed on posters."

"Like what?" she asked.

"Sorry, don't remember."

Randy spoke again. "For God so loved the world that he gave his one and only Son. John 3:16."

"Dude, you know the Bible?"

"Broncos games," Randy answered back. It was the closer man, Yamaguchi realized, the preppy looking one.

"Broncos games?" Yamaguchi asked, then sneezed and dabbed at her nose with the wad of tissues in her hand.

"It's a common verse you see at sporting events. I told you you should watch sports," said Munroe.

"Anything else you noticed?" asked Yamaguchi.

"No, sorry," McCracken said.

"Randy, you remember anything else?" Yamaguchi asked.

"Sorry," he said.

"OK, thanks, Sean. I guess that's it. Here's my card if you remember something or see the girl of your dreams again. Uh, do you mind letting us take a look downstairs?"

"No problem let me get the keys."

After he left, she noticed a door that was marked restroom. "Randy, OK if I use the restroom?" she asked.

"Sure," he said, still without looking away from his computer. She removed a few items from her belt and went to the restroom. McCracken returned after a few minutes.

"Where'd she go?"

"She went to the bathroom," Munroe's voice said from

the speakers. McCracken jumped slightly. Without Yamaguchi there, Munroe's voice seemed even more disembodied.

She came out of the bathroom a few minutes later and saw McCracken waiting. "I have a cold," she explained unnecessarily. He nodded. She disconnected the speakers from the terminal, put it back in the armband and reconnected the ear buds.

"This was neat, Alex," she said. "We should do this more often."

"I know. If we get to do more investigations, we should get some speakers."

McCracken asked, "Ready to go down?" and after she nodded, led them downstairs.

He opened the left-hand door at the base of the stairs. It was a single floor-length glass door, three feet wide, and Yamaguchi thought "fire code violation." It wouldn't be sufficient to empty the space in the event of a fire.

He flicked on overhead fluorescent lights and Yamaguchi saw the ceilings on this floor were even higher, at least 14 or 15 feet. The room was about 40 feet wide by 80 feet long and wide open except for some support pillars. Yamaguchi also noted a double set of doors with push bars and a much larger roll-up door that probably opened onto a loading dock. She revised her fire code suspicion. With the fire sprinklers overhead, emergency lighting, two fire extinguishers and the push bar doors with lighted exit signs, the room probably met the fire code, although she suspected the space often exceeded capacity.

The room was painted flat black and showed many strips of masking tape used for posters. A grid of pipes overhead probably was used to hang lights, and two doors that opened under the stairway were labeled as restrooms. Finally, a low platform would make a very small stage or more likely a place for the DJ.

"It's pretty bare," she said.

"They've got to bring all their own stuff, and they got to take it with them or the owner just trashes it."

"What kind of stuff did they bring?"

"All kinds of stuff, the usual AV equipment and posters and banners. They also brought in a lot of monitors and a lot of computer equipment. Actually, that was kind of weird."

"What?" she asked.

"Well, they bring in a lot of monitors, even a server, but they wanted to make sure there was no Internet access. Wanted us to turn it off."

"There's Internet access in here?"

He pointed to a small box hanging from the ceiling in a corner of room. "Wireless. This floor can access our DSL router upstairs."

"So you turned it off?"

"Sure, we were leaving for the weekend anyway, so we just turned off the router rather than try to get up there to turn that off."

Yamaguchi had seen enough. "OK, Sean, thanks a lot for letting us in and ... "

"I'm not done yet," Munroe said. She was surprised. He hadn't said anything for a while and she figured he'd realized it was a waste of time.

"Hey anytime, officer, you should come by ..." She held up her hand to stop him and pointed to her ear buds.

"What is it Alex?" she asked.

Munroe had been studying the space while they talked. He didn't know what triggered it, but he'd started thinking of it as a crime scene. "Give me a minute," he told her and left her side.

She noticed that her terminal displayed "No user connected." She asked the young man to wait. Two minutes later, Munroe spoke in her ear.

She addressed McCracken, "He wants to know if anyone else has rented this space."

"No, there's some kind of steampunk thing this weekend, but nothing since the 11th."

"Um, were they building anything in here?" she asked for Munroe.

"No, I don't think so. Unless they did after we left."

"Did you see them bringing in … plywood?" she asked, wondering what Munroe was thinking.

"Not as such. But they did bring in a lot of backdrops. You know, like a stage set. They were on wheels. They might have been made of plywood."

"Linda, get up on the stage," Munroe said.

"What? Sorry, Sean, he's asking me something."

"Get up on the stage, get up higher, get something to stand on," Munroe said.

"Uh, Sean? Do you have a ladder or something I could stand on?"

"Huh? Got a little stepladder," McCracken said.

"That'll do," she said. He went back upstairs.

"Alex, why do I need a stepladder?"

"You'll see."

McCracken came back, carrying a stepladder. She asked him to put it on the stage.

"Now what?" she asked Munroe.

"Get up and see if you can see anything on the floor."

Confused, she did as he asked, feeling stupid, and came back down.

"See anything?" he asked.

"Kind of. Sort of an outline in one corner, like where the walls of a room used to be."

"Go over to the outline, see if you can tell what it is."

She walked over to where she saw the outline, which was not quite as distinct close up. She bent down and rubbed her finger in what looked like sawdust.

"I think it's sawdust, maybe from plywood or particle board," Munroe said.

"Could be, I guess," she said. She turned to address

McCracken and found that he'd been looking over shoulder.

"How'd they bring the stuff?"

"Rental trucks. You know, big panel trucks like UPS uses."

"Do you remember what company … the rental trucks, I mean."

"Ryder? I think. Maybe," he said.

She heard Munroe's voice in her ear again. "Take a look at the floor a couple of feet to your right. Do those look like tracks?"

She looked and saw parallel marks on the floor that looked like tracks, the kind casters would make. She also found another set of tracks. All the tracks were parallel to what would be the long wall of the "room" defined by the dust outline.

"Sort of. I guess. And what does this prove?" she asked.

"I have no idea."

She turned back to McCracken. "Ever notice these before?" pointing at the floor.

He looked at the tracks. "No, not really. This group was actually pretty neat. The place usually gets trashed. That's why the owner spray paints everything twice a year."

"OK, we done this time, Alex?" she asked. When she got an affirmative she thanked McCracken again and he showed her out.

They returned to their car and discussed what they had learned while he also checked his email.

"So, what does any of this mean?" she asked. "Do you think there was … foul play?" She said the last words dramatically; sorry it would be lost in translation.

"Like I said, I have no idea."

"Oh come on. You're not seriously suggesting something did happen, are you? Alex, the dead get trapped all the time. What makes you think this is any different."

"Because I just got my reply back from AfterNet security. Sgt. Johnson visited the Denver entertainment forum the day before she disappeared too. I think she was here, too."

The void became light again and form and substance returned. He replayed the scene in the park but this time it didn't feel like he was moving against his will. It felt more like he wanted to go where his "dream" was taking him.

This time when the woman took his hand he felt that he was following her, was responding to her lead. He could imagine what her hand must feel like. He remembered the feel of flesh. He saw a gust of wind move the trees and he could see how it moved her dress and he knew that he could hear the sounds the fabric must be making. And when she turned to look at him and her lips moved, he knew that he could hear her say his name, "Brian."

CHAPTER 6

Excerpt from Howard Branff's *Quick Thinking, or: How I Learned to Stop Worrying and Trust my Lizard Brain,* Little, Brown, 1997

… it evolved for the purpose of staying alive. So it had to be fast. It had to be able to assimilate and process thousands of points of relevant data and make a decision. But now the brain is encumbered with lots of irrelevant data: What will others think? Do I look fat in this? I have to work with this person. What's she got stuck in her teeth? Am I going to get paid?

If you could control the data the brain gets, make it relevant to the process, you will make the right choice. If you don't think about it too much …

… because split-second thinking can often find the right answer. You will probably buy the car that's right for you by pointing at its picture on a chart, as long as you do it within two seconds. That doesn't mean you'll buy a car that's right for the planet, that will please your girlfriend or that will be maintenance free. But all in all, you'll be happy with it.

Knowing this, then, we can see why focus groups, especially marketing focus groups, often fail spectacularly. Putting some people in a room and talking for two hours might produce thoughtful, well-reasoned arguments for why a person *should* buy something, but it doesn't mean they really will or will really be happy with their choice.

It would be far more useful if you could capture someone's instant, off-hand reaction to a new product. But short of creating a race of human guinea pigs you can raise in a box, how do you achieve this?

Munroe and Yamaguchi returned to the station. She was going to call the man who owned the building and see if she could find information about who rented it. He was going to contact the church where Miller and Johnson were to meet. Once they got there, however, Munroe found a message to call the deputy chief.

He called the chief using the terminal, deciding to take the message literally.

"Clemens," the chief answered.

"It's Munroe. You wanted me to call."

"Oh, hello. Damn creepy when you call on the phone. You sound Norwegian."

"Yeah, I get that a lot."

"Is that what she hears when you talk to her?"

"Yes. Well, maybe. The terminal might use a different voice than her portable. I wouldn't know."

"Where is she?"

"She's on the phone. Should I …"

"No, that's OK. So you went on a ride along with the fire department."

"Uh, yeah. I thought it was understood that other departments could call on me if needed. And I was off duty last night."

"As soon as they get their disembodied firefighter, you're not to respond to any requests for help unless it comes through me."

"Except for an emergency, of course," Munroe added.

"Well naturally. No, you did the right thing last night. Look, I don't want to get on your case, but I got your email about helping the FD with their new firefighter. The budget's tight and I don't want them thinking we can bail them out. Let's just make sure that things go through me; don't initiate things on your own.

"The FD's paying the price for being slow to catch onto the idea of hiring the dead. So we're not going to spread our resources thin just to help them out."

"OK."

"Look, we're going to meet after the New Year on this. We've got some changes coming up on how we're going to use you and Linda, and I think you're going to like it. Don't go rocking the boat 'til then."

Clemens hung up and Munroe was left musing the implications of the conversation when Yamaguchi said, "Alex, I talked to his ... oh, are you on the phone?" she asked when she saw his monitor displayed the telephone interface.

"No, I just got off the phone with Clemens."

"What did *he* want?"

"I just got ... well not really chewed out for working with the FD, but told to cool it."

"You're kidding? I thought that was OK?"

"Not now that they're going to get their own disembodied personnel. Actually, it was kind of confusing. Apparently they're planning some changes for us after the New Year."

"Would have been nice if they'd told us."

"I guess this was their way of doing that. Heavy sigh." Munroe said. "Anyway, what were you saying?"

"I talked to Yamata's secretary and we can call him back in an hour."

"Who's ... oh, the guy who owns the building. OK, let me try and get someone at the church first."

"Actually, Alex, give me the details and I'll call."

"Why?"

"You know — church, religion, you being dead — not a good mix."

"What, now I'm the anti-Christ?" he asked, but gave in to her suggestion. He told her about Cheryl Miller and Sgt. Johnson and the church where they were supposed to have met. She looked up the number of the church while Munroe returned to his email and found another message from Rybold.

From: (Bill Rybold) Bill.Rybold@theAfterNet.net

To: jollycopper@denverpd.org
Subject: Still haven't heard from you
Date: December 21, 2004 2:11 p.m. MST

Dear Alex,
You're not going to keep me waiting are you? My secretary
says you haven't called. I know the holidays aren't good for
trying to arrange a meeting.
Speaking of the holidays, I've invited many of us dead to a
Christmas Day thing at my house. There will also be many
living friends as well. So if you and your partner find
yourselves at loose ends, feel free to stop by anytime and
stay as long as you like.
No strings attached to this offer.

Bill

Munroe stared at the email for a little while and wondered what to make of it. If I mention this to Linda, for
damn sure she'll start making jokes about Rybold making
a play for me. Munroe was genuinely puzzled. Never a
man who made friends easily, he was just homophobic
enough to be suspicious of men who did. Then he remembered he was dead and that it really didn't matter.

He also had a message from Morris.

From: (Franklin Morris) Franklin.Morris@denverfd.org
To: jollycopper@denverpd.org
Subject: WARNING!!!
Date: December 21, 2004 2:15 p.m. MST
Det. Munroe,
I think I stuck my foot in it. I heard from my captain that the
chief tried to call in that favor with the safety managers office
and was shot down.
So maybe it would be best if you back off anything official on
your end.

Which is stupid because I could really use your advice before
Sarah starts. BTW, I took your suggestion and got in touch
with her. We chatted and hit it off.
So if you don't mind, can we just sidestep the brass and work
directly? you, me and Sarah. Maybe a chat room for the three
of us?
Thanks,

Frank

Munroe sent Morris a reply and told him about the
warning he'd gotten from Clemens. He also said he'd be
happy to meet with him and his partner and that he was
sure Yamaguchi would like to join. Munroe was intrigued
that he and Yamaguchi would have a counterpart in the
FD. *Screw Clemens,* he thought.

And finally, he found an email from Melissa.

From: (Melissa Anderson) messym@theAfterNet.net
To: jollycopper@denverpd.org
Subject: Death on the Nile
Date: December 21, 2004 2:57 p.m. MST

My Dear Detective Munroe,
It was fascinating talking to you the other night. I enjoyed our
witty repartee and hope we can resume our verbal thrusts and
jabs.
See, I can talk pretty too :)
And I looked into that trip you were talking about in Egypt.
Sounds like fun. 5,000-year-old mummies might have
something to teach me (I actually did meet a couple of people
who claimed to have lived then but who can tell).
So, if you have no objections, I'd like to join you! Please don't
say no.

Melissa

Damn, I am one popular guy, Munroe thought. He replied to her and said it was OK by him. He couldn't believe how good he was feeling at that moment. *Not every day a 62-year-old man can go on a trip with a 21-year-old girl, you old dog you.*

"Alex, earth to Alex. I know you're still here."

"Oh, sorry, Linda. Daydreaming."

"Yeah, right. If you must talk to yourself, you might want to mute the field first."

"Oh, you heard that?"

"Yes, oh gift to women. What's the name of this piece of jailbait?"

"Technically incorrect, Linda. Her name is Melissa and we met while I was nursing you back to health."

"You mean while you were perusing your disgusting dead guy porn and I was puking my guts out."

"Yes, essentially, but my relationship with Melissa is on a higher plane."

"Doing it on a plane now? Kinky."

"Please, let's return to official police business."

Munroe thought he'd never seen Yamaguchi smile so broadly. It's kind of sexy, he thought, and then made sure he hadn't let that thought slip out.

"I got a hold of the pastor ... or preacher or whatever, at the church. I'm going to meet with him at 5:30."

"Hello, partners, remember?"

"You can come. I just think it would be good if we don't spring you on him until we know how comfortable he is with the dead. Just because they were meeting there doesn't mean the good reverend would have approved. You saw that story about the priest in France, didn't you?"

Of course Munroe saw it. A priest had ordered disembodied visitors to leave his church.

"OK, I'll be quiet."

Munroe and Yamaguchi tackled the few disembodied

witness reports that had trickled in that morning, and then they called the building owner together.

"Hi, is Mr. Yamata there," Yamaguchi said.

"Yes, this is me."

"Hello, sir, this is Officer Linda Yamaguchi. I don't know if you remember me. I met you at the Japanese-American Association luncheon last year."

"Of course. Yoshiko-san's daughter, right?"

"Yes. If you don't mind, I'd like to ask you a question about the building you own on 15th Street. Next to the Wazee?"

"Yes," he said.

Yamaguchi fidgeted uncomfortably in her chair. "I'd like to know if you rented space in the building on the night of the 11th for a … a party." She remembered some of the confrontations her mother had had with Yamata when she was alive. She wasn't certain if he carried a grudge that extended to her.

"Yes I did. To a Christian group, for a rave."

Yamaguchi relaxed. He seemed friendly enough. "Oh, you did. Do you have any contact information for that group?"

"Not much. I have a name and a number. Is there a problem?"

"Oh no, just checking the whereabouts of someone."

"Don't worry, the raves aren't illegal."

"Excuse me?"

"I meet all the fire codes. I have all the permits and the building is zoned properly."

"But what about … most people think …"

"No one would want to have a rave in a building with the proper permits. So most of the organizers of these events pretend they're doing something illegal."

"Oh, well that's a relief."

"Now let me get that information for you." Yamata put down the phone and Munroe and Yamaguchi could hear some fumbling. She covered the phone and spoke to Munroe. "Thank God. Yamata's a big shot in the community. He and my mom used to tangle a lot. I think …"

Yamata came back on the phone. "Here it is. The name I have is Margaret and the number I have is in Colorado Springs." He gave them the number, which did have a Springs area code.

"How did they pay?"

"With a check."

"Is that unusual?"

"Yes, most groups like to pretend that everything is under the table, even though I write them out a receipt."

"Did you write a receipt for this group?"

"Yes, made out to a group called The Explorers. There's an address." He gave them an address, also in the Springs. "The check's signed by someone else. Tracy Newell."

"Man or woman?" she asked.

"No idea. Are you sure there's no problem? For a Springs group, they seemed relatively normal, if you know what I mean."

"No problem. Uh, did you meet the person who paid?" she asked.

"No, the payment was dropped off at my office. I did talk to a woman on the phone a few times. I think she was Margaret."

"Does anyone at your office remember what the person looked like?"

"Hold on." He put the phone on hold and came back a minute later. "Sorry, the receptionist was out and when she came back, the check was on the counter. We sent the receipt by mail."

"OK, thanks Mr. Yamata. I think that's all."

"Very good. Nice to talk to you again, Miss Yamaguchi. By the way, I got an email from your mother last week. No, two weeks ago."

"You did?"

"Yes. I know we didn't always get along, but I did ... respect her. Anyway, she wanted to rejoin the association. She wanted to know who's the membership director. Is she coming back to Denver?"

"I hope ... no, I don't think so."

After this, Yamaguchi and Yamata said their goodbyes and hung up.

"Now what's that all about?" she asked.

"What, about your mother, you mean? Sounds like she's coming back."

"Oh, please, don't even joke about it," she said. "Well, what do you think about this church group?"

"You can't really say they tried to cover their tracks."

"Unless this phone number is bogus."

"Give them a call and find out."

She shrugged and dialed the first number. All she got was a default voice mail message stating the phone number and that she should leave a message, which she did.

Then she called the second number. "The Explorers. How may I help you?" a man's voice answered.

"Hi, is Margaret there?"

"Um, do you have a last name?"

"No, I don't."

"I don't know of anyone named Margaret who works here. Can someone else help you?"

"Uh, Tracy Newell?"

"Let me put you through," the man said. But after a few seconds, she heard a voice mail message, a man identifying himself as Tracy Newell and that he would be out of the office and please leave a message. She asked Newell to call her back, saying she was a Denver cop and asking about the rave.

"OK, I guess that's all we can do for now," she said. "Why don't we head out now for the church and I can stop by the drugstore? I'm really draining." Munroe agreed and they were getting ready to go when she got a call over the radio. She answered and Munroe tried to listen in but the static made the dispatcher's speech unintelligible.

"We got to go, Alex, missing kid."

She was already moving and Munroe scrambled to keep up with her. "Amber Alert?" he asked.

"Not exactly. More of a baby down a well scenario."

"Oh, shit," he said to himself. She was running down the back stairs two steps at a time now. Munroe always wondered how she did it without falling and breaking her neck. And it was impossible to keep the field of her terminal.

They made it to their car and she flew out of the parking garage. At least she had the presence of mind to confirm he was in the car before she left.

"Where are we going?" he asked.

"30th and Zuni," she said. Unfortunately, Munroe was still learning his way around Denver and since he couldn't drive, never really got to know the city like he did Seattle. "Which is where?" he asked again.

"Highlands, overlooking downtown. It's east of downtown. You know, 15th Street, once it crosses I-25, magically turns into 29th Avenue."

"Isn't that where the bathhouse is?" he asked, referring to a gay bathhouse.

"Yes, and there are apartments or condos at 30th and Zuni."

The address was only a short drive on Speer Boulevard. As they drove, they saw two other police cruisers and a fire truck ahead of them, all with lights and sirens.

They got to the intersection of 30th and Zuni at almost the same time because the fire truck had to wait on a confused driver who had stopped in the middle of the Speer and Zuni intersection.

Yamaguchi decided to park on Zuni, although the fire rescue trucks were clustered around the alley between

Zuni and Wyandot, the next street to the east. She walked to the fenced parking lot behind the building at the corner of 30th and Zuni. The building looked like it was from the 1900s or even older. A spire and dome stood on the corner of the building and she vaguely recalled that it was an old pharmacy and was now condominiums.

The lot had a retractable gate that kept the parking private for the tenants but was now kept open, probably by the police cruiser parked on the pressure plate. They found a sergeant she recognized and another officer talking with a woman, obviously distraught. They also saw a bunch of firefighters all looking at a gap between the building and its neighbor. One of the firefighters kept yelling "Jason!"

"Yamaguchi, got Munroe with you?" the sergeant asked.

"He's here. What do you need us to do?"

The sergeant answered. "Kids were playing here and we think one of them is trapped between the two buildings," he said, pointing to the group of firefighters.

"You're kidding," she said. She walked over to the firefighters and the sergeant followed. He told the firefighters, "Let her take a look."

They moved aside and Yamaguchi and Munroe could see that a crack that seemed less than a foot wide separated the two two-story buildings. This late on a winter day, very little light entered the crack and the firefighters had been trying to shine their flashlights into the crack. Suddenly a bright light appeared at the top of the crack when a firefighter on the roof of the building turned on a handheld spotlight. But even after focusing the beam as narrowly as possible, it only lit the bricks at the top and failed to throw much light at the bottom. She also realized she could see all the way through the crack when she saw cars driving on Zuni.

"I don't see anything in there," she said, when she pulled back.

"The mother said there's a … space under the buildings. Cats go in there," the sergeant said. "Can Munroe fit through, you think?"

"What do you think, Alex?"

Munroe eyed the gap suspiciously. He wasn't claustrophobic when alive, but he shared with all disembodied the fear of being confined.

"It's a little tight," he said finally. "I can probably make it. Hey, I assume they've tried calling the kid."

"They were yelling his name when we got here."

"His name is Jason. Who's she talking to?" the mother asked. The sergeant, who was probably the first on the scene, pulled her aside and Yamaguchi could hear him explaining the situation to her. When the mother heard the word "disembodied," she began crying even more loudly.

"The mother says the kid's name is Jason, Alex. Is it really too tight? I thought you could squeeze through narrower if you had to." She was right, he had squeezed through narrower spaces than this, but they always opened to a larger space on the other side. She moved back to peer into the crack.

"Never tried going through something this long before," he said. "And I don't see any space where the kid could be. How long has the kid been missing?" Yamaguchi relayed his question and said, "The mother says he's been missing two hours." Yamaguchi spoke quietly, "What's the matter, Alex?"

"Nothing. I'll try to go in. Give me some room here."

Yamaguchi told the others to back away and he'd try to go in.

When the group cleared, Munroe tried to push his way into the crack. *Think small, think small,* he repeated to himself. He only managed to get about a foot into the crack and stalled. *Think small and back out, think small and back out,* he now thought. His mental mantra accelerated as panic started to set in.

He suddenly found himself out of the crack and saw the cops, firefighters, mother and two others, probably building tenants, all looking at the crack and all starting to crowd the opening again.

He connected with his partner's terminal again. "Linda, no luck, I'll try again but tell everyone to keep back from the opening." She said nothing to him but ordered everyone away from the crack again.

This time Munroe started from much farther back and willed himself to charge the opening. He screamed the berserker scream he hadn't used since college football days.

This time momentum drove him at least four feet into the crack but he was slowing down and he could feel his stretched essence reforming itself. He came to a stop about six feet into the crack. He could see back toward the others and knew they were already blocking his exit. And he could see through to the Zuni side where another cop was shining his flashlight through the crack. But he could also look down into the gloom of the crack and could now tell that a void opened below the other building. He tried other wavelengths but saw little more than a rubble-strewn surface that appeared to be about three feet below what must have been the foundation footing of the other building.

Jason, he yelled, forgetting for a second about his situation. He couldn't help but remember the times he'd gone looking for missing kids during his days as a beat cop.

He tried moving forward and thinking small with little success. It was a weird feeling for him. Without a body and the innate sense of that body that the living enjoyed, it almost felt like he wasn't trapped. It felt more like what he imagined a paralyzed person must feel: not restrained but simply unable to move. He looked up and saw the spotlight far above him, shining through the crack. As it moved back and forth, it almost gave the impression that the crack was closing.

By now the daylight was gone and Munroe suddenly

realized he'd been stuck for several minutes. *Well this is stupid. What if there is a kid trapped down here ... along with me.*

He was still at least 10 feet from where the void began. He tried the "think small and move forward" mantra again but quickly gave up.

I just need to go from here to there, he thought, without being anywhere in-between. Which sounds just like the crap from that woman who gave the motivational talks at the Seattle PD. He'd been required to go to her seminars because the captain liked her. She liked to talk about the difference between effort and intent and how the former can get in the way of the latter. Which also sounds like the stuff Linda talks about after one of her aikido classes. *Of course, for a woman who's always talking about flowing with your opponent she sure can take a suspect down.*

So all I have to do is desire to be there and not here, he said to himself. And he moved, a little. Encouraged, he tried repeating the words with greater urgency, but didn't move.

OK, what did I do different? All I said the first time was I want to be there. And he moved again, a little further this time. He felt a surge of optimism but refrained from re-peating his thoughts.

Don't blow it. Relax. I obviously can't force it. I've simply got to desire to be there.

And he was. He was free. Or more precisely, he was now in the void below the other building, with no more than three feet of clearance, but he felt free. It was very dark and he shifted to infrared.

Now he could tell that the void extended far under the building. Above him, he could see the underside of the concrete floor of the basement of the building. Below, he could see small pebbles or little log shapes that covered the ground. *Oh joy, cat shit,* he thought.

He moved forward. The clearance dropped to about two feet and once to a little more than a foot. He could see a few hot spots above him, probably the heating system of the building or a hot water tank. One glowing line that he had to rise over was probably the sewer pipe. He lifted himself over the sewer pipe and suddenly fell because the ground dropped sharply on the other side of the pipe. He fell maybe five feet and found himself in a large pit with steeply sloped sides. At the bottom of the pit he saw a boy, lying face up in a puddle of water. He could tell the boy, who was wearing a heavy sweater and jeans, was still breathing but his eyes were closed. Looking closer, he saw the boy had smacked his head against a rock at the bottom of the pit. Drops of water fell around the boy and Munroe realized that a leaking pipe above had opened a sinkhole below the foundation of the building, aided by whatever water fell between the two buildings.

Of course, now I have to get back, he thought. It took him three tries to "jump" back up into the crawlspace. *Great, now I have to make it back through the crack.*

But when he got back to the crack he found Yamaguchi's portable terminal, still in its armband, tied to a rope that had been lowered from above. He looked up and saw her at the other end of the rope.

"Linda, can you hear me?"

"Alex!"

"The boy's down here. He's in a pit or sinkhole below the floor of the building to the south."

"Say again. Bad … again." Munroe realized that the terminal must be near the limit of the range of his partner's wireless ear buds.

"Get closer," he told her, although he didn't know how she could accomplish that. He saw her hand the rope to someone else and didn't respond. He kept repeating his message about finding the kid. Then her words appeared again. "ALEX! CAN YOU HEAR ME NOW!" She must really be shouting quite loudly for the interface to render her words in capital letters.

"I hear you Linda, loud and clear. Where are you?"

"I'm in the basement of the building to the north, standing next to the wall. Did you find the boy? Is he OK?"

"He's breathing but unconscious. He's lying in water so we have to get him out fast."

"None of us can make it through the crack."

"Yeah, look, they're going to have to bust through the floor of the building to the south with a jackhammer or something."

"How far in is he?"

"I can't tell. Not a lot to go by down here. He's maybe twenty feet from the crack, from where the terminal is hanging, just on the other side of what's probably the main sewer drain. Look, let's try this. Haul up the terminal and go into the basement of the other building. Put it on the ground and let's see if I can detect the field. Start as close to the crack as you can and we'll work out from there."

"Sounds like a plan. Let's hope the field the penetrates the foundation."

"Didn't you tell me there's a way to adjust it?"

"I've read online about people who've tried but there's no way I can do it now," she said.

"Never mind then. Uh, the puddle the kid's in seems to be near some leaking pipes. That might help narrow it down."

"All right, I'll tell them to haul up the terminal."

Munroe started to head back to the kid when he remembered something and rushed back. The terminal was still there and he hoped she was also.

The words "ALEX!" showed she was.

"Linda, I forgot to tell you to get the FD's terminal and keep it here so I can have a reference point," he said. At the same time, her saw her words, "Your friend from the FD is here. I told him to lower his terminal so we can communicate from here."

"Good thinking. Now go," he said.

Half a minute later, the terminal was being hauled up.

Munroe ducked back into the void. He was tempted to see how the kid was doing but thought he should wait for Yamaguchi.

Five minutes later, he caught a fleeting contact of the field. "LINDA!" he yelled. He kept repeating her name and forced himself to remain where he was.

"Alex!" he read, finally.

"Can you … me?"

"I got you. Not perfect but OK."

"… move three feet." He did, while yelling her name. After a few seconds they reconnected. With this method, they kept moving further toward the boy until Munroe reached the big sewer pipe.

"I'm at the sewer pipe, " he told her.

"What, didn't get that?"

"I'm at the sewer pipe. Sewer pipe. There's a drop on the other side of the sewer pipe."

"OK … on the other side … drop. Got it."

"Boy is about …" he peered over the sewer pipe and could see the boy about 10 feet away. "… 10 feet away from here."

"OK … jackhammer. Stand back. Stand back, Alex."

Munroe jumped back over the pipe but knowing what to expect, he was able to keep from rolling down the slope. After a few seconds, he noticed dirt dropping from the concrete above him. Soon a shower of dirt and then pebbles fell from above. He looked back at the kid and noticed a shower of debris falling into the water.

After about 15 seconds, the debris stopped falling, and he realized they had stopped. He moved back to where the field had been and felt its return.

"MOVE BACK, LINDA, MOVE BACK!"

"What's the matter?"

"Crap is falling off the ceiling, I mean the floor. I'm afraid it might fall on the kid. Move a couple of feet to the north."

"OK."

The jackhammer started again and dirt started falling, however, there was less falling down over the kid. The jackhammer stopped and Munroe told her they could continue safely.

After about a minute, a large chunk of concrete fell into the crawlspace and light flooded the void. A head appeared a few seconds later, followed by a hand holding a flashlight. After a second, the head retreated and a few seconds after that, one of the firefighters dropped feet first into the space, then reached back to another firefighter passing him a backboard.

"They're coming in," Yamaguchi said.

"I see that. Do they know it's a drop on the other side of the sewer pipe."

"I told them."

The firefighters had moved to Munroe's position, and he had to hug the sides of the crawlspace to let them pass. As soon as they had gone, he fled for the hole they had opened and entered the basement of the building.

He saw a small low-ceilinged room crammed with people, including two paramedics standing by with a stretcher. Munroe saw Yamaguchi lying on the floor near the hole and tried to talk to her, but she had thrust the terminal into the opening and was shouting. After a minute, she gave up and retracted the terminal. She was looking at the display when she saw "User connected" on the display.

"I'm here, Linda."

"Alex, you're here."

"That's what I said." Their conversation was stopped as more people entered the room, including the boy's mother, clutching the arm of the sergeant who'd met them. A woman with a television camera entered directly behind her.

"It's getting crowded in here. Can we go outside?" Munroe asked.

"Sure, whatever you want." She led him up from the basement and out into the parking lot. Many people were milling in the two lots, mostly the tenants of the two buildings, but also several TV news crews were broadcasting reports or interviewing people. Emergency vehicles, TV lights and work lights from the fire trucks vividly illuminated the area.

"God, what a zoo," Yamaguchi said. Munroe said nothing; he simply tried to enjoy the relative openness after being trapped underground.

"Aw, crap," she said. "We missed our appointment at the church." She took out her phone and walked away. Munroe assumed she was calling the minister to apologize. Then the door to the building banged open and the firefighters brought out the stretcher with the boy.

The crowd in the parking lot surged forward but police officers fanned out to keep them away. The paramedics passed by Munroe, who could see that the boy's mother was keeping pace with them, her hand on his brow while one of the paramedics adjusted an oxygen mask.

The procession quickly passed him and the crowd reformed. Munroe rejoined his partner who was still on the phone. A minute later, the sergeant that had greeted them clapped his hand on her shoulder.

"The boy's going to be OK," he told her. Yamaguchi quickly got off the phone and turned to the sergeant.

"Sorry, didn't see you were on the phone," he said.

"No, I just got off. He's OK?" She stamped her feet to get warm. The basement had been cold and she'd been lying on the concrete. Her head felt like a snot-filled bowling ball and now the wind was picking up.

"Yeah, he called for his mom when they got him out. That's what I like, happy endings." Another officer called out to the sergeant. He said, "Tell Munroe he did good," then left.

"Alex?"

"Yeah."

"Did you hear that?"

"I did. Happy endings."

Yamaguchi was fumbling for some tissues and could only find a used wadded one. She was doing the best she could when she noticed that the sergeant had gone to talk to a knot of reporters and TV people. He pointed in their direction and they were quickly surrounded. A flurry of questions attacked her.

"Officer, is your partner here?" "What's his name?" "Is this the same officer who was hired last year?" "Can you tell us how you made it through the crack?"

Yamaguchi shied from the lights of the TV cameras and the flashes of the photographers. She held up her hand to shield her eyes from the lights.

"Uh … yeah, he's here. He's the one who went into the crack and found the boy. And yes, he was hired last year. His name is Alex Munroe. Look, could you please stand back. I've lost contact with Alex and I think you're blocking him." She made a motion to her right and the reporters hurried to make a space while the cameras turned to point at the empty area beside her.

"OK, everyone move back, give them some room," a commanding voice said. Yamaguchi recognized the officer, who was actually pushing back some of the reporters, as Barbara Chavez, the department's public affairs officer.

Once she felt enough space had been created, she walked back to Yamaguchi, leaned close to her and whispered, "It's Linda Yamaguchi and Alex Munroe, correct?" She nodded.

Turning back to the reporters, Chavez said, "Let's ask the questions one at a time."

"Whoa, she's a take charge sort," Munroe said to his partner.

Chavez picked a reporter and motioned for him to ask a question.

"That crack between the buildings measured eleven inches. How did Officer Munroe make it through?"

"Shit, that was eleven inches? Tell 'em I got stuck a couple of times … but I realized I was only giving 110 percent so I reached down inside myself to come up with the extra 90."

"I can't tell them that," she said to him silently.

"Then tell them that there's no 'I' in team."

"Uh, Alex says that he got stuck a couple of times but that he … just thought about the kid and that once he got stuck, he thought his best chance was to just keep moving forward."

"Next question," Chavez said, picking someone at random and pointing.

"Do you think anyone other than a disembodied person could have effected this rescue? At least in such a timely fashion?" a woman asked into her microphone and then thrust it back at Yamaguchi.

"Effected the rescue? Timely fashion? She sounds like a press release," Munroe said.

Yamaguchi realized that he was going to be almost no help. She opened her mouth to respond but Chavez had already jumped into the gap. "I certainly think Officer Munroe made it possible to rescue Jason … expeditiously," she said.

"What about your role, Officer Yama … guchi?" someone asked. She couldn't see who had spoken. "What were you doing to help your partner?"

Chavez touched her on the shoulder and whispered to her. "Don't sell yourself short. Say exactly what you did."

"Uh, I … Alex went into the space between the two buildings and I lost contact with him. My terminal …" She showed her terminal to the reporters. "My terminal has a limited range. We communicate through the terminal. You must have seen these before?" The reporters and Chavez nodded and their assent gave her confidence. "OK, once he went in the crack, I didn't know if he was stuck or not. I mean, it was pretty brave going in there. The dead don't like being confined, you know. I mean, who would. But he went in and I don't know how he did ... oh, he said he had to kind of run at it and get in as far as he could. So then he was trapped ..."

They were able to leave 15 minutes later and went back to their car. Yamaguchi opened the door for Munroe, let him in and went to the driver's side, but she had to wait a minute while other police cruisers and news vehicles cleared the scene. As soon as she got inside, he asked, "So what got into you?"

"What? I don't know to what you might be referring," she said, while searching distractedly for a tissue. She found one and gave a good blow.

"You're on a high. You're glowing. And I mean that literally. Your cheeks are flushed and in infrared you look like Our Lady of the Press Conference."

"Hey, I got on a roll. They were eating it up."

"Yeah, I really liked the part where you battle the giant snake and I snatch the jewel from the statue of the monkey god."

"Oh, it wasn't that bad," she said, although she was already starting to worry that she had gone too far. "Besides, you were feeding me lines. 'I was trapped. I couldn't move forward or back and I didn't know how long I'd been stuck.'" He said nothing. "Anyway, I'm sure it was OK. Chavez seemed to like it," she said.

"I'm not sure that's a good thing, Linda."

"You sure can look on the dark side of things, no offense. Hey, I need to stop at a drug store to pick up some decongestants. There's one just up the road from here."

"OK," he said, not wanting to tell her that her nose was running during the whole press conference.

She pulled away from the curb and drove a few blocks to the Walgreen's at Speer and Federal. She called dispatch to tell them she'd be code 7.

It only took a few minutes to make it to the drugstore. She parked the car and told Munroe she'd only be gone a few minutes. She came back in five and got back into the car and took a cold pill, washing it down with a swig from a water bottle.

"Oh somebody please rip my head off." She waited for a witty response to her straight line. "Alex?"

"What?"

"I gave you a straight line."

"Sorry."

"All right, want to tell me what's on your mind?" she asked.

"Nothing."

"Once a man resorts to one word replies …"

"I'm OK."

She looked at him and nailed his location. "Spill it."

"I was damn scared in there."

"Where?"

"What do you mean where? In the crack, between the buildings."

"You were? But …"

"I was really stuck. I couldn't move."

"Well you obviously did." He said nothing. "Does it matter? You found the kid. You conquered your fear."

"You don't know what it's like if you're dead," he said. "You laugh whenever I get stuck somewhere and I laugh with you because sometimes it is funny. But there were a couple of times when I had no idea how long I might have to wait."

"Wow, I'm sorry, Alex. I didn't know. But hey, as long as I'm around … I mean, I wouldn't have left you there. You know, I'm your partner. Besides, you weren't in there all that long."

"What do you mean?"

"From the time you went in the crack to the time I heard back from you, maybe ten minutes."

"Ten minutes? God, it felt like an hour at least."

"Well, I was starting to get a little bit worried. Mainly I started thinking, 'What if he's stuck in the crack? How do I get him out?' So I had ideas like putting a plank on the end of the stick and squeezing you out. You know, like those ice cream push-pops I ate when I was a kid."

Munroe didn't respond.

"Alex?"

"I'm so stupid."

"Well, I won't disagree."

"That's what they did at that rave."

"What? Stiffs for Jesus?"

"Yes. The marks on the floor. They made a giant push-pop."

"I don't get it."

"They made a temporary room with the stuff they brought in. And one of the walls in that room was on wheels. That's what the tracks were. It's like those box traps from *Ghostbusters*. They push everyone in the room into one area and then trap them."

"That's ... that's insidious," she said. "Never get to use that word. But, Alex, you're making up this theory from a line of dust on the floor. A little thin don't you think? And we're totally ignoring the question of why a Christian group is trapping dead people."

"Your line of critical reasoning is interfering with my beautiful hypothesis."

"Can you even trap the dead with plywall?"

"You can trap the dead with a Hefty bag ... or a vacuum cleaner. Ugh, forget I said that. Bad image."

"Yeah ... well, we need to take another look at that warehouse. Let me see if I can reach the Barfly guys. Meanwhile, you will probably be checking your email."

He had been checking his email while they drove over to the drugstore. He found another message from Brian's mother, asking if he'd made any progress. He really didn't know what to tell her. His partner was right: his theory was thin and he didn't want to present it to Brian's mother until he was sure. *How do you tell a woman someone has kidnapped her dead son?*

He had also gotten another message from someone who remembered the deleted posting from the Denver entertainment forum. Not as specific as the first message, but more or less a confirmation.

"No message from the Springs woman or the guy. And no one's answering at Barfly. It's 7 p.m. anyway. I guess we can try tomorrow," she said.

"No, we have court, remember?"

"Right. OK, so we have a busy Thursday. Let's hope we hear back from the Springs. Uh, Alex, at what point do we say something to … someone up the food chain. Now we're talking about a crime, not just missing persons."

"I don't know if it is a crime. It's pretty hard to prove a crime without a body."

"That's not fair, is it?"

"Need I mention that …"

"Life ain't fair, I know. All right, how do we proceed?"

"I don't know what we do next, Linda. I think we're stuck waiting at least until Thursday. Maybe if we're lucky, the court case will get postponed or we can try to get something done over lunch."

Brian dozed with his head in Karen's lap. Funny, he found himself doing whatever she wanted, and he didn't mind. She'd always complained before that he was too selfish and they always did what he wanted to do. But obviously she was wrong. Or maybe it was him that was changing, taking time to relax instead of working so hard to get his degree. Although it was funny that he was spending so much time lazing on a park bench. *When I was alive ...*

Wow, what a strange thing to think. Of course I'm alive.

That weird thought brought him out of his reverie with a start and he was sure that he'd sat up. But here he was with his head still in Karen's lap, who was still talking. "... or do you like the Mini Cooper?"

"What?" he asked. "Sorry, I just had the strangest thought. I thought ... I thought I had died."

"That's a really weird thing to say, honey. If you'd died, how could you be here with me?"

"Is this ... is this heaven?"

"No, you dope, it's Denver. Heaven is a place where nothing really happens."

"Talking Heads. You like Talking Heads too?"

"They're kind of old, but yeah, I like them. But you know that."

Edwards, the older of the two men observing the session via their monitors, made a mental note to talk to Rachel, the woman acting the part of Karen, about the Talking Heads reference. *Stick to the script,* he thought. Thankfully it worked and the subject didn't notice but the line was just a bit too clever considering the situation.

"I guess, sometimes I forget," Brian said.

"Don't worry about it, we all forget sometimes."

"How long have we been here?"

"I don't know. Fifteen minutes?"

"Seems like longer."

"Maybe, but you still haven't told me yet what car you prefer."

"What?"

"Look over there you dope. See those three cars parked there?"

Brian lifted his head from her lap and looked where she

pointed. He saw three shiny new cars, the sun glinting off their paint.

"OK, the Ford Focus, the Honda Civic and the Mini Cooper. Which one do you like the best?"

"The Cooper, I guess."

"On a scale of one to ten?"

"Um, a seven."

"Good, honey," she kissed him on top of the head, then smoothed his hair with her hand, softly moving his head back to her lap. "Why do you like it so much? Is it fun? Is it exciting? Is it sporty?"

She kept reeling off a list of adjectives and Brian would make his choice.

Good, we didn't lose him, Edwards thought. He turned back to his monitor started checking off boxes on Brian's evaluation form: Suggestibility, Good; Malleability, High; Retention, Fair.

He found himself humming a tune. When he completed the form, he got up to stretch his legs and looked through the windows of the small office overlooking the warehouse full of beach ball-sized black spheres wired together. *I got another intake evaluation to do after this,* he thought. *I hope Rachel can wrap things up.*

CHAPTER 7

STOCKHOLM (Reuters) — The Nobel Foundation announced today that it would reconsider the prohibition against awarding the Nobel Prize posthumously.

"There are scientists, authors and politicians who remain active in their fields, even after their death. The foundation believes that to ignore their contributions would be an injustice," said Hans Erich Kleineman, speaking at an annual gathering of the board of directors.

Currently the foundation's statutes read: "Work produced by a person since deceased shall not be considered for an award. If, however, a prizewinner dies before he has received the prize, then the prize may be presented."

Antonia Simone, the woman whose invention and death led to the discovery of the afterlife, praised the decision. "Even though I'm unlikely to ever be nominated, I'm happy on behalf of the early pioneers in afterlife research, who deserve to be considered.

"But it obviously goes far beyond afterlife research. We're seeing real progress in the fields of robotics, gene therapy and artificial intelligence because of the work of disembodied researchers. And those are just a few examples."

Nobel watchers agree Simone is unlikely to be nominated. "Dr. Simone's conduct, the crimes of which she was accused, would of course, remove her from consideration," Herbert Walstrow, an editor at *Scientific American*, said. "But Dr. Olaf Bols definitely deserves recognition and it would help dispel the notion that he 'stumbled into his field.'" Walstrow was referring to Bols' accidental death at CERN, the high-energy particle research center in Switzerland. It was his work that proved the validity of "field fingerprinting," making it possible to recognize a disembodied person's unique energy signature.

It was a nice idea, trying to sneak out of the courthouse Wednesday, but it didn't work. The case was an arrest for selling fake IDs that Munroe and Yamaguchi had worked four months ago. Munroe had been asked to stake out a bench in Cheesman Park and observed a payoff between a Denver Motor Vehicles employee and the person selling the IDs. Bushes obscured the bench so only someone within 10 feet of the bench could see the exchange, which would have seemed obvious, so Munroe did the surveillance.

As usual, they arrived at the courtroom early because the assistant district attorneys always wanted to go over their testimony one last time. And although they were expected to testify in the afternoon, there was no guarantee they wouldn't be asked to testify in the morning, or at all.

They were now sitting on one of the hard benches outside the courtroom. Yamaguchi was extremely uncomfortable. She was in uniform and the various items on her equipment belt were pushed into her side by the bench. She was also practically asleep. She really required her eight hours and when fighting a cold, considerably more. Munroe was mildly grumpy because the early start meant he didn't go to his morning coffee klatch at Starbucks, which he had already made a daily habit.

"Any messages from the guy in the Springs," he asked.

"What? Oh, I forgot. Let me check my messages," she said. She used her phone to check her voicemail but kept talking to Munroe. "What did you do last night?" she asked, ready to let his drone of websites visited and chats partaken lull her to sleep.

"The usual," he said. "Caught one of the games at the sports bar next to Coors Field."

She opened her eyes. "You mean Hooters, don't you?"

"No, not Hooters. I don't go there anymore since you raised your objections."

"Yeah, right. Uh, no messages, by the way. What else did you do?"

"You'll laugh."

"Oh, I never laugh at your interests," she said, rolling her eyes. *I bet she does that so automatically now she doesn't even know when she's doing it,* he thought.

"I went to a website for disembodied cops."

"Oh, no, you got to be kidding."

"No, really. It was kind of interesting. I talked to a guy who claimed to be Wyatt Earp and someone who said he was Allan Pinkerton."

"And were they? My voice is dripping with sarcasm, by the way."

"The guy who said he was Pinkerton was pretty knowledgeable. But then, he didn't know anything about him that I didn't know. I'm a bit of a buff on historic detectives, you know."

"You don't say. And what did you talk about?"

"Well, in theoretical terms, I asked about this case — specifically if we can charge anyone with a crime. And no, they didn't have any suggestions. What about you? What did you do?"

"Used up an entire box of tissues and went to bed. I need sleep, remember?"

At that moment, the door of the courtroom opened and a bailiff called a witness, but not them.

"Crap, we're going to be here all morning for nothing," he complained.

"And our alternative is?"

"Nothing. I'm just complaining that we're going to be here all morning and I can't go on the web."

"Were you this bad alive?"

"What, grouchy in the morning?"

"No, did you go online all the time?"

"Hell, no, I never went on the web. It was still pretty new. Actually I can't even remember if I knew anything about the Internet. And I didn't do anything on a computer if I could avoid it."

"Pretty ironic then, huh?"

"Yes, thank you, it is. And I also got an email from Cheryl Miller asking if we've found Sgt. Johnson. Oh, and there's another thing. I meant to ask you ..."

"Yes?"

"Interested in going to a Christmas party? On Christmas Day, I mean?"

"I've told you about Christmas before, Alex."

"Yeah, but this will be different."

"In what way?"

"You've never been to a Christmas party thrown by a rich dead guy and attended by his rich dead friends."

"Rybold? What? He really does have the hots for you."

"We're just friends is all. No, seriously, I've been dreading Christmas, as usual. I know you're not fond of it. But this seems, I don't know, different."

"Like discovering your boyfriend is into leather different or like your mother trying to stab your father with a fork different?"

"Your mother tried to stab your father with a fork?"

"It's just one of the many reasons I don't like Christmas. As to your party, I don't like being the token fleshie."

"No, there'll be other fle ... living people there."

"Are you sure?"

"I'm sure."

"I don't know. Maybe."

Just then the bailiff called their names.

"Please state and spell your name and occupation for the record," the bailiff said.

"Alex Arthur Munroe. A-L-E-X A-R-T-H-U-R M-U-N-R-O-E. I'm a Denver police officer." He fought the temptation to spell out his occupation.

The bailiff withdrew and the deputy district attorney stood up to approach the witness stand. As usual, Yamaguchi found the scene surreal. The assistant district attorney was addressing her portable terminal, perched on the edge of the railing of the empty witness stand. It was connected to a boom box placed on an audiovisual cart.

He asked the familiar roll call of questions: How long have you been a police officer? How long have you been a Denver police officer? What are your duties with the police department? When did you die? What did you die of? In what capacity were you engaged on the afternoon of September the 13th of this year? Where were you on the afternoon of September 13th of this year?

She yawned. She'd actually had a good night's sleep, but she always yawned in court, which was dangerous. Defense attorneys often managed to sneak a "Have you stopped beating your wife?" question in a long-winded cross-examination and pity the sleepy officer who didn't notice.

She often thought of the phrase "all deliberate speed" at this point. The ADA was moving with all the deliberate speed of a zombie in a horror film. She knew the point of this slow-motion train wreck was: "Officer Munroe, is this the man you observed accepting $2,000 in cash from Stephen Andriewski on the afternoon of Sept. 13 in Cheesman Park." But if he asked a direct question, the defense attorney would accuse him of leading the witness.

Eventually, despite 10 minutes of foreplay, the ADA finally came to the point. "Please identify the person you just described."

Munroe's digitized voice sounded wonderfully doomful, Yamaguchi thought, as he said, "He's sitting at the defense table, the person in the middle."

"Thank you, officer. No further questions." The ADA sat down while the defense attorney immediately stood up.

"Officer Munroe, how do we really know you are who you say you are?"

"Objection, your honor, the identity of disembodied individuals on the AfterNet has been recognized by the courts for a year now," the ADA said, as calmly as a bored outfielder shagging flies.

"But he's not on the AfterNet now, is he? And he wasn't on the AfterNet when he allegedly saw my client accepting a payoff. He's communicating through a portable terminal, your honor, not through an AfterNet terminal with its supposed ability to detect the unique energy fingerprint of a disembodied person and match it against a database."

The ADA was sitting bolt upright and looked as if he were ready to make an objection, but then realized that he couldn't think of one. Instead, he said, "We could ... uh ... bring in a terminal, your honor?" The judge agreed and after learning it would take a half hour or more to install, ordered a short recess.

Yamaguchi reclaimed her portable terminal and was then pulled aside by the ADA.

"Why didn't you tell me about this?" he asked.

"Because ... I never thought about it," she said.

"Does he have a point?" the ADA, Feldman, asked of his assistants who acted as a screen from the passersby in the hallway outside the courtroom.

"I don't know," the woman assistant said.

"It's not as secure, I think," the male assistant said.

Yamaguchi told them, "A portable terminal, like ours, can be set to accept input from a single person by matching their energy fingerprint against a stored fingerprint. Munroe and I set that up the first time we used the terminal. But unconnected to the Internet, a portable terminal can't match that fingerprint against the AfterNet database of verified identities." She took a breath before adding, "which is what an AfterNet terminal can do."

"Great, so what do we do now?" Feldman asked of his assistants.

"Once we get a terminal in the courtroom, it'll show that this really is Munroe, right?" the woman assistant said.

"Won't do us any good," Feldman said. "The sneaky bastard's already accomplished what he wants. Made the jury doubt Munroe's identity. Next, he'll just say, 'How do we know that it was Munroe who saw the payoff?' Or even, 'How do we know the man we're talking to now is the same man who testified earlier?'"

"The judge would never allow … oh, he doesn't have to," the male assistant said.

"It's my fault," Feldman said. "I should have brought a full terminal in the courtroom. I just thought the portable terminal looked friendlier."

Yamaguchi kept quiet. She had emailed her suggestion to Feldman that they use her portable terminal the week before. She thought Munroe's digitized voice on her terminal sounded friendlier than the one that came out of a public AfterNet terminal.

The ADA and his team went into a huddle and left Yamaguchi and Munroe alone. "I hate lawyers," Yamaguchi said quietly.

"I know. You've told me. Frequently," Munroe said.

"I gave him the idea of using my terminal and the boom box."

"It was a good idea."

"I'm sure Slavin would have found something else to complain about," she said, referring to the defense attorney. "Oily scum-sucking lawyer," she said, quite a bit louder.

"You called," said Feldman, who was now standing behind her.

Yamaguchi spun around, her eyes wide. "The other oily

scum-sucking lawyer," she said. Munroe could have sworn at least two attorneys in the hallway wanted to respond to that.

"The defense attorney," she added.

"Yes, thanks for the clarification. Look, I need you and Munroe to just do what you were going to do. Don't try to fix anything."

Feldman returned to his assistants. Eventually the group broke up and they and Yamaguchi took the recess break as a chance to go the bathroom, make a phone call or raid a vending machine. Munroe ran downstairs to a public AfterNet terminal to check his email.

Yamaguchi was eating a doughnut when he came back, just in time for the bailiff to call everyone back into the courtroom.

This time Munroe communicated through a full terminal placed on the audiovisual cart. He actually had to stand in front of it to capture the field, rather than go into the witness stand. He didn't say anything because he didn't want to cause yet another delay, but it looked odd to see the defense attorney addressing the empty seat.

"All right Officer Munroe, now that we really know it's you, let's continue. Oh, but wait a minute, how do we know it was you in the park that day?"

"Your honor, this is ridiculous," the ADA Feldman said, rising to his feet.

"All right, all right, I'm willing to drop it and accept this officer's word that it was he that day," the defense attorney said. He favored the jury with a smile and a half wink. He turned back to face the witness stand.

"Now officer, let me make sure I understand how the dead ... disembodied that is, communicate." The defense attorney paused and Munroe realized the man was confused for a split second. *He's expecting me to nod so he can continue but there's nothing to see.* "Uh ... where ... as I understand it, the dead cannot hear."

"That is correct," Munroe said.

"And yet you hear me now?"

"The terminal recognizes your speech and translates it into words that I can read, either by watching the terminal's video screen, like you're doing, or by the words that appear in a virtual screen projected by the terminal that only the disembodied can see. I'm not sure how it works, but it does."

"And the dead cannot speak?"

Where's he going with this? Munroe thought. "No, we can't." He wanted to explain more but he remembered the rule: Answer yes or no.

"So the voice we're hearing now is not your real voice."

"No, it's not."

"Can you read lips?"

"No."

"So without ears to hear or the ability to read lips, how do you know my client knowingly accepted any money from Mr. Andriewski?" Munroe saw Feldman pull his tablet out of his suit pocket, tap the screen and then look up at the witness stand.

"Officer?"

"I'm sorry, could you repeat the question?" The defense attorney did so and Munroe said, "Because I saw him give the money to the defendant."

"But you were unable to hear anything?"

"Yes."

"That's not quite accurate, is it, officer. You were able to hear just like you're able to hear me now."

"Yes, that's correct."

"Because a portable terminal, probably the one your partner is wearing on her sleeve right now, was taped to the underside of the bench where my client was sitting." The defense attorney looked at the judge. "Your honor, I'd like to submit that using Officer Munroe in this fashion wasn't any different from bugging my client. The park bench that he was sitting on was in a secluded area, shielded from casual eyes and yet difficult to approach without being seen. He had a reasonable expectation of privacy under these conditions."

Feldman rose to object.

"Mr. Feldman's going to say the park is a public place, but the courts have allowed the concept of private areas, even in public places."

"Your honor, I do object for exactly the reasons Mr. Slavin has stated. And the expectation does not extend to a park bench." Yamaguchi was impressed with the amount of loathing with which Feldman could say the defense attorney's name. "The park is a public area. The concept of a private place in public has been upheld to include a phone booth where a warrant was not obtained, but when that phone is not in a booth, it's not illegal to overhear a conversation. Surveillance cameras are a common sight in airports, banks and store and even on the streets and evidence from those sources have been allowed."

By now the two lawyers had everyone's attention.

Slavin responded, "Yes, but surveillance cameras are a physical presence. We know they are there. We can see them and we can adjust our behavior accordingly. When we go into a department store, we're warned that we are being observed. But Officer Munroe does not exist, at least not in the sense that we can see, touch or hear him. If we allow his testimony, aren't we saying that we're not safe anywhere. That we can never know when someone is watching."

The judge banged her gavel and told the two attorneys to stop talking and approach the bench. They argued in stage whispers before the judge. After a few minutes of this, the judge told the attorneys that she would meet with them in her chambers and ordered another recess.

Back outside in the hallway again, Yamaguchi said, "I'm starting to feel like a yo-yo."

Munroe was about to reply when Feldman appeared. "Come on, Yamaguchi. The judge wants you and Munroe, too."

He escorted them to the judge's office, which now held three lawyers from the district attorney's office, two defense lawyers, Yamaguchi and the judge, who eyed them all with distaste.

"Bobbie, do you really need both your underlings?" she asked the ADA. Feldman dismissed the male assistant.

"OK," the judge said. "Mr. Slavin ..."

"Please, call me Edward, your honor," the defense attorney said, wanting to be on an equal footing with the ADA.

The judge gave a quick grimace. "Yes, very well, Eddie. Your tactic has been tried before and it didn't work then and it's not going to work now. Testimony from the disembodied has been admitted in court and upheld and I don't want any more crap about doubting Officer Munroe's ... you are here aren't you Munroe?" Yamaguchi said yes for Munroe. "Doubting Officer Munroe's identity."

"Yes, your honor."

"And how many more iterations of this same defense are you going to try."

"Surely, your honor, you're not suggesting that I have to have my defense strategy pre-approved, here, in front of the prosecution."

"Cut the crap. Are you going to keep pulling this stuff?"

"I will defend my client to the best ..."

"OK, we're going to adjourn for lunch and try this again in the afternoon and I want to warn you, Mr. Slavin, that this court will not be your ticket to the Supreme Court."

The judge dismissed them all and Yamaguchi and Munroe found themselves closeted with the prosecution over a working lunch. After lunch, the defense attorney continued his cross-examination of Munroe. Although he gave up his privacy defense, he still tried his death of a thousand cuts, finding a discrepancy in one of the dates in Munroe's report versus Yamaguchi's and Munroe's statement that the money was in a brown envelope when the fraud detectives described it as gray.

They were finally released about 3:30 and went back to the department. Yamaguchi had been at the courthouse since 8 a.m. and was dead tired. Munroe, however, was aching to get online. Munroe replied to Rybold, saying he and Yamaguchi would be attending his party. Yamaguchi tried to reconnect with the minister and reschedule their interview. Then they worked on disembodied witness reports.

About 5 p.m., Yamaguchi got a phone call back from the minister and they arranged to meet at the church.

— & —

Edwards tapped his pen nervously on the desk, waiting for the phone call. His report would be disappointing, he knew, and he racked his brain trying to come up with some way to color it to his favor.

He answered the call on its first ring.

"Hello, Edwards," he said. "Yes sir. No, I'm afraid the results aren't as promising as I'd hoped. But I … oh, thank you sir. Yes, I'd already said 5,000 would be needed to be statistically meaningful. Right now, 3,500. I do agree." He nodded his head several times agreeing. "You will? That would be … that would be great." More nods, then, "Yes, yes I will. Goodbye."

He hung up the phone, feeling dazed but happy.

"Well, what did he say?" his assistant asked. The younger man had been listening to the one-sided conversation and was on the edge of his seat.

"He agreed. He said he knew our sample would be too small and he gave us the go ahead for another collection."

"You're off the hook?"

"We're off the hook. Yes, he said he understood. He was very nice about it."

"Even though we missed the target ..."

"Yes, even though we missed our target." Edwards sat up straighter in his chair and looked disapprovingly at his assistant. "He knows the limitations we're working under. We're not the ones who came up with the suitability estimates, you know, so I wouldn't want to be in that group's shoes. But we're OK. He even said to say hello to you."

"He ... uh ... he knows who I am?"

"Yes, he does."

"Don't know if I like that."

"Don't worry. Let's get back to work. We've got a lot more units that have to come online in the New Year."

— & —

Yamaguchi and Munroe parked on the street next to the church in the Five Points region of Denver. They got out of their car and walked to the church. It was quite dark and she was scanning the neighborhood automatically, the way she used to when she patrolled the area years ago.

"I bet they have some good barbecue here."

"Oh please, Alex, that is such a racist thing ..."

"Hey, there's a restaurant right there, 9 o'clock."

She looked and there was indeed a barbecue restaurant cater-corner to the church.

"Oh, I'm sorry Alex. I guess I overreacted."

"You know I'm not that bad."

"No, I know you're not. I'm overcompensating." They had reached the main doors of the church, but saw a sign labeled "Office" that pointed to the side of the building. They followed the sign.

"I used to patrol here. It's historically a black neighborhood and it's high crime, especially after the afterlife. So it's easy for some cops …"

"Yeah, I know. It looks like a nice neighborhood."

They came to the office door. A sign hanging below a peephole said to knock and she did. They soon heard someone fumbling with locks. The door opened and a short black man opened the door. He was dressed in black pants and shirt, but wore a dark red cardigan sweater. His clerical collar identified him as the minister.

"Rev. Anderson? I'm Officer Yamaguchi." She held out her hand and he immediately clasped it with both his hands.

"Come in, officer."

After relocking the doors, he led them into his office, which was cramped, and lined with bookshelves and plastered with the motivational type posters she recognized from the police station. Except …

"Wow, de-motivators," she said.

The minister laughed. "You like these? They're hysterical. I really like this one."

He pointed to a poster showing a group of skydivers, holding hands to form a ring as they were falling. The caption read, "Never underestimate the power of stupid people in large groups."

"Seems appropriate for a church, don't you think?" he asked.

"Yes, sir."

"Now, what do you and your partner want with me?"

"Partner?" she asked. "You know …"

"I recognized you from the TV last night. You and your partner rescued that boy last night. That's why you couldn't make it, correct? Oh, my manners, please sit down." He grabbed an uncomfortable metal chair and offered it to her while taking a slightly more comfortable vinyl backed one. They sat in front of his desk, illuminated by a pool of light from his desk lamp.

"Yes, sir," doing her best not to wince. She'd managed to avoid the topic during the day. Because they started the day early and didn't need their car, they hadn't been to the department yet. And the courtroom intrigues left little time for small talk.

She had seen the paper that morning, however. The story was on page one: "Disembodied cop rescues trapped boy." There was a photo of the fire department carrying the boy out on a stretcher and another photo showing the crack. The story was pretty straightforward, not sensational at all. Even Munroe had said that despite the headline and the inevitable ribbing he'd get because of it, he thought they'd come out ahead.

The story was fine. The photo of her on an inside page, however, was another thing. "Denver Police Officer Linda Yamaguchi, runny nose on left, animatedly explains how she and her disembodied partner, Officer Alex Munroe, rescued Jason Acevedo from the crack from hell," the caption read, or should have read. The photo had that kind of iconic look to it — like the picture of Lee Harvey Oswald getting shot. It was taken during the impromptu press conference. She was not quite in the center of the picture because the photographer had framed it to include Munroe, represented by the odd gap between her and the public affairs officer Chavez.

But despite not being the center of the picture, she was definitely the most interesting thing about it. She had some kind of demented expression and her hands apparently had been waving so wildly they were blurred. "You look fine, Linda. I mean you take a good photo. Not like me," Munroe had offered, when she showed him the picture.

"Uh, we'd — that is my partner Officer Munroe and myself — would like to ask you some questions about a woman, a disembodied woman. She had arranged to meet someone here at your church."

"Oh, the missing Sgt. Johnson."

"You've obviously talked to Ms. Miller."

"Yes, I did talk to her. I mean we've sent e-mails back and forth. I'm afraid I can't be of much help. For one thing, it's been a number of years since Tralawna was a member of this congregation."

"Yes, sir, I ..."

He interrupted, "Call me Chuck, if I can call you ..."

"Linda. Did you know her well when she was alive?"

"I was the one who baptized her, but there's not much to say, a likeable kid, athletic. Looked just like her mother, which meant she didn't date a lot." She looked at him oddly, not accustomed to such bluntness from a minister. "I know her mother, Evelyn Johnson, very well."

"Oh, great," Yamaguchi said. "Maybe we can talk to her about her daughter."

He shook his head. "I'm afraid that won't help you much. Evelyn ... apparently she didn't want to believe that Tralawna was her daughter." He sighed. "She's one of the people who doesn't believe in the afterlife ... in the disembodied."

"Ask him what he believes," Munroe urged her. She shook her head slightly.

"So they had no contact?"

"No, that's why Tralawna had contacted me. She wanted me to talk to her mother for her. But I never knew that she had made an appointment to meet Ms. Miller here. She probably never thought about making an appointment to see me. She'd know I'm always here."

"Ask him." She shook her head again.

"Do you have anything else you can tell us? You haven't heard from her since her friend reported her missing."

"No, I haven't heard from her. Is there something wrong, Linda?" he asked when she shook her head again.

"I'm sorry. It's my partner. He wants to know what you think … about the disembodied."

"Where is he?"

"Just to my right."

The minister looked in Munroe's direction. "I don't know what to think, officer. Some of the people I've talked to on the AfterNet I knew when they were alive. They were people I've counseled, people I visited when they were sick or who helped out at a church function. I don't care if the national church officially recognizes them or not. I know they are who they say they are." He put his right arm on the edge of his desk and picked up a paperweight, a round river rock, which he rolled around in his hand. "They aren't the devil. They're not aliens. I don't know what to think.

"I've done a lot of transition counseling, you know, for some of my older members, people who were terminally ill. Maybe if I'd had a chance to work with Tralawna's mother, but a traffic accident, so sudden. Evelyn gets a visit from the Army one day and a few days later hears from her daughter. The Army really has to do a better job with counseling. If I'd known … oh, well, all I can do is learn from their mistake."

Yamaguchi stood, and then the minister. "Thank you, sir. I'd appreciate you getting in touch with me if you hear from Sgt. Johnson." She handed him a business card. They shook hands again. He walked to his office door, unlocked and opened it for her.

He touched her lightly on the shoulder before she stepped out.

"Tell your partner, he has my respect," he said softly as he handed her his business card. "I'd be pleased to chat with him sometime."

She smiled and accepted the card and stepped outside.

"Seems like he'd be pretty sympathetic to Sgt. Johnson," Munroe said.

"If they ever meet."

"Right. Hey, aren't you about done for the day?"

"Yeah, I'm bushed."

"OK, drop me off downtown and call it a day."

Munroe spent a few hours that night at Duffy's, a bar near the eastern end of the 16th Street Mall. They had recently remodeled and put in a large screen TV that the regulars ignored, so the management just left it turned on with closed captions. Sometimes Munroe would call ahead and ask them to leave it on for some show he wanted to see and every once in a great while he'd buy a round at the bar (a difficult thing to arrange through PayPal).

He'd stopped at the station to check his email, of course, and found a reply from Rybold saying he'd expect him and Yamaguchi. He also sent a message to Cheryl Miller telling her that they'd talked with the minister. As with Brian's mother, he did not voice any suspicions that she'd been abducted.

Afterward, he cleared his inbox of new disembodied witness reports and was going to see what kind of buzz his latest blog update had generated. But several uniform cops, including the desk sergeant, walked into the break room. He was curious what they were doing and followed. Munroe assumed it was something of interest to men, because all the cops were male and they had that mischievous look he associated with bachelor parties.

One of them produced a laptop and typed in the address of one of the local TV stations and played a video from a local news show. An anchorman was talking and the words "Disembodied cop rescues boy" appeared to his right. The picture switched and showed a reporter at the scene, then quick images of firefighters and cops staring at the crack, a mug shot of himself (probably taken about 1985), then firefighters removing the boy from the hole in the basement and finally out of the building on a back-board. The reporter returned, talked some more and then he saw Yamaguchi talking to the reporters.

Apparently this was what the assembled cops had been anticipating. He could tell they were laughing — actually laughing so hard one man was turning red and seemed to be choking. His friend had to slap him on the back.

He wasn't quite sure what was so funny. Without closed captioning, he was missing any obvious humor in what she was saying. *Granted, she looks kind of wild and she's waving her hands around a lot and ...* He saw why they were laughing when the desk sergeant paused the video and then replayed it frame by frame. He saw her use her sleeve to wipe her nose and the glistening smear it left on her upper lip. *Oh, yuck,* he thought, *poor Linda.* He watched as they replayed the scene again. *I wonder if I can find it online.*

CHAPTER 8

From *The New Yorker*

The heavy metal door slams shut behind him; a sound totally in place with the man, the building, the institution and the state. He's the senior warden of the Polunsky Unit of the Texas Department of Criminal Justice — the man in charge of the death house.

John Blue has overseen hundreds of executions and a few years ago, he believed that death by lethal injection was a just punishment and deterrent for crimes that required the ultimate penalty.

"Now I'm not so sure," the 53-year-old Blue said, running his hand over his close-cropped hair. He looks more the Marine he was than the stereotyped image of a Texas warden. He doesn't even own a pair of mirror sunglasses, but he does have a "Don't Mess with Texas" bumper sticker on his pickup truck.

"We're required to have an AfterNet terminal available in the visitor's center. And we're just waiting for the day when we execute a prisoner and see his name pop up on that screen 15 minutes after he stops twitching."

That hasn't happened yet, but executed criminals have logged on using that terminal. The quickest turn around time to date has been two days.

Vikki Rawlings is hoping to reduce that time. She's a registered transition counselor with the criminal justice department. Her job is to file living identity certificates for the men and women on death row, and give them basic instructions on how to use an AfterNet terminal.

"So far, no one's been able to use a terminal while alive. As you know, not many people can. I can't. But I can prepare them for the experience."

Munroe cringed when he saw Yamaguchi throw the young officer to the mat, falling on his back. *Ow! That must really hurt.* Then she appeared to cradle his arm and danced around his head, turning all 225 pounds of cop onto his stomach, then holding his hand against her leg while using her knee to lock his elbow as her foot slid under his shoulder. The procedure happened so fast the man didn't have time to resist, but he was now slapping the mat with his free hand.

Munroe guessed that it was an indication that he was completely at her mercy and starting to feel pain, but she ignored him, still talking to her other students in the arrest control class. She pulled a tissue out of the back pocket of her sweat pants and blew her nose while still keeping him pinned.

She's really in a bad mood. Poor ... oh, what's his name, Martin? Just his luck to be her victim after she's seen the video. He wasn't there when she saw it. He heard about it from Marianne, the criminal justice intern who helped out in the detectives' room.

Now she was making her victim stand back up while holding his hand almost like a baseball bat. He stood on tiptoe whenever she twisted his hand a little.

Munroe had snuck into the gym to watch his partner. He sometimes did when she taught arrest control training because he worried how his tiny, petite partner could handle herself in a real fight with an unruly suspect. He knew she was a black belt in aikido and an arrest control instructor, but it just seemed impossible that she could defend herself.

He could see he was wrong. She brought her hands

down in front of her, still holding the young man's arm. His elbow came down like a Whack-A-Mole mallet and his body followed. He fell face down onto the mat. He lay there a while before rolling onto his back to stand up.

She reached down to help him up, but he backed away as if she were a snake. *Yeah, she can handle herself. Maybe I'll talk to her later.*

He left the gym to head back to his desk. She'd be in class all day and he was left to his own amusements. Which meant another pile of disembodied witness reports.

He found his chair at his desk and started compiling mug shot lineups for witnesses. An attempted bank robbery on Colorado Boulevard a week ago was observed by at least three disembodied witnesses. Of course, there may have been hundreds who saw the crime, but subtract the ones who were insane, didn't know how to use a terminal or didn't care, and he was left with three, still a pretty good number. And unlike the living witnesses, whom the gunmen had terrified, the disembodied got a good look at them.

Detectives had identified one man as a suspect and Munroe was collecting stock mug shots from the database the FBI maintained on the AfterNet just for this purpose.

He'd scheduled chats beginning at 3 p.m. with the detectives, an assistant DA, the defense attorneys and the first of the witnesses, who was now in Cheyenne, Wyoming. It was going to be a long day.

Yamaguchi rubbed her sore shoulder as she searched the stacks of the library. *Why do most guys think arrest control requires force after they've already got you pinned? I never do,* she thought, and then made a mental note to apologize to Martin. She also made a note to use Steve to demonstrate the yankyo pin next week as he was one of those who laughed hardest after watching the video.

She found what she was looking for: *Dragged Through the Mud; The Search for the Seattle Strangler.*

The book cover was more lurid than she would have guessed: obviously staged crime scene photos that showed a large pool of blood (I thought he was a strangler) and the trademark white tape outline of a body (I've never seen one of those in real life).

She took the book over to a chair overlooking the lobby and sat. She flipped through the pages and immediately saw Munroe's name listed in the "I'd like to thank" section. She fanned through the book and it seemed as if his name was on every page.

She looked at the book jacket blurb: "Jackson Denning was the man neighbors asked to watch their kids if they had to run to the store. You gave him your keys when you went on vacation. This made him an unlikely suspect in a series of brutal killings of young women in Seattle. But author Michael Selwyn, an award-winning reporter for the *Seattle Post-Intelligencer*, unravels the clues that led police to catch the man dubbed the 'Seattle Strangler.'"

She looked at the back and saw the picture of the author, actually wearing a corduroy jacket with leather patches, backed by a wall of books. He was kind of intriguing looking, despite his little Van Dyke beard, and he definitely had an air of self-importance. She could imagine the ribbing her partner must have endured when the book came out. She'd found the first mention of Munroe in the book.

"Alex Munroe is a big man, 6 feet 3, 220 pounds, and he still looks like the linebacker he was when he played college ball at Notre Dame. He uses that size to keep people at a distance and I've seen him use it to intimidate, although I've never seen him be violent and he does not have that reputation.

"He has one failed marriage behind him and says, 'Don't tell my wife, but I'm working on my second.'

"He's blunt and when he talks, which is rarely, makes jokes like that when the conversation ventures anywhere near an emotion. But it's still easy to see his determination whenever the subject of the Strangler comes up."

That's Alex? she thought. *That's nothing like him. There are times I can't make the man shut up.* She flipped a few more pages and read.

"It's incongruous to see this man, who you'd think would have all the sensitivity of a bulldozer, finesse a crime scene. Sherlock Holmes, a detective he admires, would meet his match in Alex. He will stand unmoving for minutes, just looking, just noting the out of place element and comparing it with his memory of previous crimes.

"He noticed, for instance, that in each of the murders attributed to the Strangler, a wastebasket had been emptied and replaced with a new plastic liner. And he noticed this at only the second crime scene he had investigated (which was actually the third murder committed by the Strangler). It was even more impressive when you consider that all the murders, save one, were committed in motel rooms where you wouldn't be surprised to see a recently emptied wastebasket. But the liners that caught Alex's attention were different. They hadn't been knotted to keep them secure in the basket, unlike the liners in the other wastebaskets in the room."

OK, that sounds more like Alex, she thought, remembering his thoroughness back at the LoDo rave site. She skipped ahead.

"By this point in the investigation, Munroe had become obsessed by the case. His marriage had fallen apart. His partner had been reassigned. Co-workers (he had few friends) noticed that he'd begun losing weight. And the Strangler was now publicly taunting him, leaving behind messages pinned to the victim's clothing."

She read one of the notes:

Mr. Detective,
Lovely Carol Ann
Did you not know she was next?
Could you not guess her name?
I thought we were playing the same game, Alex.
Catch me

"Munroe's encyclopedic knowledge of crime is fascinating. He can rattle off the Yorkshire Ripper's victims as readily as Jack the Ripper's. He's privy to details held back in many of the major serial killings in this country because of his acquaintance with detectives in those cases. He knows the inner workings of the serial murderer because he allows himself to be dragged through the mud with them.

"But that knowledge is also troubling to anyone who tries to understand Munroe. How can a man retain his sanity or his morality when he understands such terrible things? Because he does understand these murderers. When he talks about the Strangler, he goes far beyond the cold, bare facts of the FBI's psychological profile. You can hear the comprehension in his voice when he reads the assessment, 'The Strangler may be the product of a broken home, deprived of the love of his mother and terrified of the presence of his father.'

"I asked why he thinks the Strangler is committing these crimes. He looked at me and said, 'I think he's lonely. I think he wants someone to play with him.'"

Oh, Alex, she thought, *I never knew you had to go through something like this.* She was absentmindedly-turning pages when she saw the photos. She saw the pictures of the Strangler's victims, crime scene photos, reproductions of some of the notes, and then Munroe. *Oh my God, I never realized how handsome he was.* The photos were in black and white and the first showed him sprawled on a diner bench, wearing the same dingy sport coat so many of the male detectives wore even today. Another photo was of Munroe crouched at a crime scene, pointing at some detail and looking up at the camera and the last was of him at a press conference announcing the capture of the Strangler. Oddly, he looked the saddest in this picture. And in all the pictures, he had a cigarette in his mouth or in his hand.

The last two pictures in the book were of the Strangler — Jackson Denning. The first photo was from a high school yearbook, showing a cherubic youth with unruly long hair and a smile that couldn't be contained. The last was a booking photo showing a man of about 30, still very recognizably the same youth and the same smile.

She closed the book and sat back in her chair. Her partner was now revealed to her as a different man. She'd always known he could be a grouch when he wanted, but in general, he was good company. And she would never describe him as a tortured soul, which considering the circumstances, you'd think he would be.

Her phone vibrating against her back interrupted her reverie. She pulled it out and saw a number with a Colorado Springs area code. The woman at a nearby chair gave her a dirty look. Yamaguchi smiled in apology and took the phone over near the escalators.

"Hello, Yamaguchi speaking."

"Uh, Officer Yama … yama …" the man said. *It's a simple name,* she thought to herself.

"Yes, that's right. Can I help you?"

"Hi, this is Tracy Newell, with the Explorers. I'm returning a call from … sorry, from a few days ago."

"Thanks for calling back. I was hoping I could talk to you about an event that took place in Denver on the 11th."

"Oh sure, let me see. Yes, we sponsored a rave that day."

"I'd like to know a little bit about it. Oh, heck."

"Excuse me? Is there something wrong?"

"I've got to get back to class. And I'd really like to get my partner in on the conversation."

"Well, I'm afraid I called you right before I was supposed to leave for the holiday. I'm sorry I didn't return your call sooner."

"No, no problem. Look, could we make an appointment to see you? Maybe Tuesday?"

"You want to come here?"

"If it wouldn't be an inconvenience."

"No, Tuesday then. Let me look … How about 10 a.m.?"

"Actually, that would be …" she said, calculating when her shift started and the time it would take to get back from the Springs. They might be starting their shift a little late. She'd have to remember to clear it with Clemens. "I'm pretty sure that would work. If I can't make it …"

"Just leave a message with my assistant or leave a voicemail."

"Fine, Tuesday then."

Naturally everyone was late getting to the mug shot lineup except for his disembodied witness.

> **jollycopper:** I'm sure they will get here soon.
> **AlfredBThomas23:** No problem detective. As I'm sure you know, I have nowhere to go. :(
> **jollycopper:** Thanks for understanding, Mr. Thomas.
> **AlfredBThomas23:** Always glad to help the police … uh, Detective … sorry, what was your name again?

jollycopper: Alex Munroe.

AlfredBThomas23: Yes. You know you really should replace that nickname with your real name. I would think a police officer especially would want their name prominently displayed.

jollycopper: You might have a point, Mr. Thomas.

AlfredBThomas23: Please call me Al.

jollycopper: So, Al, what did you do before you died.

AlfredBThomas23: I was an insurance claims investigator, for 23 years.

jollycopper: Sounds like interesting work.

AlfredBThomas23: Oh it was. And I often worked closely with the police.

janemurtagh has entered the room

fat_tony has entered the room

Paul.Rodriguez has entered the room

janemurtagh: Sorry I'm late.

Dick.Sussel.ADA has entered the room

jollycopper: OK, looks like everyone is here. If I might do the introductions. Mr. Thomas is our witness. Jane Murtagh and Anthony Cipriani are detectives. Paul Rodriguez is an attorney for the suspect. And Dick Sussell is an assistant district attorney.

AlfredBThomas23: Delighted to meet you.

jollycopper: OK. I'm sure they're delighted to meet you too. Let's start. Mr. Thomas, I'm going to show you six pictures. Look at them carefully and tell me if you recognize any of these people.

AlfredBThomas23: I don't see any pictures.

Dick.Sussel.ADA: Click the viewer window.

janemurtagh: I don't see anything either.

jollycopper: OK, everyone stop. Everyone should be using Internet Explorer, right.

AlfredBThomas23: I'm not.

jollycopper: No, you're correct Al, you should be using an AfterNet terminal. The actual physical display.

AlfredBThomas23: That is correct.

jollycoper: OK. Then look on the left hand side of the chat screen. There's a button that says Image Viewer. If you have any problems, say so.

AlfredBThomas23: Number three.

Paul.Rodriguez: What?

AlfredBThomas23: I recognize number three. From the bank robbery

Dick.Sussel.ADA: Uh, Alex, all I'm seeing is a broken link for the number 3 picture.

Paul.Rodriguez: If you're seeing a broken link, how do we know what the witness is seeing? I insisted before that this witness return to Denver. This chat is a waste of time.

Dick.Sussel.ADA: This is ridiculous. Even if we brought him here, what's the diff? We'd still be using a terminal to talk with him.

janemurtagh: Hey, Alex. Now the number three picture is the same as the number two picture.

If he could have, Munroe would have buried his head in hands. It was going to be a very long day.

CHAPTER 9

LSU PRESS ANNOUNCES
NEW TOOLE NOVEL
For Immediate Release
Contact: Edna Mayfair

When he wrote his introduction to John Kennedy Toole's "A Confederacy of Dunces," Walker Percy lamented that the tragedy underlying this vast rollicking comedy was the author's suicide in 1969 at the age of 32 — and the fact that the readers of the world had been denied a great body of work. It was a great pity, he wrote, but there is nothing we can do about it.

Little could Percy have dreamed that a little more than two decades later (and more than a decade after his own death) he would find himself writing the introduction to a completely new sequel, written by Toole himself!

Louisiana State University Press is proud to announce the March release of "A Parcel of Rogues." Yes, John Kennedy Toole is back. And so is Ignatius J. Reilly, that vast (both in flesh and mind) Gargantuan Falstaff who made the Pulitzer Prize winning "Dunces" such a literary roller coaster.

"Parcel of Rogues" picks up where "Dunces" left off. Ignatius, with the assist of his girlfriend-of-sorts, Myrna Minkoff, has fled the Big Easy for the Big Apple. You might think he'd be a whale out of water, but the beatnik folk scene of the Village in the early '60s proves a perfect place for a medieval misanthrope to thrive.

Familiar characters from "Dunces" make welcome appearances and they are joined by a fresh confederacy of more-than-colorful creations. "Parcel of Rogues" will be available in both print and as an online e-book on March 2.

Munroe and Yamaguchi arrived at the district six substation parking lot about a quarter after 2. She'd gone to the main department building downtown where they usually worked, but he'd had a surprise for her, which had necessitated the drive to the substation. He actually had two surprises for her.

"We're on patrol tonight."

"What?"

"Yeah, they're short handed. Seems everyone has your cold."

"Funny. District 6 at least, I hope?" she asked.

"We're keeping the holiday shoppers safe."

"LoDo?" she asked, referring to that part of lower downtown with shops, bars, restaurants and over-priced condominiums, and the site of the rave.

Denver was divided into six districts and district 6 included downtown. The main department building was the home of the Criminal Investigation Division, but the patrol division was scattered throughout the six substations. So they had a short drive over to the District 6 substation near Washington Street and Colfax Avenue.

"Yeah, should be fun."

"You're not actually looking forward to this?"

"I always liked patrol."

"Is that why you were a detective?" she asked, as they parked.

She walked through the lobby and went to the door that led to the secure area of the building. She had to wait for another cop to enter his code and let her in.

"Oh my God," she said after she walked through the door. The cop who'd let her in looked back at her, but she waved him on.

"What?" Munroe asked.

"Roll call." Since the rescue of the boy and her embarrassment over the photo and the newscasts, she'd been able to avoid large gatherings of cops. She'd been in court all day Wednesday and teaching the arrest control class Thursday. She'd largely been spared the mockery of her fellow officers.

"Oh, shit."

"It won't be that bad, Linda," he said. Of course he was lying. He liked her a lot and thought she was a good cop and being her partner he would have stood up for her in any situation, but the video was damn funny. Maybe the antihistamines she'd been taking had made her goofy or it was just the high you get when you save someone's life, but she looked wild on that video. Even without sound, just looking at the closed captioning, it was hilarious.

She said nothing. He couldn't help but enjoy her predicament. "Come on, you'll enjoy yourself. Christmas Eve, chestnuts roasting, carolers singing."

"Shoplifters stealing, drunks vomiting."

"We are in a bad mood."

"Sorry, Alex, I told you I don't like Christmas. Now, if you'll excuse me ..." She pointed to the sign that said "Women's Locker Room."

Munroe waited for Yamaguchi in the hallway, amusing himself by looking at some of the motivational posters on the wall that inspired the minister's poster, including the one showing a game of tug of war with the caption, "Never underestimate the power of people working together to solve a problem."

Damn, I hope it fits, he thought. *Damn, I just hope it's in the locker room.*

She emerged from the locker room ten minutes later.

"Alex, it's beautiful," she said.

"So that's it, huh?"

"Yes, can't you tell?" she asked, turning around for him to see.

"Sure. Actually, I never knew there was anything wrong with the one you had before. But you were talking to Mary a while back and I overhead your conversation. The office terminal can pick up conversations from quite a distance if it's quiet."

"Oh, good to know," she said, filing away that information for the future. "You got the right size and width. It fits perfectly. And it's a lot lighter than my old one."

"Yeah, Mary picked out the size and ordered it and I think she got one for herself."

"Thanks, Alex. It's a wonderful Christmas present. I know you and Mary don't really get along and I appreciate you teaming up. I love it."

"The real challenge was getting it sent from downtown to here."

"Well I appreciate all the effort. OK, I guess we go to roll call," she said, smiling happily. She turned and walked confidently away with a swagger.

He stayed behind to watch her. *Damn, diamonds may be a girl's best friend, but a nylon gun belt that weighs half as much, that's priceless.*

Surprisingly, they arrived early, only a few other people were waiting in the squad room, and they didn't look up as Yamaguchi entered. She silently told Munroe, "OK maybe if we hang back here we can escape the worst of it." The joy of her present had already faded.

Then sergeants Diller and Tompkins, followed by three other cops, entered the room and she knew she was done for.

"Well, who do we have here? It's Gooch!" Diller said.

"Hey sarge."

"Long time no see, Linda. Not out rescuing anyone?" asked Tompkins.

Yamaguchi actually liked Tompkins, even if it was impossible to hold a normal conversation with the man. He kept quoting lines from "Monty Python" or "Star Trek" and using his arcane knowledge of pop culture to explain policing, politics and life in general and expecting everyone to know what he meant.

Yamaguchi hated Diller, however. Not only was she the person who came up with the appalling nickname, she was its most ardent promoter. For some reason, Diller disliked Yamaguchi from the first time they met and for most of her time in patrol, Diller was the sergeant for the Five Points sector — her sergeant.

"No, apparently patrol is so weakened by disease and easy living that I had to fill the gap," she said in response to Tompkins.

"I heard you were the one who started this plague. Spread from downtown to the substations," Tompkins said.

"Greatly exaggerated, I'm afraid. I merely acted as a host for the parasite before it began infecting the rest of the crew," she said. Tompkins smiled.

"Your partner with you?" asked Diller, interrupting the witty repartee with Tompkins.

"Joined at the hip," Yamaguchi said.

The other cops started filling the squad room including the other district sergeants, so Diller and Tompkins took their places at the table up front.

Roll call was running late so the show got started while people were taking their seats.

"Good afternoon, ladies and gentlemen," a male sergeant, who Yamaguchi thought was responsible for LoDo, said. "Let's get this started so the day shift can go home. We're obviously undermanned today so let's do everything we can to stay on the street. That means only the bad guys go to jail. Everybody else gets a 'get out of jail card.' And let's keep the code 7 to a minimum, which means you Reichart. That means break starts when you call it, not when you sit your ass down.

"I'm also told to remind you that as usual people are running late on their timecards. There is no longer any way to get your timecard submitted after the 3 p.m. deadline. This comes from the embittered old bitch who we all know and love in accounting.

"Um, let's see, we're putting together the riot staffing for the New Year's Eve weekend. Special operations don't expect this year to be as bad as last year, but I'm sure most of you remember that they said the same thing last year.

"Finally, Merry Christmas or whatever because other than riots and pillaging, our crime statistics look good. Apparently our ceaseless efforts have kept the streets of Denver safer than they were last year. So good job and don't screw it up. Now to let you know about the crime we haven't been able to prevent. The irate Broncos fan has struck again in the 1300 block of Sherman Street, tagging four cars. And as this is only a block from the Capitol, it makes us look bad."

The sergeant continued reading out various crimes that had occurred in District 6 the past few days. Most of the cops looked bored because they'd heard the litany of crimes the day before and the day before that. A few conversations were going on while the sergeant, reading from a computer screen, never looked up.

"Oh my God, this is boring," Munroe told Yamaguchi.

Yamaguchi had almost nodded off and Munroe's voice in her ear caught her surprise. "What, I thought you liked patrol?"

"Yes, but I can't remember roll call being this boring. Every petty crime in the world."

"What, crime was more interesting when you were young?"

"Must have been. And you were starting to nod off, too."

"Still fighting this cold."

"So what's the deal with you and the woman sergeant?"

"She's the one who came up with 'Gooch.' I don't know what she has against me, but we've always hated one another."

"Oh, I almost forgot, we had another bank robbery, a very bad guy who pistol-whipped a cashier," the sergeant said. "Luckily, the security cameras caught him in the act and he can clearly be seen in this video."

"Hey, maybe something interesting after all," Munroe said. "Wonder why he left it for last?"

Sgt. Diller got up from the table and went to a laptop connected to the overhead projector. She turned on the projector, which displayed the newcast already cued to Yamaguchi's performance. Then she hit play. The room went wild when Yamaguchi wiped her nose with her sleeve. Diller paused the video and Sgt. Tompkins stood.

"Excuse me, apparently that was something else. OK, everyone quiet down. As you all know, we have an extra special guest," Tompkins said at the front of the room. "I'm sure you all remember Officer Yamaguchi from her days in patrol." A few people applauded. "She and her partner ... I'm sure you've all read about the exploits of Officer Munroe in the newspaper and from watching TV ... will be joining us tonight. Good job getting Timmy out of the well, you two."

All the cops in the room swiveled in their seats and looked at Yamaguchi, who slowly got up. She stood as tall as she could and hooked her thumbs in her new gun belt.

"The only thing I've got to say to you morons is ..."

Munroe was a little worried. He had seen her temper in the training class yesterday. Then she brought the back of her hand to her nose and elaborately wiped it across her face and tried to make the biggest snuffling sound she could.

"... much appreciated."

"OK, that's it. Have a good night out there," Tompkins said, once the laughing subsided.

Yamaguchi and Munroe drove around the apartment complex for the second time that night.

"What make and model did they say was popular?" she asked.

"Didn't you pay any attention?"

"It means so little to me."

"You mean make and model? You're a cop for god's sake. You're supposed to know this stuff," Munroe said, wondering how she'd ever been a patrol cop for three years without knowing car models.

"They all look the same to me. Was it a Japanese car?"

"Yes, they're targeting Acura Integras. That's a hatchback. You know what a hatchback is, right."

"Well, of course," she said, although Munroe doubted her.

"It's the one with the little round headlights. You actually pointed one out to me last month and said it looked sporty."

"Oh, yeah," she lied.

"Why are you asking, anyway?"

"Because I think I saw one a block back. It might have been abandoned."

She turned right at the corner and backtracked their car to the vehicle in question. It was a red car and was missing its back two wheels.

"That's a Celica. It looks nothing like an Integra."

"Whatever, run the plate."

Munroe entered the plate into the computer. Luckily they were in an unusually fast hotspot and the information came back quickly.

"Not reported stolen," he said. "And it's registered to a guy who lives in this block."

She started driving again. "It was worth a look."

Driving east on Speer Boulevard over Interstate 25, Yamaguchi saw a car ahead driving the speed limit, which on Speer made it stand out. The car was a 1990 Chrysler LeBaron, which she didn't recognize as such, but she knew it was an ugly American car. She couldn't quite make out the expiration tags and it held four people, all young men from what she could tell through the tinted windows. She was now tailgating the car and she saw that the plates had expired.

She called dispatch and told them she was going to do a traffic stop and the approximate location, then she flashed the cruiser's emergency lights, but the car continued. She turned on the siren momentarily and the car pulled over to the right.

"It's registered to a Hector Garcia, 21 years old, 5 foot 7, 155 pounds," Munroe said. He'd already run the plates. "No wants or warrants."

The car finally pulled off at the entrance to the Elitch Gardens amusement park. Yamaguchi called dispatch and updated them on their location.

"Want to do the honors?" she asked Munroe.

"I'll tell you if it's safe," he said.

She opened the car door and sat back as far as she could in her seat. Munroe squeezed his way past her and out the car. He approached the driver side window and looked inside. He could tell the car held four young Hispanic men, three of whom were staring straight ahead. One in the back seat seemed to be sleeping. The three looked nervous but many people do when a cop stops them.

The young men were dressed nicely. Munroe was looking more closely at the two in the back seat when he noticed that something was on the lap of the man on the passenger side. All he could tell was that it was long and black. He shifted to infrared and the heat of the man's body made the outline more distinct. It was a baseball bat.

He went to the other side of the car and looked again but saw nothing else suspicious. He went back to Yamaguchi.

She had already transferred her portable terminal to her left hand so he didn't need to reenter the car to speak to her.

"Four young Hispanic males. Rear seat, passenger side, has a baseball bat in his lap."

"A baseball bat?" she asked.

"Yes, but I think it's wrapped ... like a Christmas present. They look OK."

Yamaguchi got out of her car and approached the Le-Baron. The driver side window rolled down. She pointed her flashlight at the side view mirror and the reflection lit the face of the driver — obviously a young kid. As she came alongside, she flashed the light at the passengers and saw two more nervous faces.

"Could I see your license, registration and proof of insurance, please?" she asked.

The young driver nodded quickly and reached for his wallet — or a gun. She had no reason to believe this, but her right hand rested lightly on the butt of her gun. Then she saw the wallet in the young man's hand and relaxed. *Been a while since I did this,* she thought.

He pulled out his license and gave it to her, but then began a conversation with one of the young men in the back seat. She quickly glanced at the license and saw that it was issued in Chihuahua, Mexico. *This won't be easy,* she thought, *Mexican driver's licenses are impossible to run.*

"Do you have registration and insurance?" she asked the driver again. He looked at her nervously, nodded his head and turned to face the other occupants. A quick conversation in Spanish appeared to center around one of the men in the back, on the driver's side, who appeared to be sleeping, or passed out.

"Alex, is he dead, the one who's asleep?"

"No, he's alive. His heart is still pumping. I think he's passed out."

The other passenger in the back started prodding the unconscious man, who was now moaning, and then started rolling him. Yamaguchi took a cautious half step back. *Damn, I'm jumpy.*

"What's he doing to that man?" she asked the driver, who failed to hear her. She tapped the driver on the shoulder. He jumped and so did she. She repeated her question.

"We're trying to get his wallet. It's his car." The driver said. His English was good, far better than her Spanish.

Eventually a registration and insurance card matching the car was produced, and the unconscious man's license also matched the registration.

"What's the matter with your friend?"

"Too many beers. His boy … son died."

"What's in the back? Is that a baseball bat?"

"Yes. The Rockies. *Palo conmemorativo de béisbol.* It's for his son."

Yamaguchi was confused, but intrigued. "When … how old is his son?"

The driver asked the question to the others in the car. "Twelve."

"And when did he die?"

"Last year. On this night. *Víspera De Navidad … ¿Cómo usted dice víspera De Navidad?*" he asked his fellow passengers. They answered back "Christmas Eve," while Yamaguchi silently mouthed the words as well.

She found herself asking the next question reluctantly. "Is the bat a present for this year?"

"Yes," the driver responded. "He ask for it this year."

Yamaguchi remained silent. She was startled when she heard Munroe's voice in her ear. "Give him a break."

She looked again at the driver's license and then addressed the driver. "Mr. Rivera, you drive safe, OK? Get your friends home. And tell Mr. … uh, Garcia, to get his

160

plates renewed." She handed everything back to him and walked to her car. After a few seconds, it pulled out and continued down Speer.

The rest of the night passed uneventfully. They'd gone to back up another officer at a bar where a patron was reported as drunk and disorderly but by the time she got there, the man was just plain drunk and no longer disorderly. She left that because someone reported hearing shots fired at the Pepsi Center, but when she got there, the vast parking lot was empty. There were no events scheduled at the sports arena that night. She drove around the building and found nothing except a private security guard asleep in his car. She woke him up and he said he'd been there all night and had heard nothing. After that, she went to the 16th Street Mall to take a report about an incident involving a mounted patrol officer — a man claimed the horse bit him. But bystanders said it was more of a kiss than a bite and the man decided not to file a complaint.

"Oh God what a boring night. Kill me now," Munroe said after she got back in and they were moving again. "Can we go yet? It's almost the end of the shift and we … you still haven't had a lunch break. And we're just a couple of blocks away."

"All right you big whiner. I'll call code 7 and we can go to your thing."

She drove down to the LoDo end of the 16th Street Mall and parked the car on Wynkoop Street, not too far from the site of the rave, coincidentally.

"You could have parked closer," Munroe said.

"What? Now you don't want to … oh, of course, there's a light breeze."

"Did you say that in a sarcastic voice?"

"Yes I did. Come on, the walk will do you good."

Munroe almost felt cold moving through the wind with

his partner, occasionally ducking behind her to draft in her slipstream. In a few minutes, they were approaching the Tattered Cover bookstore, which was brightly lit in contrast to the restaurants and stores closed for the holiday.

"I wonder why they're remaining open," she said.

Munroe had regained her side. "The notice said they just wanted to do something for the disembodied that had no home to go to. It's co-sponsored by the AfterNet."

"See, Denver's a nice place, just like your Seattle. Now I'm using my treacly sweet voice, by the way."

"I bet it still sounds sarcastic. And I've never said anything bad about Denver."

The terminal reported her response as unintelligible, but Munroe guessed it was in the nature of "harrumph."

Yamaguchi held the door open for her partner, who immediately felt the store's AfterNet hotspots. She knew her partner. "Go mingle while I get some coffee."

Munroe went to the periodicals hoping to bump into some acquaintances, living or dead. Several living people were already online, sitting in comfortable chairs, banging away at their laptop computers. He logged into the field and found David, the dead TC employee, with whom he often discussed jazz.

"Alex, glad you stopped by."

"Thanks, David. Big turnout?"

"Last time I checked, more than 500 online."

"How many are you talking to?" Munroe asked. David was infamous for holding multiple conversations.

"You're number ... uh ... 24." David had been a long time TC employee. He'd been a homeless drug addict for a number of years before being hired. Since his death, he never budged from the store, except for occasional visits to the other branches. He had become the store's liaison to the disembodied world, and still worked for the store. A lot of people made a beeline for the Tattered Cover when they died.

"Hey, I've got to go in back and see if there's a package. Why don't you take over and dissuade this moron's opinions about *Tijuana Moods*?"

Within a few minutes, Munroe was deep into an impromptu Mingus chat.

Yamaguchi was on the second floor, skimming a book about AfterNet field mechanics. She'd already found Munroe in the periodicals, talking about jazz with his buddies. She couldn't understand the appeal of what she considered arcane music to a bunch of deaf dead people, but it pleased her that he still found it interesting. He apparently was defending the merits of some obscure album. He hadn't even noticed her online and was as happy as a pig in slop.

She, on the other hand, kept glancing around her. She always felt uncomfortable in stores while in uniform. Chatting up salespeople or talking to citizens she could always justify to herself as community outreach. But when you start shopping, the public saw you as a lazy cop who's pursuing personal business on the job. Of course, seasoned cops, like her partner, were forever chiding her about her scruples.

The second floor was mostly empty, however, and she had let her guard down.

"Wow, heavy reading," a man said, almost in her ear.

She turned and bumped into the speaker, dropping her book. She didn't like the fact she had let someone get that close without her noticing. And most citizens wouldn't get that close to a cop.

"Sorry," the man said. "Didn't mean to startle you." He bent down to retrieve the book.

"No, that's OK." She got a good look at him. He wasn't tall, maybe 5'7" but nicely proportioned in his black leather jacket. He had a buzz cut that clearly showed his hairline, which wasn't receding. What she could see indicated he had brown hair. And he had nice blue eyes that nicely contrasted his dark looks.

"'AfterNet Field Mechanics Explained,'" he said, while handing her back the book. "That's pretty technical." He had an Irish accent, or at least it sounded sort of Irish. It was intriguing, whatever it was.

"Is that an Irish accent, or what?"

"Mock Irish," he said, sounding more Midwest now. "It's the accent I use when I … I'm a native Coloradan, but I lived in Dublin from age 8 to 14. Sometimes I slip into it." He said the last with the accent again. She liked it.

"Are you on duty?"

"Well, I don't normally dress like this for Christmas Eve." He looked a little crestfallen at her rebuke and she regretted it. "But I'm on break now. I'm not just wasting the taxpayers' money." He rallied at her offer of continued conversation.

"So why are you here? Tonight's mostly for the disembodied."

"Well, you're alive. Why don't you tell me why you're here?"

"No, you first."

"My partner's dead. He's downstairs talking jazz."

"Oh, yeah, I peeked in on that. Kind of … well, you know, jazz heads."

She grinned and nodded.

"Oh, so you're that cop," he said. *Damn!* she thought, *he's seen me on the news.* "I mean he's that cop. Yeah, I remembering reading about it when he was hired. And you work with him?"

She relaxed and said, "Yup. So, what are you doing here? Are you with … do you know someone who's … you know."

"My ex-wife."

OK, that threw a damper on things, she thought.

"She died the day our divorce became final. Car hit her.

Her last words were, 'I'll always love you.'" His accent became almost impenetrable. "I'm having you on." She gave him a blank look. "I'm making it up," he said in a normal voice. "It's Christmas Eve and I have no place better to be and I'm friends with the owners and currently I have no woman in my life."

"Cheeky monkey," she said, trying to sound British. She regretted it immediately. She wasn't very good at accents, but he just seemed to have an unfair advantage with his.

"That's very good," he said. He pointed to the book again. "Seriously, are you interested in that?"

"Yes. I'd like to see if I can boost the range on this thing. Do you know anything about these?" She turned her shoulder to let him see the terminal on her arm.

"Well, I know a little." He took out his wallet and handed her his business card. It said "Robert Feore." He worked for the AfterNet.

"Really, uh Robert?" she asked.

"Bob," he said. "There are a few unofficial hacks to extend the field, but then it's so strong it violates FCC regs. And battery life will drain a lot faster unless you put in a pot to adjust it … and the case is held together with Torx screws so you'll need a special screwdriver …"

She looked at him skeptically. "So essentially, no. It's nothing I can do."

"I didn't say that. You can find instructions for mods on the Internet. I'll admit cutting the surface mount traces to the limiting resistor on the board is difficult and if you screw it up, you've basically destroyed it, but it can be done. Of course, as an AfterNet employee, I could never condone such a thing. Wink, wink."

"Huh? What … wink, wink?"

He looked at her as incredulously. "Monty Python."

"Oh."

"You know, Monty Python's Flying Circus."

"I know," she said, a little irritated. "I've seen *Holy Grail*. And the other one, the Jesus one." She liked Monty Python, up to a point, but the encyclopedic knowledge of Python fans could grate on her. "Anyway, what do you mean?"

"It's why I gave you my card. I could mod your terminal for you. Or perform any other services you might desire."

This was a new experience for her. Her last boyfriend, who was chased off by her mother, only asked her out after six months of preliminaries. He tapped the card she still held in her hand. "That's my email address, and my phone number, and my cell number. I could add my ICQ, but that might appear too desperate."

"Is this man annoying you, officer?" she heard from her ear buds. *Great timing, Alex.*

"I'm sure I have more than enough information to contact you, should I need to."

"Because I could make him go away. Call for backup," Munroe said.

"Is there something wrong with your ear?" Robert asked.

"I'm getting a call," she lied. "I'll just ignore it."

"Can you do that, if you're a cop?"

"He's right, you know. You're always on duty."

"No, it's a personal call. You're right, I'd better ..." She put the book back on the shelf. "It's been nice ..."

"Shouldn't I get your card?" Robert asked.

"Look, thanks, but I ..."

"Oh, give him your card," Munroe said. "I'll wait."

She took out a card and as she gave it to him, she drew in her breath and said, "OK, got to go," and left.

Feore stood there with her card in hand and watched her go away. Her equipment swayed with her body as she walked. He thought she looked a little hippy, but cute.

CHAPTER 10

INT. A BEDROOM -- NIGHT
A shadowy figure moves through room and wakes
a sleeping couple.

                NARRATOR (V.O.)
Ever have the feeling that you're being
watched? Worried that your privacy is being
invaded? Well guess what? It's true. The
disembodied are everywhere and you can't do
a thing about it. Until now. Dispelle, the
incredible ionizing Z-ray wristband will
protect you from unwanted spying.

INT. A CONVENTION HALL -- DAY
Woman stands before Dispelle tradeshow booth.

                WOMAN
I no longer have the feeling I'm being
watched. Finally I can use a restroom or
try on clothes at the store.

Man stands before Dispelle tradeshow booth.

                MAN
I've got a disembodied friend. But I still
don't want her watching me when I don't
know it.

```
INT. A BATHROOM -- NIGHT


A woman turns on a light and starts brushing
her hair. She turns around, startled.
                    NARRATOR (V.O.)
   If you're plagued by unwanted guests ...


INT. A BEDROOM -- NIGHT


The same woman is brushing her hair before a
mirror. She pauses to spin her Dispelle on
her wrist.


                    NARRATOR (V.O.)
   ... Dispelle will harmlessly push them
   away. Our patented technology ...
```

"So how long have you been a police officer?"

"Excuse me?" Yamaguchi asked the man who'd asked the question. She'd been distracted by the sight of yet another person playing with the Star Trek-like doors in Rybold's mansion.

Everything in the house bewildered her. It was the largest private home that she had ever entered, although her familiarity with the homes of the rich was admittedly limited. It was south of the Cherry Creek Mall in the Polo Club subdivision, but the rich people who lived there probably would resent the word "subdivision" to describe their gated community.

The elderly man with the bad comb over and holiday-themed cardigan repeated his question.

"Oh, excuse me, I pulled a long shift yesterday. I ... zoned out there. I've been a cop for a little over four years." The man and his friends all nodded politely at this information and she wondered again why they were all being so nice to her. She assumed rich people were always cold and calculating and uninterested in the lives of the common man, but these people were plying her with questions and listening intently to her stories. At first, she suspected that Rybold had instructed them to keep her occupied while he talked to her partner. But after a while, she lost herself to the unaccustomed experience of having a lot of rich people pay attention to her.

But every once in a while, out of the corner of her eye, she'd see a door slide open and close, sometimes in response to a person walking up to door — often just to see the door in action — and sometimes without anyone being there at all. Rybold had converted all the doors in his house to pocket doors, with detectors that slid the doors open in the presence of a person, disembodied or otherwise. As nonchalant as she was to the thought of working with a dead partner, this was the first time she really had an idea how many disembodied shared the world with her as the doors opened and closed in the house.

"Don't let it bother you," comb over told her. "They're just more of Bill's friends — no different than you or me, but look who I'm talking to. You of all people should be comfortable with the disembodied." He gave her shoulder a comforting squeeze and she thought for a moment that he reminded her of her Uncle Saul, a friend of the family who had given her a lot of counsel growing up, until she noticed the Patek Phillipe watch on his arm and realized it was probably the equivalent of her year's salary or more.

His comment sparked another round of questions directed at her.

"Miss Yamaguchi?"

She turned and found herself looking at Rybold.

"Mr. Rybold. Hello. Lovely party."

"Today I'm not Bill. I'm just plain old Derek Humphries today. See? No pin," he said, patting his chest.

He leaned closer to her and said in a confidential tone,

"But Bill did ask me to look after you." He straightened back up and said in a normal tone, "I think I found it for you. If you'd like to follow me ..." He smiled at her and made a vague hand gesture.

"Oh, yes, that's nice," she said. "Excuse me," she told the group.

He led her to the door she'd seen open and close and was delighted as it opened for them. The other room was a library with only a few people sitting in leather armchairs surrounding a low coffee table that held an AfterNet terminal.

"Hope I'm not wrong. You looked kind of surrounded back there."

"No, thanks, they were being awfully ... uh, friendly."

He laughed "Yeah, that's the word for it. Actually, they're all really curious why you're here. You're probably the poorest person here, no offense."

Yamaguchi was walking to the large French doors that gave the library a view of the garden. Humphries followed her.

"None taken. And I'd like to know why I'm here, not that I'm complaining. The shrimp's really good."

"It's pretty obvious. It's your partner. Bill's headhunting him. I don't know why, but that's it."

"He really wants to hire Alex?" Humphries nodded. "I thought that was just a way of breaking the ice at the reception."

"I'm sure it was, but Bill's hiring all the time, and not just the disembodied."

"What for? Isn't he ... retired?"

"Bill? Hardly. Yeah, he's given up trying to take back ClearView, but his next project ... look, I'm sure your partner will fill you in. Bill's talking to him now."

"But what's he need a cop for?"

"Can't say. Bill hires the strangest people. He's got an instinct about it. Sometimes he hires people just because they intrigue him. That's my guess for his interest in your partner. A disembodied cop. Very noir."

"Yes, but if he works for Mr. Rybold, then he wouldn't be a cop any longer."

"Ah hah, but if he hires him as an outside consultant, he'd be a disembodied private detective. Can't get much more noir than that."

She lifted an eyebrow, or at least tried to. "Is he drawn to the dark side?"

He did a much better job of raising his eyebrow. "No more than any other dead billionaire bent on world domination. I'm kidding of course."

"And I'm out of a partner," she said. *I've really got to figure out how to raise an eyebrow,* she thought.

"I'd bet it's a package deal."

"And what would he want with me?"

"It's pretty obvious you two work together well. You could continue being his avatar."

"I'm not his avatar," she countered, not quite sure whether being considered one to be an insult.

"Well, whatever you want to call it, it's not a bad job."

"What do you call your job?" she asked.

"Me? Personal assistant. Secretary. And from time to time, avatar."

"It's not a full-time job?"

"Being an avatar? By no means. Bill needs me to be the public face of the company occasionally. But day-to-day, I'm his assistant. When he's traveling, I make sure doors get opened. When he's entertaining, I pour the drinks. Stuff like that. I'm sure it's not too different from what you do."

"Back up a second. You said entertaining. Do you mean …"

"I've said too much already, Linda." He grinned.

"OK, but I've got this image in my mind. Well, if he wants to hire Alex, and me, what's he like?"

Humphries shrugged his shoulders. "Bill's an easy boss to work for, and he's a brilliant businessman. But I'm closer to him than anyone else, obviously, and I still don't really know him."

Munroe eased himself into the chair, which detected his presence and swung the terminal into position for him. They were in Rybold's office. He logged in and saw that Rybold was already waiting for him in private chat.

ribaldhumor: Hello, Alex.

jollycopper: Bill, thanks for inviting me … us.

ribaldhumor: You're welcome. Glad you could make it. And I really did mean to invite the both of you.

jollycopper: Nice house. Awfully big.

ribaldhumor: For a dead guy you mean?

jollycopper: Hell, big for Charles Foster Kane.

ribaldhumor: Where are you staying?

jollycopper: Anywhere I can. I mostly hang out at the department, hit the sports bars when I can, the library.

ribaldhumor: So no fixed address? Wouldn't you like a place to call home?

jollycopper: I'm not saying it wouldn't be nice, but the job doesn't pay much and besides, as long as I have access to a terminal, the world's my oyster.

ribaldhumor: I don't believe your needs are that simple, Alex. I think you're compensating for your situation.

jollycopper: Yeah, I'm dead and so are you. What's the difference if I'm dead in a house with 12 toilets if I can't piss in any of them.

ribaldhumor: Easy, Alex, I wasn't trying to rub it in. I'm not showing off my wealth to you. Instead I'm trying to see if I can help you. My job offer is serious.

jollycopper: OK, why would you want to hire me? What do I offer?

ribaldhumor: You're an example. Your work with the police department shows that the disembodied shouldn't be ignored. You and your partner show that the living and the dead working together can be powerful. But we can't allow ourselves to be treated as anything but equals, Alex, and allowing yourself to be treated as a piece of equipment dilutes that message.

jollycopper: So you're saying that working as a cop makes me your poster child, but at the same time I'm making it worse for those who might follow. It's a nice Catch-22.

jollycopper: You know a lot of black cops in the 60s and 70s had to make the same choice. They were never paid as much as white cops, but they got their foot in the door.

ribaldhumor: Stop thinking like a member of a minority, Alex. You know, I was aware of you even before the city was thinking about hiring you. The second my doctors told me I had pancreatic cancer, I started planning for my afterlife.

ribaldhumor: I tried to find out who was speaking up for the rights of the disembodied, and I found you. You made a big impression when you testified before that House committee.

ribaldhumor: You said, "Ignoring what we offer will damn the disembodied to irrelevance and neglect. And be careful what you sow here today, because I know you will be around to reap the spoils of your decisions."

jollycopper: Can I speak now?

ribaldhumor: Please go ahead.

jollycopper: You just happened to have that quote ready?

ribaldhumor: Yes I did. You're an influential man. Your blog attracts a lot of readers. I looked at your site statistics and calculated your likely ad revenues. You probably make a little from that. With that and what the department pays you, you could rent. So why not?

jollycopper: We both know where that leads ... once the dead start demanding a place to stay, we crowd out the living. It's just like your comment about my taking the job with the department.

ribaldhumor: That's why you resent my owning this house.
jollycopper: Yes.
ribaldhumor: I agree. That's why I'll be putting it on the market as soon as we break ground on the Center for the AfterLife.
jollycopper: ?
ribaldhumor: Here, in Denver. A massive project, a home for the disembodied, an advocacy group, a power base, a world-class research center.
jollycopper: Ah hah. All those Einsteins and Newtons come home to roost. But despite predictions of warp drive and personal flying machines, we still haven't seen the … ah, you're going to say we haven't had the infrastructure to support that kind of research.
ribaldhumor: Yes. Part of the problem is the insistence of the AfterNet and their certificates. Why do we require that someone prove they're Einstein or Planck or Edison? And besides, why do we require an Einstein, when an Alex Munroe will do.
jollycopper: Sorry, I'm no Einstein. What good am I?
ribaldhumor: You're just one example. Admit it, Alex, you already know where this is going.
jollycopper: I'm obviously not as smart as you think.
ribaldhumor: No, you're smarter than you think you are. The power of the human mind, Alex, unfettered by corporeal restraints, freed from the drudgery of eating and sleeping and the need to make enough money to go on eating and sleeping. Can you really tell me you've not thought about this?
jollycopper: You're saying the disembodied are smarter than the living? You've not trolled the forums much, have you?
ribaldhumor: I'm not talking about the dross of humanity, Alex. Tell me, what are you doing online right now, in addition to our chat.
jollycopper: I'm reading my mail, checking a few news sites. You've got a fast connection here.
ribaldhumor: Is that all?
jollycopper: All right, I'm updating my blog and checking my

ad revenues. And I'm searching for anything about your center.

ribaldhumor: And how long have we been talking?

jollycopper: About 20 seconds. I get the point. Some of us can think and communicate faster than we could when alive.

ribaldhumor: That's why I want to hire you, and others like you. The disembodied "who have learned to exceed the limitations of the flesh and travel the filaments of the world on electric threads." That's from the center's mission statement. A little purple, but I think it gets the point across. Be honest, Alex. What do you foresee happening, to the world?

jollycopper: The second wave. The first wave was the panic after the discovery of the afterlife … the suicides, riots, wars. A whole lot of denial. But we're in the trough right now. Next come the demands. Demands from the dead to have a voice, to vote, to own property. Demands from the living that those rights will be waiting for them when they die.

ribaldhumor: Go on. A nice metaphor, by the way. You used that on your blog.

jollycopper: You are checking up on me. Well, to continue stealing from my own writing, the living are starting to accept this is real. It's not a phenomena. It won't go away. Every time someone famous dies and can prove their identity, it makes it more real. The living get more scared. They plan a little more.

ribaldhumor: And what's the seismic event that triggers the next killer wave, to continue your metaphor.

jollycopper: China, India and the Muslim world. We've actually had breathing space because most of the disembodied are insane and won't go online. Demand for bandwidth is still low because much of the third world doesn't have Internet acces, much less AfterNet access. But once India gets over the idea that karma doesn't mean squat, once the Muslim world ends its denial, once China re-embraces ancestor worship … we're heading for a world where all you do while you're alive is prepare for death. The ancient Egyptians had it right.

ribaldhumor: Bravo, Alex. but you forgot to mention the baby boomers in the U.S. Once they start dying in numbers, the Social Security shortfalls will seem insignificant.

jollycopper: So your center will solve all this?

ribaldhumor: I hope it'll make a dent. We can't assume the living will care what happens after they die. The idea of an afterlife or heaven and hell, reward and punishment, has been a tenet of most every religion. That still doesn't mean most people live their lives in such a way that they deserve that now outdated concept. No, we, the disembodied, we've got to secure our own future.

jollycopper: And I take it that working as a cop won't be enough.

ribaldhumor: For some, it might be. There will always be a need for security guards, cops, spies, etc. … but the center will sell the amassed power of our intellect.

jollycopper: Again, I think you overestimate my intellect … and that of most disembodied … despite my ability to walk and chew gum at the same time.

ribaldhumor: Then you would be amazed at what we think we can achieve, Alex. If you've got time, I'd like to give you a run down of what we're planning.

jollycopper: I don't know. You've already taken up a whole forty seconds of my valuable time. But go ahead. Linda can probably amuse herself.

"Linda, let me introduce you to someone."

Humphries had led Yamaguchi back for more food and she was marveling at her little tray that allowed her to attach her wine glass. "I just love these …"

She looked up and saw that Humphries was standing next to Robert Feore.

"Bob, this is Denver Police Officer Linda Yamaguchi, and Linda, meet Bob Feore. He's the CTO at the AfterNet."

"What are you doing here?" she asked.

"Well, what are you doing here?" Feore countered.

"So you know each other then."

She turned to Humphries. "We met last night at the Tattered Cover."

"I offered to hack her terminal."

"Really?" Humphries said. "I have no idea what that means." He used a hand to shade his eyes, as if he were shielding himself from the sun. "Oh look, I see someone I need to talk to. I'll leave you two to talk alone."

Feore looked at her. "You seem on pretty good terms with Rybold."

"That wasn't Rybold. I mean he was, but he's not at the moment."

"Oh, is he … damn, what's his name?

"Derek."

"Right, right. Anyway, why are you here?"

"I've been asking myself that all day. I guess Rybold wants to hire Alex, my partner. And me too, I guess. What about you? And what's a CTO?"

"Chief Technical Officer. That's my title."

"That sounds kind of important. Like maybe you know more than just a little bit about field mechanics."

"Maybe just a little bit more."

"But why are you here?"

"Like I said last night, I don't know a whole lot of people in Denver. And Rybold invited me. Or rather, he invited most of the top management. I'm the only one who showed up, that I know of. The only single, unattached guy." He sighed. "Woe is me." He brought his hands to his shoulder and mimed playing a violin and hummed something that was supposed to sound mournful. She liked a man who didn't mind making himself look stupid.

"So what's a CTO do?"

He stopped his performance. "I evaluate all the coming technologies that might impact the AfterNet and I make sure the day-to-day technologies continue to work."

"So, super nerd."

He smiled. "Yeah, that's me."

"A pretty important job, I should imagine."

"Maybe, definitely a pretty busy one. Part of the reason I don't … uh … know anyone I could spend Christmas with."

"I bet you're another rich person like them," she said quietly, vaguely gesturing at the other people in the room.

"No, not in their league, I'm afraid."

"Oh yeah? Here, hold this." She gave him her tray, which he accepted in his right hand, and with her right arm, she grabbed his left wrist and lifted his arm. She slid back his sleeve and exposed his watch: a Swiss Army watch.

"All right, you're a regular guy." She took back the tray.

"What was all that about?"

"Nothing. You want to sit?" she asked. The rich food, the wine she'd been drinking and the sense of intrigue were starting to catch up with her.

She started walking back to the library and Feore followed. She sat on a window bench and he sat next to her.

"Are you OK? You look a little beat."

"Just getting over a cold. And I'm not used to all this."

"All this what?" he asked.

"Wealth. I mean this guy is seriously rich."

"So I take it you come from poor but humble folk."

"Well, not poor exactly. They're both college professors. And my dad still is."

"What about your mom?"

"She died a while ago."

"I'm sorry."

"Not as sorry as I am. No, I shouldn't say that. Or should I say that? It's hard to figure out. I love my mother, but she can be a colossal pain in the butt."

"So, you still keep in touch?"

"Yes, but right now, my mom's in Japan, torturing my dad. He's alive. What about you?"

"Both my parents are dead. My dad died when I was 18, my mom when I was 20. I haven't been able to contact them. So actually, I'm a little envious of you. It'd be nice to talk to them again."

"Be careful what you wish for."

"My, we are being bitter."

"I'm sorry, Christmas brings it out in me."

"What's the matter with Christmas?"

"That's when my mom killed herself." She'd said it before she realized. She'd never told anyone this.

"I'm so sorry," he said. He didn't know what else to say.

Oh what the hell, she figured. *In for a penny* ... "In '97, the Christmas after the discovery. You know, people were killing themselves right and left. And my mom, she was always threatening to kill herself while I was growing up. It was her way of getting what she wanted. Whenever my dad and her would argue, she'd try to kill herself — take some sleeping pills, but never enough to really do it. But after the discovery, I guess she figured, why not. Look, I'm sorry. Suddenly I start spilling my guts out to a perfect stranger."

"Perfect, huh?" he asked her. She could see in his face that he was doing his best to amuse her. *I guess I know how to charm a guy. Tell him about my dead mom.*

"Just a phrase, doesn't mean anything," she said with a smile.

"Well, I'm going to consider it a compliment. So, other than the fact that you're mom's dead and your partner's dead and you're at a dead guy's party, what else is bringing you down this Christmas."

"Well, Safeway is not stocking the Dickens Toffee coffee I like."

"I know. What is up with that? And you know they

closed that little deli shop at Sixth and Grant. Another burrito shop took its place."

"Which deli? Cushman's?" She decided not to mention she ate at the burrito shop two days ago.

"Yeah. I always ate there. Best pastrami in Denver."

She laughed. "The world is going to hell, isn't it?"

"What are you two laughing at?" Munroe's voice asked her. She was startled for a second.

"Oh, Alex, I'm sorry, I didn't see … Alex, this is Bob, Bob Feore. Bob, this is Alex Munroe, he's my partner."

"The one Rybold's after. Pleased to meet you, Alex."

Munroe was impressed. Unlike most people introduced to a disembodied person, Feore didn't appear uncomfortable, and he automatically looked to Yamaguchi's right, about where Munroe was standing.

"This is the guy from the TC last night. What's he doing here?" he asked his partner.

"Alex says hi. Bob works for the AfterNet. He's a big shot there."

"Sorry, Linda, forgot my manners. But ask him what he's doing here."

"Alex is curious why you're here," she told Feore. She looked back to Munroe. "He got invited same as us."

"Rybold's a pretty big player. I met him through the Tattered Cover; the owners introduced us. You know, he was actually trying to steal the sponsorship for last night's party away from the AfterNet. Anyway, I must have made an impression and he invited me."

"Bob was trying to cheer me up," she said out loud. Privately, she told him, "Stand down Alex I like him."

"OK, OK. Just seemed like a weird coincidence."

"Maybe U want to move along, mingle?" she told him.

"Hey, wait a minute," Feore said. "Are you the same Alex Munroe with the blog?"

"He says he is."

"You're quite a celebrity."

"He is?"

"Oh yeah. He's causing quite a stir. I have no idea where you got those projections but they're dead on."

"What projections?" she asked.

"About the challenges we're going to have in the third world, getting the AfterNet accepted and the need for a cheaper, simpler public terminal. We'd just signed a deal with Red Hat for a stripped down OS and he knew about it. How did he find out?"

"Tell him it's amazing what you can find if you look hard enough."

She relayed this and Feore responded, "What, you're saying you found that out by a search?"

"Tell him I found an RFP that the AfterNet put out a year ago and ..."

"Wait!" she shouted. "Look, you two should get a room. Why don't you go sit at that terminal over there? You won't have to go through me."

"Do you mind?" Feore asked.

"No, no problem at all," she said out loud. "Bring him back when you're done, Alex," she said to him privately. "I'm not done with him yet."

"Where will you be?"

"By the food. I think I'm getting my second wind."

"I'm not going to use the cat door, Linda"

"But I can't leave the door open. Look, I turn down the thermostat, leave the flap on the cat door up and you can come and go as you please."

Munroe and Yamaguchi were arguing over her offer of letting him stay at her apartment while she was in Winter Park skiing Sunday and Monday.

They'd left Rybold's party around 6 p.m. and Munroe had taken her offer to stay the evening. She had plugged her terminal into her home entertainment system and she could hear him in five-channel surround sound while watching the old Alastair Sim *Christmas Carol* movie with closed captioning. Yamaguchi was on the couch and she'd run an extra long patch cord between the terminal and the audio equipment to allow Munroe to sit with her.

"A lot of the places you might hang out will be closed anyway," she argued. "I just don't want you wandering the streets. And since you're not interested in skiing …"

"No, I'm definitely not interested in skiing." He thought the sport a monumental waste of time when he was alive, doubly so dead. He also didn't know how to ski or how he could do it dead. "Besides, I know how much Mary likes my company."

She was glad he didn't want to go with them on their trip. Mary was a fellow officer from district 6 and she didn't feel comfortable around Munroe, always referring to him as "that dead guy," or "creepy, dead guy." She was pretty surprised they had collaborated on her Christmas present.

"I'm sure you two could get along," she said, not believing it for a second. "I just feel bad … you know, the holidays, being alone … maybe it would be a good idea if you came." *Oh please, don't believe me.*

"Liar," he said. "OK, if it'll make you feel better, leave the cat door open and if I'm desperate enough, I might use the place."

"I guess that's a compromise. Oh, here comes that stupid commercial again." Munroe looked up at the screen and saw a bedroom at night, with two people asleep. They awake, startled, by someone, probably a burglar, lurking in the shadows. Like most commercials, there was no closed captioning.

Some kind of burglar alarm? he wondered. He was going to ask Yamaguchi what it was when he noticed her lips were moving and she had that glassy-eyed stare television can induce. Then she laughed and said, "Finally I can use a restroom or try on clothes at the store."

"What?"

She looked at him. "Huh? Oh, sorry, you haven't seen this? It's a hoot."

"What is it? A burglar alarm? One of those arthritis bracelets?"

"No. It's Dispelle, the incredible ionizing Z-ray wrist-band."

"Yeah, so what's it do?"

"It keeps away the dead without harming them."

"No, really? People actually believe these work?"

"Not intelligent people, but stupid people. Oh, what's his name, graveyard guy, kind of good looking, tall, got a scar on his cheek, dumb as a brick … Tomás. He wears one."

Munroe searched his memory and tried to recall the officer in question. "I don't think I know him."

"Of course you wouldn't. You can't get within a mile of him. So you've never seen one of these? They're on TV all the time."

"I mostly watch the news. So people are really scared of the dead?"

"Well, some people are. I don't know what the big deal is."

"So it doesn't bother you how many disembodied there are?"

"Of course not," she lied, remembering the doors opening and closing in Rybold's mansion.

"It doesn't bother you that there might be a hundred other dead people in this room right now, watching you?"

"No. But *you're* creeping me out."

"Even if we were to set your terminal to anonymous access and see how many hits the field might record?"

"Ew, no. Let's not. What's got into you?"

"Just thinking about some of the things Bill and I talked about."

"Oh, so that's it. You and Bill. What were these things?"

"Just … the tensions between the living and the dead, what we might … what he's trying to do about it." He couldn't even begin to summarize their talk. He realized their conversation lasted ten minutes, but it reminded him of those late-night bull sessions in college or the instant friendships he made in the army. He felt a connection to Rybold, but oddly not a personal one, more the friendship of two people worried about the same problem. "He really wants to hire me."

"Why?"

"I think he wants me as a poster child of what the dis-embodied can accomplish. He wants to create a center or foundation to help the disembodied." He felt guilty not telling her more. He really had no intention of taking the job but somehow he felt like he'd been caught going out with someone else.

"That sounds like a good idea," she said, reluctant to encourage him. She decided to change the subject. "I read that book about you and the Seattle Strangler."

"What? Aw Linda, that book is a pile of crap."

"Well I hope it was."

He remained silent, trying to discern some meaning from her statement and reluctantly found himself asking, "What do you mean by that?"

She looked at him again. *Damn, sometimes she knows exactly where I am,* he thought.

"I mean the book makes it sound like you were a bril-liant self-destructive loner who covered up his feelings by either making jokes or bullying those who were close to him."

He said nothing.

"Alex?"

He still said nothing.

"OK, I'm sorry to bring it up." She turned back to watching the TV and the silence grew heavy. *He started it with that stuff about all the dead people in the room.*

She drew her knees up and hugged her legs close to her body.

"Why are you bringing this up now anyway?" he finally asked.

"I just couldn't believe what that guy was writing about you."

"Damn straight. The guy got nothing right." *Why the hell was she reading it?* He realized that, except for that email from Sunderland, he hadn't thought about Seattle and the dark times he'd gone through. Now that he wasn't specializing in serial murderers, he found that he actually enjoyed being a cop again. It was a whole new job, being a disembodied cop. *Granted I have to suffer Denver's penny-ante, cow town crime and rescuing Timmy from a well, but overall, I'm enjoying myself.*

Shit, I'm happier dead than alive. I can't believe it. I'm a happier person dead than alive —not that I wouldn't gladly trade being a ghost for a chance to get laid or eat a steak or even a bowl of Ivar's clam chowder.

"So, why were you reading the book?"

"Rybold mentioned it. I was interested," she said, without looking away from the TV. "I just … I just wanted to know more about you, what you were like."

"When I was alive, you mean?"

"Yeah."

"I was a prick." That got her attention and she turned to look at him and grinned.

"Yeah, you were. But you're nothing like that now."

"Thanks. Can we move on?"

"Sure. As long as you're not really considering working for Rybold."

"I'm a cop. And being a cop makes you pretty useless for anything else." Too late, he remembered that she had aspirations beyond being a cop. "You, of course, with your computer degree, you still have a fall back."

"Nice save, but you avoided answering my question.

No more disembodied witness reports. No more traffic stops. No more slimy trial lawyers. Who wouldn't want to quit?"

"What, and give up showbiz?"

— & —

Brian relaxed in his easy chair. So relaxed he was unable to get up. He knew he had things to do, but he just couldn't find the energy to get going. It was just so nice to spend a long Sunday afternoon watching TV on the mega-enormous flat-screen TV his wife had bought him for their first anniversary. Karen was the best. She had such a great job that allowed her to work at home and still make a lot of money. He felt a little sheepish about not going back to school or finding a job, but she persuaded him that he still needed time to recover from the surgery to correct that problem he had.

Oh, that's funny, he thought, when he saw a commercial with the talking orangutan buying the lawnmower. He dutifully pressed the button on the remote to record that he liked it. "Just press the button when you see a commercial that you like, honey," Karen had told him. "You'll be helping me with my job at the ad agency. I just don't have the time to watch all these shows, so whenever you see a commercial or a show you like, press these buttons on the remote from one to five."

What's not to like about this job? So much better than those other jobs she had, like when she worked for that aerospace company, or when she worked for that nuclear power lobby, and she was always asking his opinions about things that were boring and so complex he couldn't even begin to understand them. Now I'm watching TV and helping my wife. Life can't get any better.

186

CHAPTER 11

By Alvin Feathers
Outside Magazine

I watched while all the other skydivers left the DeHavilland Super Otter twin-engine plane. All six stepped out and were whisked away without a moment's hesitation, even the 42-year-old mother of two who made her first solo jump this day.

It had been a long time since my last jump. Illness had kept me from a lot of things and it felt good to be in an airplane again, ready to take that last big step.

I looked at Marcy, my wife, and at Bill, the jumpmaster. Bill gave me the thumbs up and Marcy said something, probably "Love you honey!" and opened the box. It took a few seconds for the wind to really catch and swirl inside the box. Marcy gave it a good shake and I was sucked toward the open door.

Suddenly I was out, expecting to feel that wonderful first gulp in my stomach. But, of course, it wasn't anything like I remembered. The other disembodied I talked to said it would be like stepping off a fast-moving train onto a platform and that's just what it was like. I had just joined one of the newest and weirdest sports: disembodied skydiving. And people are just dying to try it out. But although you obviously do have to be dead, you don't have to be crazy.

Floating lonely as a cloud

And you could say I was a crazy thrill seeker when I was alive. Before the climbing accident that ended my life, I skied, mountain biked, flew hang gliders and I even raced a snowmobile on water, in the summer. You could say the acceleration of gravity was my friend.

But disembodied skydiving is a completely different formula. Just a few seconds after leaving the plane, all motion stops. You're like a little cloud, hanging motionless. You don't feel the wind whistling past your ears. You feel the most blissful peace. And you get to enjoy it.

A beginner's tandem freefall lasts 45 to 50 seconds before your chute opens and another six to eight minutes before you land. You can obviously change the proportions depending on how experienced, brave or stupid you are. But my first jump after my death lasted about five hours and I ended up in the next state.

Munroe, she assumed, was already up when the alarm woke her at 5:30 a.m. She'd prepared a little nest for him in the living room before going to sleep. The TV was set to CNN with the closed captioning turned on. She had brought her laptop and portable terminal to the coffee table and had booted the computer into the AfterNet OS. And she had already left the cat door flap up, afraid she might forget in the rush to leave in the morning.

She wandered into the living room, still groggy from lack of sleep and unaccustomed to waking this early. She put on her wireless ear buds so she could talk to him while she was getting ready to go.

"Morning Alex," she mumbled while brushing her teeth. She heard no reply and thought the brushing had garbled her voice. She looked at her laptop, then the terminal and saw that he wasn't connected.

"Where the hell is he?" she asked herself out loud.

She went back to the kitchen to start making coffee and saw that the door was closed. She remembered she got up in the middle of the night to go to the bathroom, felt a draft coming from the kitchen, and closed the door.

She went in, rinsed her mouth at the kitchen sink, and

started making coffee. While grinding the beans, she thought she heard something and stopped. Hearing nothing further, she continued grinding when she again thought she heard something.

"Alex?"

"You closed the damn door, Linda."

"What? Oh. Were you … you were in the kitchen?"

"I went out last night. I thought I saw something outside in your backyard."

"What, like a burglar?"

"Yes, like a burglar. So I went outside to investigate."

"My hero. And?"

"Must have been dogs or something. Or maybe there was somebody. I took a look and saw your neighbor's dogs barking."

"It was probably just another dog or a raccoon. They get into the trashcans on the porch. Drives Pepe and Pepito nuts. Stupid Labs. I think they woke me up."

"Yeah, and then you closed the door."

"Oh, Alex, I'm sorry. Gosh, that was around three. Have you been waiting in the kitchen all that time?"

"More or less. Not many places open Sunday morning after Christmas. I tried using the public terminal at your post office, but it wasn't working."

"Poor baby. But why were you prowling around the kitchen like a watch dog?"

"I got bored, wanted to stretch my legs."

He can't stop being a cop, she thought. *He probably checks to make sure I lock up and looks out the windows like a night watchman. Just like my dad.*

She'd been making the coffee during the conversation and now the little coffeemaker was finished. "Well, I'm sorry. Look, I've got to hurry. I told Mary I'd pick her up." She took her coffee into the bedroom while she added last minute items to her backpack. He was still next to the terminal in the living room.

"I hope my lapse won't discourage you from using the place while I'm gone."

"I'll probably hang out at the department," he said, then thought it sounded a little ungrateful. "But I might spend some time here, too."

She was assembling her belongings by the front door getting ready to leave. "Whatever," she said. "See you at work Tuesday if you're not here when I get back. Remember, we'll have to leave by 8:30 if we want to make it to the Springs on time. I'll try to check my email when I can."

"Have a good time," he said. But she was already removing her ear buds and was placing them in a little basket on a table by the front door and was gone.

He felt a little sad when she left and still a little irritated after waiting in the kitchen for three hours. It had taken such a short time for him to feel possessive about her place, and he really was grateful that she had let him stay. When he really thought about it, he was most mad that she had left so quickly and not given him enough time to bitch and moan. *What a miserable human being I am.*

He felt contrite as he went online and checked his email. Melissa had responded to his reply that he'd be happy if she accompanied him on the Egypt trip. He tried to find her online somewhere on the AfterNet but had no luck. She'd mentioned that she would be staying with her brother's family over holidays and hoped she was well.

His conversation with Rybold weighed heavily on his mind. Rybold's center sounded like a wonderful opportunity, but he just couldn't get past the utopian commune sound of it: dead people working together for the common good, using their wisdom for the benefit of all mankind, but making a home for themselves away from the living. And he was inherently suspicious of any club that would want him as a member.

He turned his attention back to his surfing. He was

reading a thread in a World War II forum started by a guy who claimed he was a Marine who died at Guadalcanal. His own father was in the Navy and was at Guadalcanal, serving as a deck gunner on a troop transport ship. The dead Marine admitted to dying when he took a bullet while still in a landing craft — not particularly glamorous. His reminiscences had the ring of truth about them and several other "devil dogs," most dead but a few still living, had contributed their own stories. Munroe kept checking the details of the stories with online references and confirmed most of the details. He noticed that almost all the dead posters did not have certified identities. But they were either the real deal or like him, had done excellent research.

It wasn't often that he allowed himself to be drawn in so completely. He was touched by the Marines' recollections of Christmases spent away from home. He added a story told to him by his own father.

It was almost 11 when he surfaced from the drama of the Pacific island and went back to checking his mail. He looked up at the TV and CNN and saw that they were talking about a tsunami that had hit Indonesia. He went to the CNN website and caught up on the details.

Wow, sounds bad, he thought. *You read about tsunamis but you don't really appreciate how dangerous they are.* He couldn't help but recall his talk with Rybold and his remark about the second wave.

Yamaguchi stood in the long line waiting to board the lift while Mary yammered in her ear.

"… and Sanchez steps in front of me again. I really should just shoot him. The man has no sense of self-preservation. He's definite proof that evolution doesn't work."

She nodded and agreed, which was all the encouragement Mary needed to continue.

I guess Alex really isn't as bad in comparison. What if I had Mary as a partner?

Actually, few Denver cops had partners unless they were training recruits or working with a rookie. Some of the detectives worked in pairs, but by and large, most cops worked alone. She'd known Mary since the academy and although they were good friends, her talkative friend could get on her nerves.

"Are you listening?"

"Yeah, sure, Sanchez. No sense of preservation."

"You're worried about Alex, aren't you?"

"I'm not worried, but I am thinking about him."

"Creeps me out." They moved onto their lift.

"Yes, so you've told me. But you did get along enough to get me the present."

"Well, it was a good present. And I ordered one for myself. I noticed the one Alex got you didn't include the snap in pad. You might want to order one of those. It makes all the difference, makes the belt ride the hips better. And did you look at the catalog I put in the box? I wrapped it you know."

The lift was already high and Yamaguchi looked down at the ground. "Yes, really nice. I appreciate it."

It was their last run and the shadows were getting long. It was also getting colder and she wanted to call it a day. She was ready to go back into town, eat somewhere nice and retire to the hotel, but she figured she owed her friend one more run.

They'd taken the Winter Park Ski Train from Union Station (which looked a lot friendlier when you weren't looking for an armed suspect). They got to the station in plenty of time for the 6:30 boarding time, and the train left at 7:15 as scheduled. But their train was delayed while still in Denver because of switching yard problems. So they arrived an hour and a half later than scheduled. Mary had actually been pretty understanding, considering Yamaguchi had been the one to suggest taking the train, rather than drive Interstate 70.

They got off the lift and made their way to the run, an advanced intermediate. She wasn't a great skier and it looked intimidating, but Mary was already saying "see you at the bottom." *Oh well*, she thought, *the sooner I get down, the sooner I can find somewhere to get online.*

CHAPTER 12

From: "PETER ENELI" [peter_eneli@dcemail.com]
Reply-To: peter_eneli@jumpy.it
To: rosemary.p.frankforth@theafternet.net
Date: Sun, 18 Apr 2004 17:53:55 +0000
Subject: From Peter Eneli

Abidjan Cote D'Ivoire With Due Respect Dearest Beloved

Sir,

I know you will be surprised to read from me, but please
consider this as a request from a family in dire need of
assistance. First, I introduce myself, I am the late Mr. Peter
Eneli from South Africa and am the first and only son of the
late Dr. Stephen Eneli. Our untimely death impossible made it
to transfer our family wealth of US $5 million.
I am presently residing in Abidjan Cote D'Ivoire In West Africa.
The brutal and repressive regime of this country does not
recognize the property rights of the disembodied and we hope
to help my sick mother Mrs. Susan Eneli whom the doctors
have confirmed that she will die before few months. We
cannot obtain our funds that remain languishing.
I got your contact from Business Directory in Cote d Ivoire
Chamber and Industry and know that you are friend to the
people of South Africa and to the plight of disembodied
peoples everywhere. Will you help our mother, his wife by the
expediency of transferring to your bank or your companies
bank the sum of US $5 million, which I deposited in one trunk

box with a Security Company in Abidjan Cote D'Ivoire In West Africa.

Before my father's death, he was in charge of many positions in my country as you can confirm from this sites below

http://www.polity.org.za/html/govdocs/pr/2001/pr1003b.html
http://www.gov.za/projects/procurement/yengeni.htm
http://news.bbc.co.uk/1/hi/world/africa/1577682.stm

For your efforts, I am prepared to offer you 25% of the total fund while 5% will be set aside for local and international expenses and 70% will be kept by my family and me. Finally, modalities on how the transfer will be done will be conveyed to you once we have established trust and confidence between ourselves

Please, treat as urgent and have it in your mind that the security company never know that the content of the consignment is money, it is just a secret between you and me.

Best regards, the late Mr. Peter Eneli

Yamaguchi left Interstate 25 at the Garden of the Gods Road exit. "I go west, correct?" she asked Munroe.

"Yes, toward the big mountain-like thing."

"Funny man," she said.

They had been driving an hour and a half already and Munroe was getting irritable. Leaving Denver, Interstate 25 southbound was a mess because of a traffic accident and as usual, his partner insisted on driving the speed limit. Add to that spotty Internet access, and Munroe was getting cranky.

"Sure is a nice day," she said, trying to get her partner talking.

He said nothing.

"You're just not going to be pleasant today, are you?"

She smiled broadly and even glanced at herself in the rear-view mirror to see her smile. The drive was pleasant and she enjoyed any day when she could work in plain clothes.

"Not a lot to be pleasant about," he said.

"Suit yourself," she said, and turned on the radio. "Where do you get NPR in this town?" she muttered to herself. "All you get is Christian radio."

Munroe finally had some success getting Internet access. "Death toll's up to 15,000 in Sri Lanka," he told her.

"Oh my God, it just keeps getting worse. Sorry, Alex, I forgot." She'd only learned about the tsunami last night, after getting back from her ski trip. In fact, she never did go online the entire time or read a paper or listen to the radio. She'd allowed herself a distraction from the world. In a way, she'd also escaped from the afterlife. In a ski town, there were few signs of the disembodied. She only noticed one public AfterNet terminal, although there were probably more. She had read in the paper that disembodied instructors were helping in the skiing for the disabled program, but she and Mary were never near the runs where they practiced. Several times she noticed people wearing white plastic boxes on their arms, but they were always music players or phones. After a while, she stopped noticing.

Munroe had followed news accounts of the tsunami all day Monday. The number of missing, the number of dead and the projected numbers of missing and dead increased steadily. He'd updated and checked his blog several times already. One man, living, who claimed he worked for Doctors Without Borders as a sanitation specialist (not a good choice if he was trying to impress), said he thought the death toll could climb as high as 100,000. That posting, somewhere around 3 a.m. Monday, was ridiculed, but now it looked not impossible.

Just like many living people who announced their intention to fly to Indonesia to help, he wished he could do something. In fact it occurred to him that disembodied volunteers might be able to offer a lot. An influx of unorganized living volunteers would need housing and food that the region just couldn't afford, but disembodied volunteers would need neither. They could work tirelessly, going into places too dangerous for their living counterparts. And they would have little to fear from oppressive regimes or civil unrest. Disembodied Without Borders? The thought appealed to him. It seemed more practical than Rybold's grand schemes for his center.

He couldn't help but wonder what effect 100,000 new disembodied would have. In some ways, it's really just another drop in the bucket compared to the number of people already dead. But in another respect, it was huge. Many of them would know about the afterlife and they would be demanding access to the Internet at some point.

"Oh, I finally found it. Looks like it's on FM, a college station," she said.

They listened to the report, coming from Madras, India. NPR reported the death toll in Sri Lanka at 12,000 and the reporter in India talked about the devastation there.

"Here, we go, 30th Street." She turned their police cruiser south. Despite the delays on the interstate, they were still on time for their meeting with Tracy Newell at the Explorers.

Munroe had never been to Colorado Springs and it had been a while since she had visited. "That's the Garden of the Gods?" he asked of the red rock formations he could see in the distance.

"Yeah, but it's a funny angle here, wait till we get closer," she said.

"They're like Red Rocks," he said, referring to the city park and amphitheater west of Denver.

"Kind of. The rock formations are kind of straight up instead of at an angle like Red Rocks. Oh, here's where we want to turn."

She turned east and drove up a road that climbed a small bluff. She could see lots of housing developments surrounding the bluff, but they were on a private road, following a sign that said "To castle."

"Castle?"

"That's what it said. Jeez," she said. The road ended in a circular drive in front of a castle. Not the medieval kind with arrow slits and battlements, but more the *Sound of Music* kind. She parked their car in one of the few visitor parking spots.

"I really should have looked this up before we came here," Munroe said. "Too busy following tsunami stuff."

They walked to the arched entrance into which the words "The Explorers" were carved. Seals on either side showed a covered wagon with a mountain in the distance and a sailing ship headed toward a sunrise or set. The thick wooden doors were left open and when they entered they saw closed modern glass doors that kept out the cold.

Inside they walked up stairs to a reception area. An older man, a security guard, was seated behind a beautifully carved round desk.

"Hi, can I help you?"

"Yes, I'm here to see Tracy Newell. I have an appointment."

"Sure, let me ring him and if you wouldn't mind signing in?"

She signed the visitor book. She decided not to sign Munroe's name. When she was done, the man said, "Up the stairs to my left, one flight up. Go down the hallway, all the way to the end."

They followed his directions. At the end of the hallway another reception area served a ring of offices. A woman typing at the reception desk looked up at Yamaguchi.

"Mr. Newell's on the phone right now. If you could take a seat?"

She nodded and sat down. Munroe sat beside her.

"Hey, Linda, pick up that magazine," he told her. She didn't like his tone but she picked it up anyway. It was the official Explorer's magazine, glossy and professionally done. She thumbed through it and saw that it was published in the Springs at Explorers Press, the publishing arm of the organization. The photos and stories were all about fresh-faced kids doing good works around the world. She privately thought, "Young Republicans for Christ," then felt guilty about it.

"They've got that Hitler Youth look, don't they?" Munroe asked. She was always worried when their political views coincided.

"He'll see you now," the administrative assistant said, without looking up from her typing.

Yamaguchi put down the magazine and got up. She muttered under her breath, "Shut up now." The receptionist looked up at that but Yamaguchi smiled, pointed at the door and nodded, pretending she hadn't said anything.

She entered Newell's office but stopped in the doorway, the door handle in her hand.

"Impressive, isn't it," the man said. "Best view on the planet."

She nodded. Newell's office had a large picture window that showed the Garden of the Gods, backed by Pikes Peak. The sun was shining between scattered clouds, dappling the white shoulders of the mountain. Colorado Springs was much closer to the mountains and Pikes Peak carried a weight that the comparatively distant foothills outside Denver never could.

"Please come in, have a seat."

She nodded and said, "Thank you. That's beautiful."

"You're welcome, not that I had anything to do with it. But the Explorers built this place knowing the effect the view would have on our members, and our visitors."

"I'm afraid I don't know very much about your organization. Could you fill me in?"

Newell went back around his desk and sat, then realized he was blocking the view and moved aside.

She finally sat, pulled out her notebook and gave her attention to the man. He was tall, attractive, in his 40s and quite blond. He looked like he'd been quite athletic but was now starting to enjoy middle age spread. He didn't strike her as the sort to be kidnapping the dead.

"So officer …"

"Uh, please, just call me Linda. And this is Alex, Alex Munroe, my partner," she added, vaguely waving her hand in his direction.

"Your partner?" he asked, looking confused. *Damn, I forgot to tell him Alex's dead.*

"Did you forget to tell him I'm dead?" Munroe asked.

"I'm sorry, I should have told you. My partner, Alex Munroe, is disembodied."

"Ah, I see."

"Any problems with that?" she asked.

"None whatsoever." He turned in Munroe's direction. "Alex, if I'd known, I could have had a terminal brought in."

"I never said he could call me Alex," Munroe said, which she ignored.

Newell continued. "Well to answer your question, the Explorers is a Christian organization, as I'm sure you guessed by now, started in 1925. We have ministries around the world. In fact, I'm sure our outreach program in Southeast Asia is pretty busy today. Here in the Springs, we run camps and workshops for our younger members. And we've always had a strong connection to the military. We have ministries in most of our country's military bases."

"That sounds nice," she said, ignoring Munroe's comments about the camps and workshops. "But how does sponsoring a rave in Denver fit in with your … mission?"

"We regularly sponsor youth outreach programs, but

many kids find those programs a little too tame. They like the excitement of finding out about an event from friends, feeling that they're in on secret knowledge. We wanted to give them that same kind of excitement, but without the enticement of sex and drugs, but leave the rock 'n' roll. So, we put up posters, talk about it in chat rooms, etc., but we make sure that they don't hear about it from their church group."

"So they dupe them into thinking they're going to have good time," Alex said. "Ask them if they resent it."

Newell noticed her expression. "Does your partner have a question?"

"I'm sorry, he wants to know if you get kids who … didn't know they were going to a religious meeting … and resent it."

"Oh, I'm sure some do, but I don't think it's a problem. These events are professionally … OK, 'managed' for a better word," he smiled and held his hands outspread. "There are no Bible readings and Christian rock really has come a long way since the days of Amy Grant. There are incredible amounts of caffeine and sugar, and I'm afraid a lot of them smoke, but we don't serve alcohol. We have chaperones … young Explorers … who are on the lookout for any drug use or sex, and they do their best to discourage that behavior."

"Ask him about the dead. Ask what they do to attract us."

"OK," she muttered. "What about the dead … the disembodied? Are you trying to attract them?"

"Yes, very much so, it's a stated goal of our ministry. I'm afraid our early attempts to attract the disembodied didn't go very well, however. So we had to separate the two groups."

"What, separate entrances? A disembodied entrance?"

Newell composed a serious face. "We're not bigoted about the dead here, Linda. We don't believe they're a sign of the Apocalypse or an instrument of the devil. Look, the Explorers have had a presence in the Pikes Peak area for more than 75 years. We didn't start in the Reagan years … we don't have anything to do with … I'm sorry, now I'm apologizing for being in Colorado Springs and it's a great city."

"I hit a nerve," she said.

Newell slumped back in his chair. "Yes, you did. And to answer your question in a more sane tone, yes, we have a separate disembodied entrance. We set up terminals and a special area for the dead to enjoy the party."

"A special area? The dead and the living don't mix?"

"No," he gave a lopsided grin. "We tried that at first and the dead … the disembodied … they freaked. They don't like crowds you know. What am I saying, you have a partner. So, we had to have a separate area."

"OK, specifically, about this party in Denver on the 11th. Anything unusual about it?"

"No, not really. I think we had a great turnout. Yes, we had to hustle a few kids out of there who were trying to score drugs, but that was it. Please tell me, what's this about?"

"We're trying to track down a disembodied kid, Brian Thompson. He might have attended the rave and no one's heard from him since."

"You're trying to track down one disembodied kid? I didn't know the police would do that."

"It is unusual, but his mother wants us to find him. And there's another person who might have attended the same rave. Neither of them have been on the AfterNet since. Do you have a way of knowing who might have attended the rave? I mean among the dead."

"No, I'm sorry. We provided the terminals and a local network, that's all. We don't try to capture any personal information. Maggie convinced us that it would be seen as intrusive."

"I'm sorry, who's Maggie?"

"She actually arranges the events."

"Oh, I thought you did?"

He laughed. "Well, I don't mean to sound pompous, but I am a regional director here. I'm responsible for the events that occur in my region, but the raves are a very small part of our overall mission. Maggie's an outside consultant and she's responsible for the square states: Colorado, Wyoming, New Mexico, Arizona, Utah and Nevada. She was a young Explorer herself. She does all the planning and set up. I just sign the checks."

"What's Maggie's full name? Can we speak to her?"

"Sure, let me call her cell phone. And it's Margaret Duggan, two 'Gs.'"

"If I could get that number as well?"

He wrote it out and handed it to her. She sat back while Newell dialed. "think hes telling truth," she asked Munroe silently.

"I guess. But I wouldn't be surprised if Maggie is a case of plausible deniability."

"uur so cynical."

"Maggie, this is Tracy," said Newell, obviously leaving a message for Maggie. "Can you call me …"

"Actually, if you could ask her to call me," Yamaguchi said, sliding him her business card.

Newell left the message and hung up. He patted the top of his desk with both hands. "Now, is there anything else I can do for you?"

He waited while her partner was prompting Yamaguchi. "Yes, Mr. Newell. I have to ask this. Are you … are you kidnapping the disembodied?" She felt really stupid asking the question.

He laughed — a quick, loud laugh. "NO!" he said. "That's ridiculous. Why would we do that?"

"Religious organizations have had a hard time dealing with the discovery of the afterlife," she said. "It could be your way … I'm sorry, I know this is a crazy question. I just had to ask it."

"Like I said earlier, the Explorers is an old, established, respected organization. We work with inner city kids. We dig wells in Ethiopia. Hell, I dug wells in Ethiopia. I … wait a minute."

He swiveled in his chair and faced his laptop and pressed the spacebar to wake it up. When the screen reappeared, he turned it to face her. "There," he said, with a flourish.

She looked at the screen. It was an email Newell had been writing.

Dear Uncle Ted,
Glad to hear you're adjusting and again, no need to thank me for

"I'm sorry," she said. "I don't understand."

"Look at who it's addressed to."

She looked. The recipient was theodorenewell2@theAfterNet.net. "Oh," she said. "Your uncle. He died recently?"

"Yes, five, no six months ago. Like me … actually, the other way around … I chose service to God because of his example. Dying and finding himself on the AfterNet … that really tested his faith. He was lost, but I suggested he accompany one of our missions to Nepal. He's now acting as chaperone to a bunch of kids and he's enjoying being at 13,000 feet without being afflicted by the emphysema that killed him.

"Look, officer, I don't know what the afterlife is, but I have no difficulty accepting this as part of God's design, and the Explorers as an organization doesn't either. If you look on our website, you'll see our mission statement, which includes our position about the afterlife and … OK, you might have to go back two newsletters, but we have a profile about two of our disembodied volunteers."

Newell was standing by this point and Yamaguchi had shoved her chair back.

"Are we done now?"

"Yes, thank you," she said and stood. She walked backward to the door, keeping her eyes on Newell who now seemed even taller.

"Uh, if Maggie calls … you know, ask her to call me." Newell nodded. His lips were now a thin, tight line. As she opened the door, the sun broke through some clouds and through the window she could see Pikes Peak and the full panoply of heaven adding an Old Testament rim light to Newell.

She stepped through and closed the door. "Shit," she said after the door closed. The assistant looked at her. "I said shit," she told her. The assistant looked away.

"He could have had it prepared," Munroe said, as they were walking down the stairway to the main hall. Yamaguchi stopped at the reception desk to sign out. She didn't care at this point what anyone thought of her behavior, so she spoke to Munroe out loud, not caring if the guard would notice. "Are you just deranged? What do you mean?"

"I'm saying he knew we were coming. Wanted to make it look like some of his best friends are dead and typed that email just before we walked in. You got to admit, it was convenient."

"He was acting?"

"I'll check when I can get on the AfterNet."

"Look, Alex, reality check here. I realize you want to help, but let's face it, a lot of the dead can't handle being dead." She walked to their car and opened the door for Alex, then got in herself. "You know, they lose it after a while. Maybe our missing kid and the sergeant are just sitting around dribbling ectoplasmic goo somewhere."

"Yeah, maybe. Or maybe the castle has a dungeon."

"That's just crazy talk. Why are you so paranoid?"

"Why don't we try to find Margaret Duggan?" he asked, ignoring her. They were driving south on 30th Street after leaving the private road.

"What?"

"We're already here. We should look up this woman, she if she's home."

She was already worried about their long drive back to Denver. "I don't know. We should get back."

"It's on our way. We just stay on 30th, don't turn onto Fontanero. She lives on Kiowa Street, 2800 block."

"You already looked it up?"

"Just now. Come on, if we see her now, we don't have to come back down later."

"If she's not home we just leave, correct?" She was dubious but she had to admit it made sense to see if Duggan were home.

"Anything you say. You're driving."

She followed his directions and they were soon driving down Kiowa Street. Most of the homes were classic bungalows, with the occasional Victorian. The neighborhood seemed nice but slightly messy, betraying the habits of younger families just starting to have kids and slightly overwhelmed by the effort.

"Looks like your kind of neighborhood," Munroe said as they passed several houses in a row displaying "Re-elect Gore/Lieberman in 2004" signs.

She said, "The west side of Colorado Springs is fairly urban and liberal. The suburbs are in the east, just like Denver and Aurora. I think this is her house."

They parked in front of a two-story house, very similar to a Denver square. It stood out from the bungalows on either side. Because the house was multi-story, its footprint was fairly small, leaving a lot of yard in front and back.

"Let's go," he said, but she didn't move. Instead, she said, "We go up to the front door and knock. If she's not home, we leave, right?"

"You got it partner."

She opened her door. She guessed that he would leave from her side, afraid she might change her mind and his "I'm here" in her ear told her she had guessed correctly.

She walked up to the gate in the chain-link fence that enclosed the yard. The gate wasn't even latched, giving her no excuse not to enter. She entered the yard and walked toward the porch. A few newspapers, still in their plastic wrappers, were scattered around the yard. None had made it to the porch. The mailbox beside the front door showed at least a day's accumulation of mail.

"Doesn't look like she's at home," she said, and then knocked on the door. She saw a doorbell button and pushed it. She could hear the chime.

"Make sure we have the right address," he urged her.

"And how do you propose I do that?"

"Go through the mail."

"I'm not going … wait, I don't have to. I can just see her name on this letter," she said, peering through a crack in the mailbox. She looked through a large window into what was obviously the living room. The room held old unfashionable furniture, a mishmash of styles that included a few Arts and Craft pieces and chrome chairs from the Fifties. No lights were showing. She went back to the front door and pushed the doorbell button again.

"No one's home, Alex. I say we leave."

"Let's check around back," he said.

"What's the point?" she asked. "Alex … oh you bastard." A look at her terminal confirmed he'd left her side. She sat down on the porch step. "You can just look on your own and I hope you fall down a well," she said out loud.

Munroe was already checking out the back yard. A rusted, broken swing set and a detached garage were the only things of interest. The back door was part of what seemed to be a later addition to the house and it was open.

Yamaguchi still hadn't followed him. He assumed she was out front sulking. He went in.

The addition was basically an enclosed back porch, a place to take off your muddy shoes before going in and a pleasant room to enjoy the summer. A sturdier door provided access to the kitchen. It too was open. He went in.

The kitchen looked like it had never been renovated since being built, but it was in good condition, despite being untidy. The sink, made of heavy soapstone, contained a load of dirty dishes. The refrigerator was bulky and rounded and avocado green, but it looked appropriate against the ancient wallpaper. The stove matched the refrigerator and was clean. The food stains on the microwave on the counter indicated that it saw more use.

The door into what was probably the dining room was open. He went through the doorway and into the dark room. The décor was definitely odd for a young woman who produced raves. The dining table looked Old World: dark, claw feet and heavily carved. Lace curtains covered the narrow windows, which looked southeast.

He moved into the living room and saw an upright piano with lots of photos. At first glance, the photos seemed to picture a young girl with her grandparents. But photo after photo on the piano and the walls seemed to indicate the older people were her parents.

He was puzzling out the story the photos told when he noticed a small change in the light behind him. Looking back through the dining room, he realized the kitchen door was closed.

Yamaguchi had gotten one of the newspapers and removed it from its wrapper. It was dated Dec. 23. At least if she had to wait on Munroe, she could read something. She'd give him a few more minutes because she didn't really like the idea of wandering around the yard hoping to bump into him. She'd started reading a national story about a disembodied man who'd won the "Match 5" Powerball lottery when she thought she heard a door slam.

Maybe she is home, she thought. She put the paper down and walked around the house to the back yard. She saw no one, but she did notice that a door on the back porch was open. "Hello," she said. "Anyone home?" She leaned against the doorframe and poked her head in. The porch was empty. She could see that the door to what was probably the kitchen was closed, but a door in the floor of the porch was open. It probably led into the cellar and might have been a way to get coal into the house.

"Alex, where the hell are you? If you went down there, you are in so much trouble." She stepped onto the porch. She decided to look through the glass of the kitchen door before checking out the open door when she heard "LINDA!" through her ear buds. She jumped back all the way to the porch door and her hand automatically came to rest on her gun.

"Alex, you dumb ... where are you?" She heard nothing in reply and looked at her terminal. It said no one was connected. She moved closer to the door and heard "Linda, I'm inside the house."

"Where?"

"I'm in the kitchen looking at you."

"Did you go down into the cellar?"

"What? No, this door was open. Somebody must have closed it."

"Oh sure. Liar."

"I swear, Linda, the door was open. I went in and when I went into the dining room, someone shut it."

"There's no one here now. Maybe they went into the cellar."

"What cellar?" he asked.

"There's a door in the floor of the porch. It must lead to the cellar."

"How did you find it?"

"It's wide open, hard to miss."

"It wasn't when I walked in."

"OK, well let's not argue. I'll just open the door … damn, it's locked." She jiggled the door handle for dramatic effect.

"Big surprise. She trapped me in here on purpose."

"Don't be stupid. How would she know?"

Munroe had no answer to that. *How could she know?*

"Why don't you see if there's another way out." she said.

"OK, let me look. Be right back." A couple of minutes passed before he returned. "I've looked around the first floor. There doesn't seem to be a way out. I might have found the door to the cellar, however."

"Why didn't you go up to the second floor?"

"I did go up to the second floor. There was only one open door, a bathroom. The window's closed."

She put her head against the door and considered banging it. "Maybe an attic?"

"I didn't see stairs or a door. And what would I do, jump?" She decided against saying it would be unlikely to hurt him. "Maybe you could go down into the cellar," he added.

She sighed and in a mocking tone parroted him. "Maybe you could go down the cellar."

"What did you say?"

"Nothing. All right, let me look." She went to the cellar door and looked. Stairs led down to a darkened space. *Oh yeah, go down into the dark cellar where there's a homicidal madwoman who wants to wear my flesh as clothes.* "Hello," she yelled. "Anyone down there? I'm a police officer. I'd like to talk to you." She felt really stupid. It was that kind of day. She took a deep breath and took her gun from its holster. She held it pointing down and prayed that she wouldn't find anyone in the basement. Shooting an innocent homeowner in Colorado Springs would not look good.

"I'm coming down your cellar stairs." She carefully walked down the dark, steep stairs, using her outstretched arms to guide her. Instead of touching brick, she realized she was touching dirt. It wasn't a finished basement, just a dug out space under the house. There were no windows and the only light came through the open door. She reached the bottom of the stairs, straining to see anything in the gloom when she heard a sound above her. She turned and saw shadows being cast through cracks between the slats of the porch above. Someone was walking on the porch. She ran up the stairs just in time for the door to catch her outstretched arm and throw her backward.

She landed on her butt and thumped down the stairs, sliding headfirst. Luckily she kept her head tucked into her chest and avoided banging her head. She remained sprawled at the bottom, did a quick body inventory and determined that nothing was injured, other than her pride. "Hello, you closed the door on me, you asshole," she yelled, "and I'm a cop and I'm very mad right now." No one answered.

She stood up carefully. She hadn't dropped her weapon but as she didn't plan to shoot blindly through the door, she returned it to her holster. *Besides, maybe she's deaf,* she told herself. *Right, that's why he left a phone message. Duh.*

With the door closed, the only light came through the cracks in the flooring. She got out the LED flashlight attached to her key ring and shined it at the cellar door. She walked up the stairs again and pushed at the door, but it wouldn't move. She shoved at it with her shoulders, but all she did was hurt her shoulder. She walked back down the stairs. The flashlight showed a room about 20 feet square. A gigantic metal octopus took up a major portion of the space. It was the original coal furnace and next to it was a more modern gas one. A water heater, the main sewer drain, two supporting pillars and another set of stairs were the other things she could see in the light of the flashlight.

She walked to the stairs and went up to the door at the top. She turned the handle. Naturally, it was locked. "Argh!" she screamed. "I can't get a break, can I?"

Munroe saw his partner walk down the stairs through the cellar door. *She is going to be hell to live with after this,* he thought. *And how could I have been so stupid as to get myself trapped ...*

A movement in the yard interrupted his litany. He saw the door on the detached garage open and a young woman stepped through it. She walked to the back porch and went directly to the cellar door and slammed it shut. Then she locked it, walked back to the yard and into the garage. She never looked at the house. A few seconds later, he saw a car pull out from the garage and drive down the alley behind the house.

He looked back at the cellar door on the porch. He thought he saw it move a few times. He realized it must be his partner trying to get out. Then he went over to the door in the kitchen that he also thought led to the cellar. *I hope I'm right.* A few seconds later he saw the door handle move and he felt the AfterNet field return just in time for her scream of frustration.

"Linda!"

"Alex!"

"I'm stuck down here," she said.

"And I'm stuck up here. I saw her do it. I saw her close the door."

"Who?"

"Duggan. It was her. And before you say, 'Are you sure?' Yes, I'm sure. There are pictures of her all over the place. And she matches the description we have."

"OK, already. How screwed am I with this door? What can you see?"

He got as close to the door as he could. "There's a deadbolt but I don't think it's thrown. I think it's just the latch."

She jiggled the handle again. "I think you're right," she said.

"Try 'loiding the lock?"

"Try what?"

"Use a credit card or something," he said. "See if you can push the latch back enough to open the door."

"OK." He waited and a few seconds later he saw a sliver of plastic appear through the crack of the door against the frame.

"A little higher," he said. The plastic disappeared and she said "damn!"

"What happened?"

"Dropped it. It fell off the stairs. I've got to find it."

She returned a minute later and resumed her efforts. After five minutes, she gave up.

"I'm never going to get it," she said.

"Don't give up. 'loiding a lock is easy," he lied, "you just need to slide the card …"

"Just shut up, Alex. Let me think." He shut up.

"The door opens inward, right."

"Yes," he said.

"Maybe I can just force my way in. If I get a running start …"

"I don't know. It looks pretty solid."

"I don't fucking care, Alex."

"OK, bust it down." She didn't reply and the field disappeared. A few seconds later, the door moved, slightly, the field reappeared and then it was gone. A few more seconds later, the sequence repeated, although this time the door seemed to move a little more visibly. He stepped back, realizing that if by some miracle the door opened, he'd be squished flat against the wall like a cartoon character. Nothing happened for about half a minute when the door shook again. Behind him, a dirty glass perched on the edge of the sink fell to the floor and broke. The door, however, held.

He waited by the door for several minutes. Finally the field reappeared. "I can't do it. The stairs are too steep. I fell back down the stairs that time."

"You hurt?"

"Only my pride for the second time. Well, and my butt."

He said nothing, afraid to irritate her further. "I guess I can try the lock thing again," she said.

"Do you have anything more flexible than a credit card?" he asked.

"Let me look. No, that won't work. Hey, I have my Miranda card. Forgot I even had this. That's a little more flexible."

Thirty minutes later, after a great deal of coaching from him, and a lot of cursing from her, the door opened and she staggered into the kitchen. *She looks mad,* he thought. Her face and clothing were smudged with dirt and she'd been sweating from the heat of the furnace and the frustration of trying to open the door. Strands of hair had been pulled from her ponytail and were flopping around her face.

"Now that I'm out of there, I can tell you what a complete and utter moron you are."

"Hey, I'm not the one who locked you in the cellar. And don't forget she trapped me, too."

"How the hell would she be able to trap you? She can't see you."

He really had no good answer for this, so he diverted her attention. "But I bet she knew you were there."

She had no good answer for that. Whoever slammed the door must have heard her, must have been aware she was in the cellar. It's conceivable the person, whom she did not see, thought she was a burglar. But then the person would have called the Colorado Springs police.

The thought scared the crap out of her. "Let's not argue about it. Let's get out of here and out of this town as quick as we can."

He agreed readily because he'd followed the same line of reasoning. They let themselves out the back door and she walked as quickly as possible without actually running to their car.

It wasn't until they had gotten onto U.S. Highway 24, heading east and back to the interstate, that she allowed herself another chance to chastise Munroe.

"If she had called the Springs PD, I can't even begin to think how much trouble I'd be in," she said.

With the immediate threat behind them, however, Munroe said, "Yeah, but they didn't. I'm sure Springs PD would have responded pretty quickly to a homeowner reporting that she'd trapped a burglar in her cellar. I think Duggan got Newell's message and decided to leave ahead of us. I think we interrupted her."

"And somehow she knew that you had entered the house? She's some kind of psychic who can sense your presence?"

"No and cut the sarcasm. I'll admit that seems unlikely. I think I went inside and she came back to shut the door before leaving. She didn't know I was there. She went back to the garage to get her car, heard you and decided she didn't want to stick around to answer questions. You go down the trap door, she seizes the opportunity. It was just a delaying tactic and it worked."

She had to admit it made sense. "You might be right. I guess she, if it was Duggan, doesn't want to talk to us. If that's the case, she played it nicely. We might find her behavior suspicious, but we can't do anything about it. If anything, we're the ones who'd have to explain why we were in her house." She kept herself from adding "thanks to you."

They had reached Interstate 25 and were now heading north.

"Finally got a signal," Munroe said. At the same time, Yamaguchi's phone rang.

"Oh damn," she said. "I should pull over."

"Just answer the phone, Linda."

"I don't like driving and talking, you know that."

"You are such a … hey, wait a minute. Uh … you better pull over now and answer that phone. Right now."

"What's the problem, Alex?" she asked, as she pulled over into the breakdown lane.

"I think there's a SWAT call in Denver."

She got out her phone and saw that the screen showed she had five messages. The phone rang again.

"Yamaguchi," she answered.

"Linda, where the hell are you?" It was the voice of the watch commander.

"We're in Colorado Springs. We're just heading back."

"What are you doing in the … never mind. Get back to Denver as fast as you can. We have a tactical in Five Points. Kid with a gun holding his family hostage."

"Yes sir, I …" He'd hung up.

The drive back to Denver was a nightmare. Traffic out of the Springs was busy and the lights and sirens didn't help that much until she got past Academy Boulevard. The whole time, Munroe was giving her the play-by-play whenever he was able to get a signal and access one of the television channel web sites.

"Channel 7 has the best view," he said. "Looks like your standard bungalow … oh, just caught sight of a sniper. They're really close. Smart cameraman, I think he's on the roof of a house the next street down. I think this is the neighborhood where we interviewed the minister. Damn, lost the signal again."

Munroe's commentary was making her anxious, but she knew they would need the information once they arrived.

"OK, got it back. They're in the newsroom now. Looks like they're talking about … that doesn't make sense … oh, bad closed captioning … they must have a neighbor talking to them on the phone. Sounds like they heard arguing, the kid has some history of mental problems, cops are always being called out to that location."

"Oh, God, is the family … Williams, I think it was?" she asked.

"Yeah."

"We always had to go there on domestics. No one ever charged anyone with anything, never anything real serious. They had a son … how old is this kid?"

"Can't tell. TV camera only got a glimpse of him. Maybe 15, 16."

"Yeah, that'd be about right. He was mental."

"Damn, lost it again."

"We're coming up on 470. Should be better in a bit."

As she said this, the static on the police radio began to fade and she could make out the occasional word on the tactical channels. Munroe also got a signal and was able to see the TV feed again.

"They're getting closer to the house. Why are they still showing this? All he'd have to do is see this on TV and he'd know where SWAT is. No, they stopped showing it. Somebody had some sense. They switched back to the reporter. Uh oh, she ducked."

At the same time, she heard the words "shots fired" on the radio.

"I think they're going in," he said. "They're showing the house again, from a different camera on the street. God, how many cops can fit in that house? Somebody just pushed the cameraman back.

"Now we're back in the newsroom. Everyone's looking concerned. Now we're back to the camera on the rooftop. SWAT's leading people, must be the family, out of the house. Aw, Jesus, they got blood all over them. Paramedics are going in."

Yamaguchi gripped the wheel tighter. It was obviously over. They were still miles from downtown. She kept the lights and siren going and was still driving fast, but she knew they weren't going to be needed.

They arrived at the scene at the same time that some of the emergency vehicles were leaving. The onlookers outside the police barricades were also starting to disperse although the police presence was still strong. An almost full moon, emergency vehicles and crime scene lights illuminated the area.

After leaving their car, they located the SWAT leader, the same lieutenant with whom they'd worked at Union Station. He saw Yamaguchi approaching.

"Kind of late, aren't you Gooch?" he asked.

"Sorry, we were in Colorado Springs," she explained. "We didn't get the message until 4."

"Well, we sure could have used you. There's going to be hell to pay on this one." He walked away before she could offer another apology.

"So what do we do, Linda?" Munroe asked.

"Hell if I know. I doubt there's anything we can do."

"I wouldn't bother sticking around," a voice said behind them. She turned and saw Sgt. Tompkins. "Hey, Linda." She nodded.

"What happened?" she asked.

"We can't find a weapon and the family's already on TV blaming us."

"Aw, hell. The kid's dead?"

"Yeah. We thought we had a chance of making him

give up, then somebody yelled shots fired and they put him down. We can't find a weapon. Why the hell were you in the Springs?"

"We were following up a missing persons report." He looked at her skeptically. "I know … I know," she said. "Any of the brass around here?"

"Chief's already left with Clemens. You probably should just go back to the department and stay in a crouched position."

She agreed with him and said goodbye. Munroe, however, said he'd like to look around the crime scene.

"What for?" she asked.

"I've got X-ray eyes, remember? Maybe I can find a weapon."

"Whatever. I'll hide out in the car."

Fifteen minutes later he returned. "Couldn't find anything they haven't already found. Damn it, we might have made a difference. I'm sorry I talked you into going."

"It's not your fault. It was bound to happen anyway. There's only the two of us. Sooner or later we wouldn't have been available for something like this. If the department would just hire more disembodied …"

"I know. I just … I'm just really sorry," he said. "Let's go back to the department and hope no one sees us. If we're lucky, it'll blow over."

CHAPTER 13

WASHINGTON, D.C. (AP) – Another "Open Your Door for the Dead Day" still remains an unofficial holiday, despite thousands of emails deluging lawmakers.

"The U.K. has it on Boxing Day, Canada has it on Canada Day. Why can't the U.S. have something? We know there are millions of the dead trapped under sinks, in attics and God knows where else," said Elise Compton, whose organization, Bring Out Your Dead, has been lobbying for an official Day status.

The first Monday of the new year has been an unofficial day to open wide the doors of little used closets, basements and other storage areas in which the disembodied might be trapped. It's a somewhat tongue-in-cheek holiday that gained new currency since Dr. Olaf Bols, a disembodied scientist, was briefly trapped after a press conference in Tokyo.

Every session of Congress, a bill is introduced, usually by Colorado Congresswoman Deena DeGroot, but "it's usually laughed out of the House and nothing gets done. I know it's a relatively minor problem, but one of my constituents found himself in this situation after he died and so it is a real problem."

Yamaguchi and Munroe waited nervously in the reception area of the chief's office. "Do U think were in trouble?" she silently asked Munroe. They could hear raised voices behind the closed doors.

"I doubt we're sitting here because we're about to be congratulated for clearing disembodied witness reports."

220

Because of tsunami news, the story was pushed into the corners on page one of the local papers. TV news had covered it extensively. The mayor had held a press conference in the morning, while the family had held their own on the front doorstep of a relative's home. The city councilman for the district, a political opponent of the mayor, joined the family in suggesting that race played an issue in the shooting. Fortunately for them, no one had asked why the disembodied officer who'd played the hero before Christmas hadn't been available to do so again.

The door to the office opened and they saw the manager of safety leave, followed by the city attorney. Half a minute later, they heard the chief say, "Yamaguchi, Munroe, get in here."

Inside the chief waited with deputy chief Clemens. Yamaguchi entered and stood awkwardly. She felt like standing at attention, but the last time she did that was at the academy.

"Sit down. Munroe with you?" the chief asked.

"Yes, sir," she said.

"Close the door, Paul," the chief instructed his deputy. "Now, want to tell me why the hell you were in Colorado Springs yesterday."

"We were interviewing a witness, sir."

"In the Springs?"

"Yes. Sir. We have interviewed witnesses before," she said, regretting her poor choice of words instantly.

"Oh have you. And what crime was involved that required you to interview this witness. In the Springs."

"A missing person. Persons, actually," she said.

"We do have detectives whose job it is to investigate missing persons. Why weren't they interviewing this witness?"

"It didn't really fall under their … it's not really … well, they're dead."

The chief slapped his hands onto his desk.

"We don't investigate missing dead people. My God, if we investigated all the missing dead people ... we'd ... we'd be doing nothing but investigating missing dead people. And for damn sure, you don't go off without telling anyone." Clemens, standing beside the chief's desk, took a small step back.

She swallowed, trying to keep a sour feeling contained in her stomach. "We ... um ... I ..." She looked at Clemens.

"She told me she might be running a little late," Clemens said.

The chief faced him. "You knew where they were?"

Clemens shoulders inched upward as he said, "She ... yeah, she mentioned something about it. It slipped my mind that's where they were. They were supposed to be back in time for their shift."

The chief looked at Clemens without speaking for a few seconds. "Sit down, Paul. You're annoyingly tall." Clemens sat. The chief continued. "OK, I don't want to bust anyone's ..." He looked at her. "You're not in trouble, Linda. Or you, Alex, if you are in fact here. Damn, this is one crazy world.

"Let's face it. You two can't be everywhere all the time and this was bound to happen. It just shows we need more disembodied officers. And it also shows we need to use them better. I know we've been dicking around what role you play. We've got you doing everything from rescuing kids to tactical to solving shed burglaries. Thanks, incidentally. I realize that's a long way from being a homicide detective.

"So here's the deal. We're planning to get two more disembodied officers in the next budget. The FD's going to add two. The situation's a lot better than when we hired you ... is there a way I can speak to him?" he asked her. "This is driving me nuts."

She explained they could go back to the terminal in the

detectives' room or she could steal the speakers from his computer. He told her to do the latter and a minute later she had placed her terminal on his desk and attached the speakers.

"Are you here?" he said, looking at the terminal.

"Yup," Munroe said.

"Where, exactly?"

"Kind of sitting on your desk next to the terminal. Your desk is … annoyingly large. If you'd move the terminal closer to the edge, I could sit." She moved a chair next to the desk and slid the terminal closer. She also removed her ear buds to eliminate the stereo effect.

"Comfy?" the chief asked. When Munroe assured him he was, the chief continued. "Anyway, we've decided the way we're using you is a waste of resources. We'd planned to announce this the first of the year, but with this shooting … well, we're going to announce it now before the press or somebody starts asking why you weren't involved."

"Announce what?" Munroe and Yamaguchi asked together.

"We're moving you to SWAT," the chief said. He waited for them to say something. "Well, you could thank me or something." They remained silent. "What, you don't want to be part of SWAT?"

"It's not what I signed up for," Munroe said.

"What the hell does that mean? You wanted to be a homicide detective again. You knew that wasn't going to happen. We told you you'd be working with SWAT when we hired you."

"Yeah, from time to time. But when I was hired, we agreed that I'd work with the disembodied community, that I'd be the initial investigator when a disembodied witness was involved. And that from time to time, I'd work with patrol and the fire department."

The chief was confused. "Yes, but …"

"I don't want to go to SWAT either," she said.

"Huh?" The chief had forgotten about her in his efforts to convince Munroe. He looked at her. "Why not? I wouldn't have thought you'd object. You've got a pretty gung ho reputation. There're a lot of cops who'd jump at the chance to join SWAT."

She crossed her arms and said, "I like patrol. And I like working with Alex. And if he doesn't want to go, I don't either."

"If it's your safety, don't worry. We wouldn't be putting you on the line immediately. You'd still have to go through the same training as any SWAT candidate."

"So then I'd just be his handler until you're ready to use him. And if I wash out, what happens then? Back to patrol?"

The chief settled back in his chair. He let out a breath and looked at Clemens. "We thought you'd be onboard with this." Clemens nodded, but didn't risk saying anything.

"Look you two, maybe this isn't a perfect plan, and maybe we have to rethink who goes where and when, OK? But let's just say we play along for now."

"Maybe a trial period?" Clemens suggested.

"Yeah, excellent idea, Paul. You give it … three months. If you don't like it, you go back to what you're doing now. By that time, we've got our new hires. We've already got one dead SWAT officer who we might be able to sign if Phoenix doesn't grab him first."

"We've got to be able to announce something to the press today," Clemens added. "We need you onboard for this."

"Linda, what do you say?" Munroe asked. The chief and Clemens glanced at Alex's empty chair, then at her.

"There's already a lot of people who resent me having this job. If I get attached to SWAT …"

"We can deal with that," the chief said.

"Three months. We don't like it, we go back to what we're doing now," she said.

"And if you screw with us," Munroe said, "we raise so much stink with the press …"

Damn it, Alex, don't get us fired, she thought, afraid he went too far, but the chief said, "It won't ever come to that."

"It's OK with me, Linda," Munroe said.

She thought a few seconds before answering. While in the academy, she thought SWAT was a possibility, but after just a year on patrol, she knew she'd hate it. As an ordinary officer, she was responsible for herself. When something big happened, a sergeant came out and took the responsibility. She didn't doubt her ability, but she did know her limits.

In her four years, she'd never had a situation where she thought she might really have to shoot someone. She'd trained her gun on an armed suspect several times, of course, but so far either the suspect had put down the weapon or had been hit with a TASER or she was just one of a number of cops. So she'd never shot anyone or been in a situation where she was about to pull the trigger. She'd trained for it and was fully prepared to shoot to pro-tect herself or others, but she hoped she might go her whole career as a cop and never have to do it. If she joined SWAT, however, she knew her chances of shooting some-one certainly would be higher.

And she had to admit, the risk was an issue. It didn't make sense, but she could accept that every day on the job, she could get killed at any time. But it was a small chance spread out over a large period. A SWAT officer's risk of injury or death, however, occurred in very small periods of time but the risk was very high. They were called to do any hazardous entry, remove barricaded suspects or raid meth labs. She wasn't that eager to become a disembodied cop herself.

"For three months, OK," she said, regretting it already.

The chief smiled and Munroe regretted it when he saw the smile. "Now, let's talk about the press conference," the chief said.

"So I didn't look weird this time, you're sure?" she asked Munroe later that evening.

For the third time, he said, "You looked fine. You were great, very professional. No snot, I swear." She'd not had time to pack a lunch, so they had stopped at the Sixth and Grant universe of fast food restaurants so she could get a burrito and she was eating it in their car. She was trying to eat quickly so they could get back to the station and catch up on the disembodied witness reports that had piled up over their weekend. Beans and rice were squished out of the tortilla as she ate and plopped to the napkins on her lap and from there to the floor of the car.

"It's not that I'm vain or anything, you know that. But after that last time," she said, talking as she ate. Not every word was intelligible to him, but he got the gist of it. He wished she would stop worrying about her appearance and onto more important matters.

"Did I do OK?" he asked. For the press conference, they'd again hooked up the terminal to speakers so he could address the reporters directly. It had been a challenge to get the reporters to ask their questions one at a time, so she'd taken their questions and relayed them to him.

"What have you got to worry about? Sorry. Yes, you handled the press very well. I wish you could have been like that last week." She was impressed by Munroe's careful answers. He must have had a lot of experience with press conferences when he was the famous Strangler detective, she assumed. He worried that he'd slipped into official police jargon and cringed when he remembered that he'd used the word "re-purpose."

They'd both been energized by the press conference and had tried to make the best of their re-assignment and not voiced any doubts.

She stopped in mid-munch. "We're so totally screwed, aren't we?"

"Yeah, we are. I think we oversold it. I mean when you get on a roll, you're pretty hard to stop."

"Me? What about … well, whatever. The problem is that it does make sense."

Munroe had to agree. If you only have one disembodied officer, it makes sense to use him on SWAT. *It's just my hard luck if it doesn't fit in with my wants and desires.*

She got out of the car to dump the remains of her burrito and returned. "We'd better get back and work on those reports. And who the hell's going to do them when we switch?"

He thought the answer was obvious. "I am, of course. Or at least, I'll be the one who sorts through them. I won't be able to follow-up any of them."

She was driving up Lincoln to get back to the department. "I don't understand," she said.

"You're going to be too busy because of training, which should be just about done when the three months are up, you know. So then they'll say, give it another three months because you really haven't had a chance yet."

"Or I wash out."

"I don't think you'll wash out. But I won't need any training. Yeah, I'll have to learn their names, their procedures. I'll be involved in exercises. But you know SWAT. Most of their time is spent either training, cleaning weapons or stupid crap like nuisance abatement and community involvement. I won't need to be around for that stuff so I'll probably have time to sort the reports and route them."

"Oh, poor Alex. Meanwhile all I have to do is hundreds of pushups and hours of playing commando."

She parked their car and they went into the department. After entering the secure area, they passed by a couple of cops talking in the hall, the hated Sgt. Diller among them. Yamaguchi prepared herself for the inevitable nickname.

"Hey, it's supercop," Diller said. "Your meteoric rise continues, I hear."

She stopped and said, "Hey, sarge. Yeah, I'm moving on up. Probably be a lieutenant before too long, or maybe a deputy chief. Don't worry, I won't forget about the little people. Bye."

She continued down the hall and heard laughter from the other cops and Diller say "Fuck you, Gooch."

"Oh God, I'm dead cop walking," she muttered to Munroe.

"No, that would be me," he said.

She left work around 11 p.m., a little early but she'd started the day with the noon meeting with the chief. She said goodbye and left Munroe alone in the detectives' room. It had been a busy day and he'd had little time or opportunity to get on the Internet, so now that he was alone he went online.

The tsunami news continued its depressing toll, with most news organization talking about a hundred or hundred and fifty thousand dead. It remained the topic of conversation of most of the chat rooms, forums and blogs frequented by the disembodied. There were already thousands of postings by people who claimed to have died in the flooding, but he found most of them implausible. Many of the countries where the death toll had been the worst had little Internet, much less AfterNet access. The irony was that the political and social upheaval that resulted from the discovery of the afterlife had made it difficult to install the infrastructure needed to support the sudden arrival of so many disembodied. The timing of the discovery, coming on the heels of the broader Asian economic collapse, didn't help.

So Munroe knew that many of the postings were from poseurs. Still, a handful of postings seemed genuine. Not surprisingly, most of those postings were from Westerners, the few tourists brave enough to travel to the region. And most of them had accessed the Internet from the few AfterNet terminals shipped there by international relief efforts. The postings were often garbled as the newly dead struggled to use the field interface.

He felt a little chastened after reading all the news and postings, realizing his woes were pretty trivial compared to what the survivors and the dead would have to face.

He thought he'd better check his AfterNet email account and found the expected hundreds of messages. He gave them a quick look after running the filters that would separate them into neat piles: blog related, friends, whackos, spam, cop related, etc. He was about to consign the majority to the trash when he saw one that caught his attention. It wasn't forwarded from his blog and so didn't use the header "Re: The next big wave of disembodied is happening now." Instead, the subject line was: "Who's kidnapping the dead in Colorado?" He opened it.

You don't know me and don't try to find me. It would be bad for me if you did.

I want you to know that I don't believe in what they're doing anymore. Not since my wife died and a more kind, loving Christian woman I have never known. If she couldn't go directly to heaven, then no one can.

I know you've been in the springs looking into the abductions. I don't have any new info but I still know some people who are starting to think like me. I left them after she died because I knew they wouldn't trust me and I'm scared what they will do to us.

Maybe I can make up for what I did. We both do.
There are more raves they're planning for New Years Eve and its going to be big. And not just Colorado but all over. I don't have any more information for you now, but if I find anything else, I;ll let you know.

He checked the sender's username and was surprised to find it was his own: (Alex Munroe) jollycopper@theafternet.net. It appeared to been sent at 6:31 p.m. Denver time.

He'd gotten spam messages before where his own address appeared in the from field. He didn't know how it was done but he did remember that he could reveal the crap at the start of an email that normally gets hidden. He revealed the long headers and saw that the email had been bounced around several times, including an email server in Romania, judging by the ".ro" at the end of the address.

Maybe Linda could figure out who really sent this, but no way I'm able to, he thought. *Maybe I can forward it to her.* He realized it was 2:30 Thursday morning, however. She wouldn't even read it until much later that morning.

OK, maybe I'm not a cyber geek, able to trace this email around the world. But maybe I can find some evidence of what they're planning. The game's afoot.

CHAPTER 14

From *The Washington Post*

WASHINGTON, D.C. — The Pew Forum on Religion and Public Life released today a survey that shows 65 percent of Americans believe in the afterlife, as it has come to be known since 1997.

The forum is a project of the Pew Research Center, a nonpartisan organization that regularly conducts opinion surveys. The figures released today show a 3 percent drop in the overall average since the same time in 2003 and are in contrast to similar surveys in Europe, where the numbers that believe in the afterlife are increasing.

Vance Edmonds, principal researcher on the survey, said, the results "follow the same nationwide trends as the years before. If we look at the South, 60 percent believe in the afterlife, which is down 2 percent from the year before. Of those without any college experience, 58 percent believe. Consider yourself 'a devout Christian' in the South, 48 percent. In the Pacific Northwest, on the other hand, 75 percent believe in the afterlife."

Claire Redmond, a spokeswoman for the group MovedOn, responded to the figures. "These numbers might make it seem that a divide is opening between those who believe and those who don't. But less than 50 percent of Americans believe in evolution, yet they don't mind receiving a new flu vaccine every year necessitated because flu viruses evolve. And I don't think people will refuse to take the new vaccines that will come online next year, even if they are based on research from disembodied scientists. And we don't believe in global

warming, yet we finally approved new cap and trade legisla-
tion. Americans have always been able to believe and accept
contradictory things."

In Europe, the acceptance of the afterlife and the disembodied is increasing, according to a poll conducted last year
by the Pew Global Attitudes Project. Surveys conducted in
Britain, France, Germany, Spain and Italy show a 9 percent
increase in belief, although the methodology of that survey is
different from this recent U.S. survey.

"I admit, it really does sound like someone is trying to kid-
nap the disembodied," Yamaguchi admitted to Munroe,
"but this isn't proof anyone's going to accept." She was
looking on her phone at the email that he'd forwarded to
her.

"I know. We need something more solid," he said. They
were sitting on the 16th Street Mall, not too far from his
favorite Starbucks where she'd gotten a hot chocolate. Few
people noticed the woman sitting on the bench talking to
herself.

"I'll go in early and start searching too, see what I can
come up with," she offered, although she really didn't
want to. She'd had a restless night and woke far too early,
in time to get a call from him asking to meet her at 10
a.m.

"It won't make a difference. We need something
faster."

"The department's …"

"A lot faster than the department," he said.

"Where're you going to find that?"

"Feel like calling your boyfriend?"

She had no idea what he was talking about. "Who?"

"Bob Feore, the guy at the party."

"Him? He's not a boyfriend. Hell, I think you talked to
him longer than I did."

"Half the time he was pumping me for information about you," he said. *A little bit of a lie, but not much,* he thought to himself.

"Really? What did he want to know?"

"No time for that, Linda. He told me about a new search technology they're working on. Then he clammed up when he realized he shouldn't have said anything. He said it was like a supercomputer search engine for the dis-embodied. I think he was trying to impress me so he could ask more about you."

"Oh," she said, looking down at her cup of hot choco-late. "I was kind of mad at him … and you. I thought I was being neglected. And when I went to find him later, he was gone."

"No, he was definitely interested in you. The point is, this search technology might help find what I'm looking for."

"OK, tonight when I go home, I'll look up his number …"

"I already have it. Call him now." He gave her the num-ber. "Go on, call him."

"I hate pushy dead guys."

"Just do it."

She dialed the number and it was answered in two rings.

"Feore. It's not my problem," he said.

"Hello? Bob?"

"Who … Linda, is that you?"

"Oh, you remember me. So nice."

"Oh, God, the party. I'm so sorry. I wanted to talk to you again."

"That's why you disappeared?"

"Sorry, I got called to the office on an emergency. I've been fighting bears all week." He let his Irish accent slip into his apology. "You must know how it is."

"Get on with it," Munroe said in her ear.

"Yeah, I guess I do."

"Maybe I can make it up to you? How about dinner sometime?"

"What's he saying," Munroe said. She covered her phone with her hand. "Shut up, Alex."

"What's that? Who're you talking to?"

"It's just my partner," she said.

"Alex? Hey say hi for me. I wanted to talk to him …"

"How about making it up to me right now?" she said, a little annoyed that he wanted to talk to Munroe.

"Sure, if I can. How?"

"Alex wants to use your search technology. Can we come over?"

"The search … no, I mean … I shouldn't have said anything."

"What's he saying," Munroe said again. This time, she told him, saying it loud enough for Feore to hear.

"Sorry, Bob," she said, getting back to him. "Alex said he needed to get more information to put on his blog."

"Blog? No, you can't … you're just messing with me, right. You wouldn't do that, would you?"

She did a pretend conversation with Munroe, begging him not to post the blog. "I don't know, he sounds pretty determined. I think the only way I can keep him from posting is if you let us come over and use it."

"OK, OK, come over. Next week when …"

"Today," she said.

"What! Do you know how busy I am?"

"I'm sorry, Bob, it has to be today. Look, Alex won't really write anything whether you show us or not. But it is important. I can't say lives are at stake, because it only concerns the disembodied, but I thought that's what the AfterNet was about."

Feore remained silent a beat before he answered. "Come on over. You know where it is, don't you?"

She looked up from her bench on the 16th Street Mall

at the skyscraper that housed the offices of the AfterNet. "I think I can find my way."

Yamaguchi waited patiently while the revolving door decided to let her pass. "Please exit the revolving door and welcome to the AfterNet," the cheerful, recorded female voice told her.

"Linda, hi," Feore greeted her as she stepped through the door.

"Hi, Bob," she said, as she shook his hand, while looking distractedly around her.

"He's over here," he said, motioning for her to follow. She followed him to another entrance, also a part of the large glass wall that bisected the lobby of the building. Glowing neon outlined the disembodied entrance.

"The neon doesn't do anything," he explained. "It just looks cool. The real deterrent is the coil that runs around the frame."

She looked more closely and saw that a twisted band of copper wires, making an eighth of an inch bundle, was embedded in the glass that surrounded the entrance.

"That?" she asked, pointing. "Doesn't look very thick."

"It doesn't take very much to stop the dead. A weak negative field prevents unauthorized visitors. You walked through the same field when you entered the Orgasmatron … the security carousel. It detects any disembodied who try to sneak in."

"So, there aren't any dead people in the building?"

"Oh, no, there're lots and lots of disembodied employees. But everyone is authorized to be here. That probably results in the lowest dead-to-living ratio on the planet."

"I'm here," Munroe's voice told her in his ear.

"He's here," she told Feore.

"I know," he said, patting the left breast pocket of his leather jacket. "I can hear." Yamaguchi saw that Feore seemed to be listening to Munroe's response, but she heard nothing.

"I still don't appreciate being blackmailed," he said, apparently to Munroe.

She glanced at her terminal and saw the "No user connected" message.

"I seem to have lost Alex," she said to Feore.

"He's out of your field. My terminal's got a lot wider field than yours. I hacked mine. Here, Alex, why don't you go on Linda's right and I'll walk beside you."

"… made her do it," she heard Munroe say, as he reacquired the field of her terminal.

"If you don't mind, let's wait to go up to my office before we talk."

Feore led them to the bank of elevators, careful to keep a gap for Munroe to walk comfortably between them.

I don't think he's as charming as Linda thinks he is, but I got to admit he has good disembodied etiquette, Munroe thought. *Must be all the dead people he probably works with.*

The elevator stopped on the 27th floor. Feore had a corner office with windows facing northwest and a beautiful view of the Front Range.

He closed the door, then went behind his desk, said, "Take a seat," and sat. He took his terminal out of his coat pocket and plugged it into a dock on the desk.

"Alex, we can hear you on the speakers." He took off his ear buds and nodded to her, and she took off hers.

"Bob, I'm sorry I asked Linda to call you," Munroe said, "but we don't have much time."

Feore looked at her. "You said something about lives being at stake. What was that about?"

She and Munroe spent five minutes telling him about their initial missing persons reports, their investigation of the rave and their trip to Colorado Springs.

"That's the craziest … trapping people with plywood

236

and moving walls? It's like the garbage compactor scene in *Star Wars*. But what do they gain? You can't hurt … is it even a crime?"

She sat forward in her chair. "I don't think it matters if it is. It's still wrong. Can you help us?"

"How? It sounds like you might already know when and where the next … kidnapping might be."

Munroe said, "We need more proof than an email to justify … look, you must have heard about the Williams shooting?"

"What Williams shooting?"

They explained to him about the shooting and their new role in the department.

"Sorry, first we had problems with the network Christmas Day, then the tsunami."

"What's that got to do with you?" she asked.

"Relief efforts," Munroe answered for him.

"That's right. Soon as we found out, we started sending as many portable terminals as we could find to send to Buckley Air Force Base. Including a couple of prototypes of the new terminals you predicted in your blog. From there, the military got them to Guam and then out where needed. So I really haven't paid any attention to anything except the tsunami. Today's the first day I've been able to breathe. Then you two make trouble for me."

"Well, at Rybold's party, you mentioned this new search engine technology," Munroe said.

"Yeah," he said, making a face and rubbing the back of his neck. "I was really full of myself that day. I shouldn't have said anything. It's something that really should have been covered by a confidentiality agreement. If you went public right now …"

"We were never really going to do that," she said.

"I'm … we're willing to sign one," Munroe said. Feore looked up. "If we could use it today," Munroe added. "The department's Internet connection is too slow and the terminal's ancient. We need a lot more evidence fast. If this search engine is what you said …"

Feore drew back, his body language making it clear he wasn't likely to agree.

"Help me Obi-wan, you're my only hope," Yamaguchi said. Munroe was surprised. She didn't often make movie references, but she had judged its effect on Feore quite accurately.

"OK … let me make a call." Feore said. "She's quite a piece of work."

"Sly move with the *Star Wars* reference, Linda," Munroe said.

"I can still hear you, Alex," Feore said.

"Damn," Munroe said. "I got to stop doing …" Feore held up a finger to silence him as he talked to someone on the phone.

Munroe and Yamaguchi looked at each other. They were used to being able to talk privately at times like these.

"It's OK," Feore said. "They're quiet in the lab because of the holiday and Shel's there so she can operate the chamber."

"Chamber?" she asked.

He smiled. "Follow me. I'll explain on the way."

He retrieved his terminal and put on his ear buds. She did the same and then he led them out of his office and toward the elevators.

"Lab's two floors down."

"Bob, I thought you told me about a search engine, not a … chamber."

"It is a search engine … sort of. And it's a whole lot more," he said, saying the last in a salesman's pitch. The elevator doors opened and they got in. Another person was in the elevator and Feore stopped talking. They rode the elevator down two floors. On getting out, they were in a small room that contained a security guard, his desk and chair, two revolving security doors, a disembodied entrance and two large double doors that were marked emergency exits.

"Hi, Bob," the guard said.

"Hector, hi. I've got two guests. Can I use your computer?"

"Sure thing." The guard got up from his desk and Feore sat down.

"OK, I'm adding you two as visitors and I'm …" — he waited as a printer sitting next to the computer produced a form — "… printing out a non-disclosure for you to sign, Linda. And Alex, I'm …" — he manipulated the mouse and keyboard "making a form online for you to sign. If you'll just log in."

Munroe moved closer to the computer and felt the AfterNet field. He saw that Feore had sent him a secure PDF to sign electronically, which he did. Meanwhile, Feore collected Yamaguchi's form.

"On its way," Munroe said.

Feore checked his email. "OK. Sorry, Alex. I'm afraid you have to go through the disembodied entrance again. And Linda, I'm afraid you have to give your phone and terminal to the guard. And whatever else you have."

"OK, but if the phone rings …"

"Hector will answer it and page us."

"And how will I hear Alex?"

"There are hotspots throughout the lab. We don't need the terminals." He gave the guard his terminal. "Shall we?" he asked, motioning them toward the entrances.

They went through the revolving doors and waited while Munroe made it through.

"I'm here," Munroe told them, as he acquired the strongest AfterNet field he'd ever felt. It was almost like basking under a warm, tropical sun.

A speaker in the ceiling produced Munroe's words. It was in an almost normal accent, the best digitized voice Yamaguchi had ever heard.

"OK, that will be Munroe's voice from now on. It was generated just for him. No one else can ever use it and if he ever visits this building again, it's the one you'll hear. It's the new speech algorithm we've been working on. It's also spatially oriented. Alex, walk to a different part of the room and say something."

"How much wood could a woodchuck chuck if a woodchuck could chuck wood?" he said.

His voice traveled across the room. Once it stopped, she saw that she was looking at a vast open area, broken only by the supporting pillars and the central core of the building's elevators and other services behind them. Glass walls divided some parts of the space, and through them, she saw several large, white spheres, possibly six feet tall, dotted around the floor.

A woman, wearing the lab coat of mad scientists everywhere, came walking toward them.

"Hey, Bob," she said. She was only an inch taller than Yamaguchi, with medium length blonde hair pulled back in a ponytail. She had the rosiest cheeks Yamaguchi had ever seen without the use of cosmetics. She looked to be 15 years old.

"Shel Younger — Dr. Shel Younger — meet officers Linda Yamaguchi and Alex Munroe."

"Hi," Younger said, extending her hand to Yamaguchi. "Dr. Feore said you were interested in the search chamber." She emphasized the word doctor, dragging it out artificially.

Yamaguchi shook her hand, impressed by the grip, and decided she liked her, despite thinking: *She's like me, but an inch taller, cuter, smarter and blonde.*

"Yes, we'd like to find out if ..."

Younger held out a hand, tilting her head slightly in the process and looking like a school crossing guard. "Please don't tell me. I'm not interested in the search parameters. Might skew the results. Now, where's the test subject?"

"Uh, is that me?" Munroe asked, suddenly regretting this.

She turned to the voice. Munroe had joined their group. "Follow me," she said, and marched off.

"Linda?" Munroe asked.

Feore looked at her and nodded. "Don't worry, it'll be OK."

"Uh … yeah. Go with her Alex. It'll be OK." She turned to Feore and started to speak, but he stopped her.

"It'll take about 15 minutes for Shel to get the readings from Alex's signature. We don't have this part of the process automated yet. Let's go into the break room."

Munroe followed Younger, feeling deserted by his partner. *What the hell have I gotten myself into?*

"Been dead long?" she asked. He hurried to catch up. For a short woman, she walked quickly.

"Since '96."

"How old when you died?"

"62."

"Hmm. You're a little old for this, I'm afraid. It might not work as well, but we'll see."

"Is this going to … hurt?"

Younger stopped and turned to where his voice came from. "Oh you big baby," she said in a comic voice that was unfortunately lost on him. But he saw her smile.

"Come on," she said, resuming her march. They were now at one corner of the floor, screened off from the rest of the space by more glass walls. One of the large white spheres dominated the space. She entered the area through a gap in the glass walls. He followed.

"Is that the chamber?"

"Yup," she said. "But before you go in, I've got to get some readings from you. OK, now stand over here, in this mesh, like so." She kept her hands about shoulder width apart and motioned that he should enter a wire mesh ball about two feet in diameter. The ball was split down the middle and apparently hinged. He entered the ball and she promptly closed the halves of the ball together. He could easily see through the mesh.

"Are you in the middle?" she asked.

"Yes."

"All right, don't move. You can talk except when I tell you not to. Just try to stay in the middle."

"Jawohl, Frau Blucher," he said.

"Huh?"

"I won't move."

"OK, I'm just going to record your field. This will probably feel … good."

She flipped a switch on a piece of test equipment. Munroe was about to object when he felt the nicest experience he'd ever had since dying. It was a combination of the smell of warm apple pie, Mom tucking him into bed, a woman stroking his crotch, his first taste of really good Scotch, the first time he proposed and the first time he used the AfterNet, all rolled into one, with a thousand other shifting good emotions fighting to get in.

"Fine, that's enough," she said, turning the switch off.

It was a few seconds before he could talk. "I love you Dr. Younger, and I want to marry you."

She smiled quickly. "Yes, they all say that. OK, this next part … well, it'll probably feel bad."

In retrospect, he should have seen it coming.

"I never knew the AfterNet did so much research," Yamaguchi said as Feore poured himself coffee in the break room. He came back to sit with her at one of the tables.

"I know. Most people just think we run the forums and install terminals. But the mandate was to make 'life better for the disembodied and improve relations with the living.' So, we keep trying to improve the user experience."

He reached for his coffee cup and said, "You know, I am sorry I ran out of the party."

"I was a little … annoyed at you. You basically dumped me to talk to Alex."

"But I'd be willing to take you to dinner. I wouldn't do that for him."

"Well, he's really not into food. Wait, are you saying that you're not mad we forced you into this?"

"No, I'm still pissed about that, thank you for reminding me. But it was my own fault for bringing it up in the first place. I was trying to impress Alex."

"And why were you doing that?"

"Well, if you want to … date old Reilly's daughter."

"What?"

"It's an old song you sing when you're really drunk on St. Patrick's Day. Forget it. I just thought if I could impress Alex, he might say a nice thing or two about me."

"You could have just asked me out."

"What a good idea. Would you …"

He was interrupted when she heard what she thought was Munroe's new digitized voice, very loud.

"OK, the worst is over. Let's rejoin your partner," he said.

"Bitch!"

"Calm down. It's over now. Everything's OK. I'm sorry, that was the worst part. Everything's neutral now. I just need you to be quiet …"

"You fucking bitch! What did you do to me?"

"They're never quiet," she said, sighing. "It's the only way to get a real reading. Look, the chamber is going to interface with you like you've never experienced. I've got the baseline reading now. All we have to do now is get some neutral readings, so please, just be quiet for a minute and we're done with this part."

Munroe had been ready to kill. He knew if he'd still be alive and armed, the bitch would be dead. But already the anger was flowing out of him. The experience itself had drained it out of him. All that remained was resentment.

"OK, Alex, please. You're moving around in there and thinking too much. Try to relax." She went to one of the glass walls, which suddenly became opaque and lowered the lighting in the room.

The darkness helped. He avoided looking into other wavelengths and he tried recalling the pleasure feelings, especially the warm apple pie. Sometimes he thought he missed food the most. Never a real glutton, happy with simple fare, he never thought food played such an important part of his life. He could eat almost anything put in front of him and he never really understood how some people could go on and about a particular flavor or …

"OK, and we're done. You can get out now." She was opening the mesh ball.

"You OK, partner?" Yamaguchi asked. He now realized that she and Feore had rejoined them.

"Yeah, I'm OK."

"What did you do to him?" she said angrily to Younger.

Younger was about to answer but Feore cut her off. "We have to get pretty precise adjustments to make the interface chamber — the big ball behind you — to work as closely as possible with Alex. We're hoping the shipping technology won't require such … precise alignment," he said looking at Younger, who tried to ignore him.

"If you ever want repeat business," Munroe said.

"Yeah. OK, I think we're ready to put you inside." As Feore said this, Younger walked up to the chamber and pressed a button on a panel. An eighth section of the chamber, like an orange slice, opened, one half swinging upward, the other downward. The inside of the chamber was a featureless gray. Yamaguchi walked toward the opening and peered inside it.

"It's empty," she said.

"Actually, the entire inside surface is an organic display. OLEDs."

"It's a big computer screen?"

"Oh, it's a whole lot more than that," Feore said. "Now if Alex will just step inside …"

"No. He's not. Tell me what this is, tell me what it does."

"We really don't want to prejudice the subject," Younger added, she thought helpfully.

"Stop calling me that," Munroe said.

"It will not hurt," Feore said. "Alex, I promise you it will not hurt. You will probably enjoy it. Hell, you'll love it. I can't really tell you too much about it, because that will color how you will perceive the interface."

Feore leaned close to Yamaguchi and whispered something in her ear. She nodded, an odd expression on her face.

"Now, Alex, if you'll step inside," Younger said.

"I think it's OK, Alex," Yamaguchi said.

"All right. Linda, promise me you'll kill these people if they do something to me."

"I promise."

After a few seconds, Feore asked Younger, "Is he in?" She nodded, flipped a switch and the sphere closed. "Linda, we're going to sit over here." He led her to some chairs flanking a double row of monitors. Younger joined them in the center chair and started typing.

Once the chamber doors closed, it was dark and Munroe was cut off from the AfterNet field. He tried infrared but couldn't make out anything except a fairly uniform glow cast by the organic LEDs. He switched back to normal light and saw that a message had appeared on the walls of the chamber.

"Alex, this is Bob. We're going to get started. You might not experience anything for a while. You might hear a woman's voice. Just relax."

Hear a woman's voice? That'd be nice. Soon he faintly felt an AfterNet field, far weaker even than his partner's terminal.

"Alex," a woman whispered in his ear. He spun around. The voice came from behind.

"Alex, don't be frightened." The voice was familiar, but he couldn't quite place it.

"Who are you?"

"Don't try so hard. Just speak normally, like you did when you were alive."

Speak? he thought to himself. *As if.*

"Yes, that's better. I can hear you quite clearly."

Who are you? He wasn't visualizing his thoughts as words like he normally did with an AfterNet field. It was more like talking.

"I'm whoever you want me to be. But I know what you really meant. I am the new AfterNet interface or agent, coupled with a greatly improved field."

You're an artificial intelligence?

"No, I am not self aware, although I have been programmed to so appear. I am merely your guide to explore the AfterNet and the Internet. Would you like to experience the new search engine technology?"

Are you reading my mind?

"Yes. Would you like to experience the new search engine technology?"

Yes, show me.

Munroe couldn't explain it. He just felt it. He didn't need to struggle to enter search parameters. He simply desired it. And the information was relayed to him not as words and numbers painstakingly visualized, but as ideas and thoughts. At first, it came too fast, but then he realized he was still trying to translate the ideas into words, instead of simply comprehending the idea.

"So, exactly how does this work?" Yamaguchi asked Feore.

"Huh, oh well, I guess it won't hurt telling you." He tore himself away from looking at the various screens and addressed her. "Remember when you first learned how to use your terminal to communicate with your partner directly?"

"Yeah."

"Has it gotten any easier?"

"Sure."

"Be honest. Can you really hold an extended conversation with him?"

"No. If I wanted to do that, I'd just speak out loud."

"Exactly. Because it just takes way too much concentration. You see, some people think the terminal is reading your thoughts, but in reality, what you're really doing in order to make the terminal understand, is projecting your thoughts into the field. You're really doing the mental equivalent of screaming out loud to project your thoughts."

She nodded. She recalled her early days of using the terminal without speaking. She couldn't walk at the same time she was trying to form her thoughts. It took that much concentration.

"I don't know about you, but the mental image I was taught is a chalkboard. I imagine I'm writing really large letters on the chalkboard, writing with the edge of the chalk rather than the point, to make the letters as big and fat as possible. I'm still pretty bad at it. I have to write one letter at a time."

She nodded again. That was the first method she was taught and it was painstaking. The method she now used was to imagine the Japanese brush script writing her father had taught her. It let her flow the letters together to form words at a time instead of a letter at a time.

"And that's how the disembodied start out. They go through the same process, imagining a letter at a time, then a word. The good ones, however, like your partner, I suspect, have gone way beyond that. They translate their internal speech directly into text, like someone taking dictation from themselves.

"But the next generation of the AfterNet field does away with that. It really is reading thoughts, and it projects thought, too."

"Why'd you ask me if he was straight?"

He laughed. "I just wanted to suggest something to him. That's why I said he might hear a female voice. Chances are, that's what he'll hear."

"He can't hear."

"Technically true. But his brain or mind or whatever it is the dead have, will trick him into thinking he's hearing."

"One other question. Why's this chamber so big?"

"It doesn't really have to be. We could probably make it as small as a ... I don't know, basketball. But it's designed to be used for hours at a time and a lot of disembodied will not willingly go into something that small."

"He's doing better than any other subject," Younger said, interrupting.

Feore turned to her. "Throughput?" he asked.

"Phenomenal. He's ... he's waiting. Processors are ... it's slowing down. Damn, two of the machines are down because I was upgrading them over the holidays."

"OK, let's start using the processor farm in lab B. I don't think ..." he took out his tablet and scrolled through a schedule. "Nope, nothing going on in there today."

"What's wrong?" Yamaguchi asked.

"Nothing. This is great. Alex is doing ... he's great. This confirms what I thought. Look, Alex, is he ... can he do more than one thing at a time? I don't mean regular stuff, like browse the web while holding a conversation. Most everyone can multitask. Can he, can he hold more than one conversation at a time?"

"How would I know? I'm the only one he really talks to." Suddenly she remembered when he'd talked about his chats at the Tattered Cover or at his Starbucks.

"All right, the processor farm is kicking in," Younger said.

I want to compare these IP addresses and these, Alex said.

"I'm sorry, Alex, that information is unavailable."

You had it a second ago.

"I'm sorry, Alex, that ..."

Suddenly the information appeared. Alex grabbed it.

How do I open a spreadsheet? Oh, thanks. Wow. That's different. OK, I strip away ... yeah ... that just leaves ... right, that's a match.

Munroe found himself talking to himself rather than the agent. He seemed to understand what he wanted better if he said it out loud.

OK, that's it. Now how do I get ...

The doors to the chamber parted and hinged outward. He felt the field of the chamber dissipate. He exited and reacquired the field of the lab. After the subtle quality of the chamber's field, the lab's field felt loud.

"Alex? How was it?" Yamaguchi asked.

"I know what I want for next Christmas."

"What was it like?" Yamaguchi asked Munroe again, back in Feore's office.

Munroe was distracted. Since leaving the chamber reality seemed a little drab.

"Huh? Oh, it was ... well, I'd say it was like an out of

body experience but, you know … I was surfing the web without needing to use screens and icons or even words. It just came into my brain. It was like … it was like a waking dream."

Feore returned to the office. "Sorry, Shel and I had a lot to talk about. Alex, you were amazing. You accessed about as much info as a living person can digest in a week. Did you find what you were looking for?"

"Yeah, I did. Can I use your computer?"

"Sure." Feore turned his computer around on his desk to face them. "Have at it."

Munroe called up the web addresses he remembered.

"First, I found this notice in several of the entertainment forums. Actually I found it last night … or this morning rather. It wasn't too difficult to find."

No drugs, no booze but plenty of soul-altering music, lots of food and drink. If you're a Jesus freak, this is the place New Years Eve. It's an abandoned school. You'll need the password: flower-rainbow. Yeah, we know its lame. We're Christians. Whaddya expect. Beelzebub. Click here for map.

"It seems to be in Weld County, a town called Gilcrest. Next, I found Margaret Duggan's blogs."

"Who's Margaret Duggan again?" Feore asked.

"We think she's the one arranging the actual abductions. The one with the church group … in the Springs," Yamaguchi added when he looked blank. "Wait, Alex, you said blogs?"

"Yeah, she's got several. This one is her journal." Munroe had called up the relevant page. Feore and Yamaguchi leaned forward to read.

Mom's feeling a lot better today because Dad's a lot more lucid. The Aricept seems to be working, and he was really alert. Dr. Jones warned me it's just a short-term thing but I'm

just thankful hes not aggressive anymore. But he's a lot more
perceptive, too. I think he knows that the dialysis isn't working
for her as much as before.

The entry was dated April 13, 2002. Munroe skipped
forward to an entry a few months later.

Just got back from the nursing home. Dad was really well
behaved and I just gave up trying to tell him that it was Mom's
funeral. He just kept saying it was Grandma's funeral.
It wasn't until I was leaving that he knew. Oh God, why?
That's what I don't understand. Give him the peace of
forgetting. Why do you make him remember?

"She was taking care of her mom and dad, going to
school and working," Munroe said.

"Yeah, I know what it's like," Yamaguchi said.

"Her dad died in December," Munroe said. He advanced through the blog.

I haven't been keeping this up and I just want to thank
everyone for their kind words. As some of you know, my Dad
died last week. He was pretty peaceful and thought I was
Mom.
The hospice people were great. I just resented them trying to
get him to sign that Afternet bullshit. Sorry. Please forgive my
earlier rant. It's all over now anyway. What does it matter?
I have to admit I was kind of glad. I am so sorry to feel that
way, but I was kind of glad. I came home from work yesterday
and I realized I had time if I wanted and I went to a movie. It's
the first movie I've been to in years. I just had the extra time. I
felt so guilty, but I knew I had the time.

"The poor kid," Feore said. "This is your villain?"

"Not everything is as it seems," Munroe answered.
"There's a big gap after this. I don't know why."

"I think for the first time in a long time, she was enjoying herself," she said.

"Could be. Anyway, here's the last entry."

Please just leave me alone. I don't know what kind of game youre playing at. I don't believe in any of you. My Mom and Dad are dead and in heaven. Dad would never have signed anything for the Afternet. He didn't believe in it and Mom didn't either. Our church doesn't believe in it and I don't believe in it so just stop tyring to contact me. Don't email ever again.

"She turned off new comments and hasn't updated it since," Munroe said.

Yamaguchi let out a small sigh. "Oh, God, that's really sad. Someone pretended to be her parents."

"Again, not quite. I found this on the Forgive and Forget forum on the AfterNet."

Dearest Peg,
Your mother and I love you so much. Please, please respond. We were wrong about the afterlife. It's obviously not heaven but your Mom has no pain, no suffering and I can think clearly again. Maybe we're not ready for heaven yet. Maybe God has other plans for us, like looking after our little girl. Please let us into your life. We watch over you and see that you've made questionable choices after we left you. Let us give you that love and understanding and help put you back on the path.

The username on the posting was Joshua.E.Duggan. "It's a certified identity," Feore said.

"He filed one before he died," she said.

"I found the website for his nursing home," Munroe said. "They strongly encourage every patient to file a certificate. I guess he filed one before the Alzheimer's got too bad. I also found a username for her mother. She doesn't have a certified identity, but I found a posting in Lost Love where Joshua met a woman claiming to be his wife. Obviously he accepted her."

Feore and Yamaguchi both sat back, looking stunned. Feore said, "You said she had other blogs."

"Yeah, right here. She started this one last year."

God is not testing the faithful. He wants to challenge our commitment. He wants to see if we can recognize Satan in his works, or if we will be dissuaded from the true path that is the word of God.

That path does not lie with the mealy mouthed protestations of collaborators who embrace the legions of Satan's demons. If they fail to recognize the threat posed by these false voices who claim to be the souls of those who have gone before, then it is up to those of us who heed God's call to expose them for what they are.

And it is not enough for us to stand idly by and merely protest. It is up to us to act and expose these vile creatures for what they are.

"Wow, that's a little nuts," Feore said.

"I agree, but it's hardly proof of anything," she said.

"I know, but take a look at this. Google found this as a forum posting. A website called 'Recognize Satan.' The posting's been deleted, but it's still in Google's cache."

Our plans to show the world and seek salvation for those who do not deserve it have taken another step forward.

We have developed a way to trap these vile creatures and expose them for what they are. Heed this call. We're looking for people who will not stand idly by. We need volunteers across this country. We will give you the tools you need. Download these plans.

"So, how do you know it's her," she asked, "other than some similar wording?"

"It's another thing we can't prove," he admitted, "but the username of the person who posted this is magdalene, which is also the username Duggan used for her personal blog. And I found the same avatar in this posting and at her blog: a jpeg of a painting of Mary Magdalene by Bernardino Luini. I've found a lot of postings at a lot of forums similar to this by a user named magdalene and the exact same avatar. The same dimensions, the same file size and cropped identically."

"What's the stuff about the plans?" she asked.

"Woodworking plans, an exploded view of a simple box. Basically, a cubic foot box with a simple sliding shutter."

"And you think those are for capturing the dead?" Feore asked.

"Or rabbits. It's not as if it's labeled 'Disembodied Trap Plans.' They're just specific about the dimensions because they're designed to be stacked. Bob, I sent you an email. Can you get it and open the attachment?"

Feore went to his email and found it. In a few seconds, they were looking at a spreadsheet.

"All right, I admit that what we're looking at isn't really statistically significant. I visited as many forums and Twitter postings and chat rooms as I could. Bob, being on the Internet backbone is a little addictive. Anyway, I tried to find as many mentions as I could of someone missing an appointment, have you seen so and so, whatever happened to. Then I tried to find the last time these missing people were recorded as visiting those chat rooms or whatever. I also sent emails about these people to AfterNet security to see when they last used a terminal, but I'm guessing it'll be a while before I get a response."

"I'll light a fire under them," Feore said.

"Good, thanks. So here's the spreadsheet."

"Oh my God," she said, looking at a table with hundreds of thousands of names.

"I never would have been able to find this much using the terminal at work."

"There are 125,000 rows here," Feore said.

"No, it's not that bad. Here's the list after I crosschecked it. Unless someone has found a way to duplicate a dead person's field signature ..." Feore shook his head "... we can remove most of the names off this list because they've been on the AfterNet or Internet at some point after someone wondered where that person was. And we're left with this list."

They looked at a list with 10,700 names. "This isn't much better," she said.

"We further narrow it down to people who last accessed the AfterNet while in the western United States ... all the square states ... and we're left with this." Munroe clicked another worksheet and they saw the list had dropped to 1,700 people.

"Now we plot these disappearances by date on a line chart."

"It's a flat line," Feore said.

Munroe loved showing off. "We change the scale of the chart, compress it a little ... *et voilá!" Yes, definitely showing off,* he chided himself.

"It's got little bumps to it," she said.

Feore leaned closer to the screen. "Each of these bumps represents no more than a two to seven increase in disappearances."

"And then we superimpose the days that the Explorers hosted their events."

Yamaguchi looked where she guessed her partner to be. "How do you know those dates?"

"They were posted on the wall of Tracy Newell's office. You see, but you do not always observe, Watson. Look at the screen."

The dates were mostly within two to three days and no more than a week away from the bumps on the chart, and all the dates were before the bumps.

255

Feore was stroking his chin. "Well, I guess that's a little more than coincidental."

"But wait, there's more, isn't there, Alex?"

This is why he liked working with her. "You are correct. If we compare the locations of the raves and the last location these missing people used the AfterNet: we have a 99 percent match for people whose physical location was within a 10-mile radius of the raves. This is going on and has been going on all over the Southwest. And for all I know all over the country."

He waited while they digested the information. After a few seconds, Feore said, "Let me call security. We'll send out traces on all these names."

Yamaguchi stood up from the computer and walked away from Feore and motioned Munroe toward her. She used her own terminal and ear buds to talk to him.

"Alex, you were in that chamber about 20 minutes."

"Yeah."

"How did you find all this in 20 minutes? How many forums did you visit?"

"Thousands. And I pulled up transcripts from chat rooms, Twitter postings, Facebook, usenet groups, Google Groups. Admittedly I didn't search any foreign domains. And half of the forums and chat rooms I checked were hosted directly on the AfterNet, and since that's where we are, access was instantaneous."

"You're like a machine."

"I sing the Body electric / The armies of those I love engirth me, and I engirth them."

"Huh?"

"Walt Whitman. I looked it up while I was in the chamber. In my spare time."

They left the offices of the AfterNet and went to the department. They had little chance to discuss their findings

256

because Clemens and the SWAT commander grabbed them to discuss their new assignment. Like most meetings that were only supposed to last an hour, it lasted two and a half. And they weren't involved in most of the debate. The SWAT commander assumed they would be in his chain of command, but Clemens still wanted all the disembodied and their partners to report to him. And because they had again connected the terminal to speakers, they weren't free to pass smart remarks back and forth.

When they were finally released, she went in search of what food was available in the break room's vending machines. Munroe had gotten her out of the house before breakfast and now it was 5:45 p.m.

She had already deposited her money to get a microwave beef stew when another cop found her and said they needed her at a traffic accident. She left the beef stew behind, found Munroe at his desk and they went to the accident scene.

A hit-and-run driver had plowed through three people in wheelchairs crossing busy Speer Boulevard at Colfax Avenue. All three were seriously injured. Traffic wanted them to canvass the area and find any disembodied who had witnessed the hit and run. Taking statements lasted several hours and it was 9 p.m. before they returned to the department.

When she went to the break room again, for grins she pressed the button for the beef stew and it plopped out. No one had bought anything from the machine, a testament to the popularity of its offerings.

She took her steaming Styrofoam cup of beefy goodness back to her desk and with the aid of several packets of hot sauce and crackers from her desk, ate while they discussed their options.

"What are we going to do, Alex? Do we go to Clemens?" she mumbled while slurping stew.

Munroe, glad for once that he no longer needed to eat,

said, "You've got to be joking. Tell him that someone is kidnapping the disembodied? And even if we can convince him, then he has to convince the Weld County Sheriff's Office. They're going to say it's not even a crime."

"It's got to be a crime."

"Not a state crime. There's an executive order, signed by the president in 2002. Basically it's just to keep the U.S. in step with a decision by the International Criminal Court. It makes it illegal to do any research into trying to dissipate the energy field that makes up the disembodied. I found it while I was in the search chamber through Lexis/Nexis. From what I could see, it's never been used. No one's ever tried to trap the disembodied before and I don't know if the order would even apply. And there's no way Weld County is going to try to enforce a presidential executive order … on New Year's Eve."

"So we don't do anything? These are your … people. All right, that sounded stupid, but you know what I mean."

"Of course we do something. But it might be a case of going there without asking permission and seeking forgiveness later. After all, this is part of an ongoing investigation. We haven't been told not to investigate."

She opened her mouth to protest but he cut her off. "Think about it. No one ever said we should stop." She closed her mouth.

"And until Jan. 1, we're still officially responsible for processing disembodied witness reports," he finished.

She threw away her empty cup. "Speaking of which, back to work on these statements," she said. They spent the rest of their shift corroborating the identities of the disembodied witnesses to the hit and run.

CHAPTER 15

DAYTON, Ohio (Bloomberg) — Dayton company Allaire Systems yesterday announced that they are now selling disembodied detectors in the under $1,000 range.

Although the military and intelligence agencies reportedly have installed detectors at sensitive locations, the common knowledge has been that those detectors were quite expensive to produce.

"Our models are affordable because we're not making something that can cover an entire room or building," explained Tom McClane, marketing manager for the company. "As you try to cover larger and larger volumes, the price increases exponentially. Instead, we aim our detectors in a narrow radius that can monitor a standard doorway or window opening.

"So a medium or small company can now afford to have a room with a single door protected for under $1,000."

The company sells a wide range of detectors that offer coverage from three to seven feet in radius, ranging from $799 to $999.

Allaire's products do not actually prevent a disembodied person from entering a room equipped with a detector, it merely detects and records their presence.

"No, we're not on the list," she told Munroe at the start of their shift Friday. She was looking at riot patrol duty and their names were not on it. It was the one thing that would have kept her from going to Gilcrest that evening.

"I guess we fell through a crack," he said. "Nobody thought to put us on the list. For once being part of the equipment budget worked in our favor."

She felt slightly better about their trip, but she still hoped this New Year's Eve would be quiet. She remembered the riots in 2001, her first full year on the force. Every available officer was needed that year.

"We still head back to town if we hear anything on the radio," she said.

"Agreed," he said.

They spent the rest of the day continuing their follow-up on the reports from the previous day's hit and run. The accident made the papers and television news. Many of the stories mentioned their involvement trying to find disembodied witnesses. Probably because of the news coverage, they had a half dozen more reliable disembodied reports.

"What an asshole!" she said suddenly.

"Who is?" he asked.

"This person claims to be one of the victims," she said. He looked at the report and saw that the report definitely came from someone the AfterNet verified as disembodied, but who obviously couldn't have been one of the victims. None of the three victims had died, although two were listed as critical.

"I'm definitely going to report this," she said. She sent a message to AfterNet security. She would prefer that person be banned from the AfterNet and the Internet for eternity, although that was, of course, impossible. The Supreme Court had already ruled that preventing anyone from accessing the AfterNet was cruel and unusual. Still, the jerk would have a red flag warning everyone that the person had attempted an imposture.

"You know, Alex, this is important work."

"Yeah, I know."

"Even this. Yeah, it's a false report, but I got to catch a creep and identify him. Very satisfying."

"Nice job, Masked Avenger," he said.

"Thank you. What time do you think we should leave tonight?"

"Heavy sigh, Linda. Stop obsessing. We've been over this."

They'd actually debated their plans all day. She would take a video camera and document what she could and they'd try to prevent anyone from being kidnapped. They also decided to transfer the terminal from their regular car and transfer it to an unmarked car from the motor pool. It would be a lot easier to take statements from any disembodied kids using the car terminal than her portable one.

Except for the riot duty issue, she never talked about backing out, but she was the kind of person who wanted to do things by the book, even when she was doing something that wasn't in the book. They'd agree they would call dispatch before they started for Gilcrest and would call regularly throughout the night. They would leave a little before 9 p.m. and arrive around 10, figuring any kidnapping attempt would happen after midnight.

"I think it's the one on the left," she said, turning down the car radio. They'd long since left the range of the police radio. She'd been listening to coverage of the downtown fireworks on a local radio station. It was the first time since before the riots that the city had a downtown celebration. The 9 o'clock display had gone off without any problems.

They were at the crossroads of nowhere and nowhere; two county roads without names, just numbers, meeting at a neat 90 degree angle. The intermittent wipers smeared the light snow across the windshield. The headlights illuminated the flakes but did nothing to dispel the darkness.

"No Gilcrest is straight ahead," Munroe repeated.

"You're sure?" Yamaguchi asked.

"Pretty sure, I think."

She looked at the empty passenger seat and sent him looks that would kill.

"I thought guys were good at this sort of thing. And you're the one who gives me directions when we're working."

"Google maps, Linda. Why do you think I instruct you to drive 3.4 miles and turn east on U.S. Highway 85? Anyway, I looked it up before we left. I'm sure." He didn't add that he'd lost Internet access for about five minutes and couldn't reconfirm the directions.

"OK, we go straight ahead," she said.

Another couple minutes of driving brought them to Platteville and the intersection with U.S. 85. She flicked her turn signal indicator left. She hadn't seen any other traffic for half an hour, but the gesture seemed a good way to indicate her annoyance at Munroe's directions. After five minutes of driving, however, she saw a sign indicating they'd entered Gilcrest's city limits.

"Oh my God, people live like this," Yamaguchi said.

"I'm sure it's a nice little town if you're not looking for soul snatchers on a dark, snowy New Year's Eve. Besides, I lived in a town not much larger than this."

"And slept in a bed with your twelve brothers and sisters to keep warm, I'll bet."

"Yeah, and we … wait, OK, that's Elm, turn left."

Yamaguchi drove to the end of the street.

"That must be the school up ahead," he said.

Yamaguchi saw a three-story building that looked quite old and forbidding. There were no houses immediately near the school, which looked like her idea of a Dickens' orphanage. Many of the windows were broken and a high chain-link fence surrounded the building.

"This is where they go to school here?"

"Where they used to go to school. I looked it up. Hasn't been used for 10 years," he said.

She parked their unmarked police car slowly, and took time to put the car into park, set the brake, turn off the engine and turn off the headlights. She put her hand on the door handle and paused.

After a few seconds, Munroe asked, "Something wrong?"

She answered after a beat, shaking her head and saying, "I don't think anyone's here."

Munroe had already looked at the building in infrared.

"Nope, there are people here. Most of the building's cold, but there's quite a lot of heat from the south end of the building and I can see two shapes moving around."

"OK," she said, but her hand still didn't pull the handle. She laughed, a quick little sound. "Kind of creepy." Then she pulled the handle and stepped out of the car.

Once outside, she confirmed Munroe's observation. There was music coming from the direction of the school and once standing, she also saw a few cars parked on the other side of the fence. She went around to the other side of her car to let Munroe out.

"Can you see the people now?" he asked her.

She said "uh huh," which the terminal translated as unintelligible. She was busy getting her video camera and a flashlight. She put the flashlight into a pants pocket and put the small camera into a coat pocket. She was in plainclothes and her coat covered her gun belt. She locked the car afterward.

"Let's go," she said.

She approached the chain-link fence and saw that the gate was still locked. She wondered how the cars had ended up on the other side of the fence, thinking it unlikely the kids had a key, or that they would lock it up after each car.

She walked to the south along the fence and now saw five young people, teens and twenties standing in a circle, shoulders hunched against the cold. Then she saw how the cars had gotten inside the fence. Someone had simply mowed down the fence, but whether it had been done recently she couldn't tell.

One of the kids had seen her, and he walked up to her.

"Hey," he said.

"Hey," she answered back.

"What's up?"

"I'm here for the …" she let her voice trail off, confidentially, nodding in the direction of the music.

He looked at her, thinking she looked a little older, but also thinking she looked really fine.

"Is that your car?" he asked, pointing to the white Dodge Neon they'd used.

"I got out of it," she said, not sure why she said it that way, but the response made him smile.

"Cool, but we're supposed to park it inside the fence."

A young girl from the group called out to him. "Forget it, J.D. no one's gonna see it. Nobody's alive in this hick town anyway."

"Rache says no one's gonna see it."

"Yeah," Yamaguchi said. "I heard." She made a move toward the building.

"Wait a minute," J.D. said. "You get the password off the site? Cause if not, you know, I can tell you what it is."

"Just let her go in J.D.," the woman said.

For a split second, Yamaguchi had an image of herself playing out a scene in a movie: hooking a leg around this acne scarred twenty something, flicking her tongue against his ear and whispering something like "fellatio" in the throatiest voice she could manage, when she heard Munroe's voice in her ear say "flower rainbow."

"What?"

"That's the password, Linda. 'Flower rainbow.'"

"I said I can give you the …"

"Flower rainbow," Yamaguchi said, thinking it the stupidest password she'd ever heard.

"Oh," J.D., said, looking crestfallen. "Yeah, go on in."

She stepped past him and his four friends. The young girl who'd admonished J.D. gave her a look as if to say "men are idiots."

"Are you spacing out on me, partner?"

She ignored Munroe until she passed beyond earshot of the group.

"They're just kids. I don't think we got this right, Alex. They don't look like an international gang of soul snatchers."

"International?"

"Pardon the hyperbole, but you know what I mean."

"Yeah, and I was thinking the same thing. But those kids might just have been window dressing."

They were standing outside two double doors. From this distance, the music was quite loud. She could understand the young woman's indifference to subterfuge.

She opened the door and the heat, light and sound hit her in the face. At first all she could see were the outlines of bodies against the strobing lights. The room, probably a gymnasium for the old school, was packed with kids dancing.

"Shut the door!" someone yelled. An arm reached out to pull the door closed and Yamaguchi jumped quickly to enter.

"I CAN'T GO IN THERE LINDA!" Munroe shouted as she slid through the closing gap of the door and was left alone.

Yamaguchi was immediately pushed against the walls of the gym by the rhythmic convulsions of the crowd. Inside the gym, the sound was so loud she could feel her chest thumping to the beat of the music.

"I'm going to see if I can find someplace where I can see better," she said to Munroe, unaware she'd left him outside. She jammed her ear buds tight to her ears with her hand to hear his reply, but the noise was deafening.

She squeezed her way through the crowd and found a little space a quarter of the way around the perimeter of the gym. An eddy had appeared beside a collection of boxes that were probably used to transport the audio and computer equipment for the rave. She pulled herself up onto the biggest box and stood.

She took the video camera out of her coat pocket and brought it up to her face. Through its viewfinder she could see out over the crowd and saw that the gym had been partitioned. A long, narrow room had been created in one quarter of the space, it walls nothing more than two-by-fours framed like inside out ribs to support plywood panels.

The sides of the walls facing outward weren't covered by plywood. It looked like a movie or a stage set. The walls were sitting on platforms, braced by angled two-by-fours. The platforms sat slightly above the gym floor and she guessed the platforms were on casters.

She could only see a single opening, a glass door that allowed access to the temporary room. A chain-link fence, maybe using some of the fencing from outside the school building, created a corridor leading to the door. She realized that with a crowd this packed, the dead wouldn't want to — "Shit!" she said.

She rolled her right arm toward her face to see the tiny LCD screen of her portable terminal. "No user connected" the display said. Of course, Munroe wouldn't want to enter such a crowded space. He was still outside.

Munroe immediately tried to regain the field of Yamaguchi's terminal, but it was gone. He realized he could wait until the door opened again to admit another partygoer, but he knew he still wouldn't want to enter the crowded gym.

He'd be buffeted left and right and make no progress through the throng. Being insubstantial had its drawbacks.

He looked to his right. The gym was at the south end of the building, which was aligned north-south, and the doors Yamaguchi had entered faced west. He walked around the corner and saw the uninterrupted south wall. No way in here. But then he noticed someone standing, facing the building. The figure hiked his shoulders and Munroe realized the person was a man who had just pulled up his zipper after peeing against the wall. The man, really just another young kid, started walking away from Munroe, who followed as quickly as he could.

The man rounded the southeast corner of the building. Turning the corner himself, Munroe saw him moving into position beside two open double doors, the mirrors of the doors on the west side of the gym. The man stood beside a sign taped to one of the doors: "Disembodied entrance only." He was probably just there to prevent the living from using the entrance.

He immediately thought of the cartoon that showed a dog trying to lure a cat into a clothes dryer with a sign above it saying "Cat Fud."

He also noticed a small box above the double doors that looked like the boxes at Rybold's house that detected the presence of a dead person. A small LED on the box had turned green as he had approached. He backed away and the LED darkened. He looked at the young man guarding the door, who appeared unaware of his presence. Perhaps it was a counter and not an alarm.

He moved closer to the open doors and could see that the partiers inside were kept away from the disembodied entrance by a chain-link fence, although there were many dancing bodies pressed against it. The fence led directly to a box-like room constructed of two-by-fours and plywood panels, just as he had imagined. An opened glass door provided the only entrance to the room.

He approached the doors again. He realized the fence was about seven feet high — high enough to discourage the living from climbing it. And he doubted he could vault it; the narrow space wouldn't give him any room to get a running start. He might be able to fling himself at the chain-link fence and squeeze through it like Jell-O, but the thought didn't appeal to him.

But as long as I don't go into that room, I should be OK, he thought. He stepped through the double doors.

Yamaguchi looked at the fenced corridor and thought, *Alex, I hope you're not stupid enough to go in there,* and tried to determine her best course. *If you're separated from your partner, you should go back to where you last saw them,* she dimly remembered from her Girl Scout days. *Of course, I also remember: "If you're lost, stay in one place until your parents find you."* She didn't think that advice applied here.

How the hell could I lose him? OK, let's go back to the door we ... I came in. Maybe he's waiting outside. She started climbing down the box when she noticed someone trying to climb onto the top of the room or trap. She stood back on top of her box and realized that two men were climbing either end of the room trap.

Oh God, they're starting. Alex will just have to take care of himself. She got down off the box with the help of two boys who then tried dancing with her. She shrugged them off and slowly made her way toward the room. She tried to record the men on top.

All right, what the hell am I going to do? she thought to herself when she reached the room. It was taller than she'd realized and she couldn't get close enough because the kids were backed up against the room. She put her camera back into her coat pocket and decided she needed help.

"Excuse me, can you help me get up there?" she asked a well-muscled kid, pointing at the top of the room.

"What? Can't hear you," he shouted over the music. The young girl who was clutching his arm yelled at him. "What does she want?"

"I want to get on top … on top of this room!" she shouted.

"Why?" he asked.

She couldn't think of a good answer. "I want to dance!" she screamed and waved her arms in a pathetic pantomime of dancing. It was all she could think of.

"All right!" the kid answered. He bent down, grabbed her by the waist and picked her up. His strength startled her. She yelled at him to put her back down.

"What are you doing?" his girlfriend screamed at him, pulling Yamaguchi back down to the ground. "You can't just pick her up like that."

"She wants to go up there."

"Put her down and just give her a leg up," his girlfriend said.

"All right, keep your pants on," he said, grinning widely. He put Yamaguchi back down, laced his fingers together and waited for her. As soon as she put her foot there, he lifted her straight up. She used his shoulders to steady herself and clambered onto the roof of the room.

She was in the middle, equidistant from either of the men already on the roof. They were both bent down, attending to some task. She walked to the man at the funnel end of the fenced corridor, careful to step on the two-by-four framing, which looked a little rickety and seemed to give slightly under her feet.

All right, what the hell am I going to say? I insist you stop this at once. Yeah, like that'll work.

She decided her best course was to flash the badge and use her "voice of command" and maybe the man wouldn't ask what a Denver cop was doing in Weld County. However before she could say anything the man, somehow alerted to her presence, stood up, turned and looked straight at her.

They were both surprised. "What you doing up here?" he shouted.

She tried to think of a good answer, but the man was impatient and grabbed her right wrist with his left hand. Training kicked in and she immediately made a small circle outward with her hand. The circle now put the little finger side of her hand on the inside of the man's wrist, making a nice *nikkyo* pin. Then she brought her right hand down and dropped until she was almost squatting on the two-by-fours. The unexpected move brought the man straight down and his chin whacked into the plywood roof.

She stood back up and was hoping to get him into a pin long enough to slap her cuffs on him when she saw someone else clambering up the side of the room.

Oh great, reinforcements, she thought, but then saw that it was the kid who'd helped her up onto the roof. Once on top, he reached down to bring up the girl who'd been clinging to his arm.

"Get off the roof!" she yelled at them, waving her free arm while still trying to control the man who'd attacked her. They waved back. "Get off the roof! Police officer!" she yelled again.

The man at the far end of the roof now noticed the other people on the roof and had stopped what he was doing. He was advancing toward them with long, halting strides matching the spacing of the two-by-four ribs. She thought he was carrying either a weapon or a tool.

The well-muscled kid now reached down and pulled up another person and she saw more hands grabbing the edge of the roof as others tried to pull themselves up. At the same time, the man she had dropped tried getting up. She shifted her position on the two-by-fours to get a better position to handcuff him, but stepped on a knot that splintered under her feet. She lost her balance and fell backward, coming dangerously near the edge. The edge of a two-by-four hit the middle of her back. Her vest cushioned the impact somewhat but the air still whooshed from her lungs. She saw her opponent advancing toward her at the same time she felt hands clawing at her — the hands of other kids trying to get on the roof.

Munroe was inside the fenced corridor when he saw a man climb onto the roof of the room. *Oh crap, they're going to start. Linda, I think it's up to you.*

He went through the door of the room. Inside it was dark except for the light coming off displays that ran the length of the room. The panels either showed live video of the rave outside or the chat conversations of the people inside. He also realized the field inside the room very slightly pulsed, probably in time with the music outside.

He logged in and realized the room was just local, not connected to the AfterNet or Internet. *Just like the LoDo rave. They can't call for help.*

He made up a screen name, this time going for an official tone.

WeldCountyDeputy has entered the room
WeldCountyDeputy: ATTENTION EVERYONE. There is a fire in the school. I want everyone to leave now.
jbruner: ? the hell do I care
wendy.cisneros: whose idea is this
shaggerific: there are no cops in this room
WeldCountyDeputy: I'm dead just like you. Alex Munroe, I'm a sheriff's deputy. Please leave the room now.
wendy.cisneros: hey somebody just closed the door

Munroe hadn't noticed the door closing. He now saw

that the man who'd guarded the disembodied entrance was standing on the other side of the glass door, looking in.

Yamaguchi tried kicking the man who advanced on her, but he simply grabbed her foot. With her free foot, she tried scraping his hands off her foot. She considered going for her weapon, but shooting a man she didn't know to be armed with all the kids around would be difficult to explain. Just then, hands grabbed at her shoulder and started to lift her. She glanced upward and saw the faces of several kids looking down at her. *These stupid kids think I want to go crowd surfing. Lame ass Christians!*

A cluster of kids now surrounded her, lifting her to waist level. Two more kids grabbed her other leg, joining the man holding her foot. Suddenly a sickening crack sounded underneath her and she felt the people holding her stagger and then she was dropped onto the two-by-fours again. With the impact of her body, the cracking turned into the scream of wood being stressed too far. Someone screamed. The entire roof dropped a foot and she slid along a two-by-four until her gun belt caught in the splintered wood.

Inside the room, Munroe noticed that the man on the other side of the glass door looked up just as the glass door shattered outward, showering him with the shards. Then he noticed that the ceiling above looked dented in places. A two-by-four pierced the black painted plywood and one of the displays crashed to the ground.

Above, more people were screaming as the roof lurched and tilted. The man who'd grabbed Yamaguchi's foot now fell backward, off the edge. More people fell as the roof suddenly dropped again, several feet this time. Munroe felt the air pressure in the room change and he noticed that he was several feet closer to the shattered door's frame. He headed toward the opening on his own as the ceiling dropped even lower. The pressure forced him completely out the door.

Yamaguchi's gun belt finally slipped off the splintered two-by-four as the roof tilted sharply. She slid to the ground, hit her head, and lost consciousness.

CHAPTER 16

Yamaguchi woke to the pounding of her pulse. She put her hands to her head to try to stop the rhythmic beat but when her fingertips touched her scalp she felt the warm stickiness of her blood. The lights above the dance floor, now empty, still strobed and in the lightning bright flashes she could see the blood, far too much of it, on her hands.

A pain in her back helped her realize she was lying on her back on the floor. Looking around, she saw a confused tangle of overturned chairs and tables and smashed glass. Her vision was blurred but she realized it was the blood that had dripped into her eyes and she wiped it away with a sleeve.

She knew she had to stand up but when she put her right hand on the floor to push herself up she felt more wetness and feared that she had bled enough to cover the floor. Then she saw that her hand was in a puddle from a spilled bottle.

She stood up, unsteadily, and remained unmoving until equilibrium returned. Her hearing was confused as well and only now did she realize that the music — "What a friend I have in Jesus" to a techno beat — continued after the partiers had left.

Actually, not everyone had left. She saw a body lying on the ground, covered by debris from the collapsed room trap. She staggered toward the body, but the pain in her back increased. She probed her right side and realized that falling on her phone had bruised her. She removed the phone from its holster on her belt and finally the thought occurred to her that she could call for help. But even before she could dial she saw that the screen of the phone was cracked and that the display made no sense. The display was a puddle of colors. She dialed 911 anyway and put the phone to her ear but she heard nothing. She tried hanging up and dialing again but either the phone or she refused to work. She let the phone drop from her fingers and onto the floor.

She continued toward the body but realized there was nothing she could do. A cracked two-by-four had speared the chest of a young girl. She was obviously dead.

"Munroe," she yelled. "Alex!" She didn't care who heard. She had had enough. "God damn you, Alex, where are you?"

She looked around the room and in her confused state she almost expected to see him, which is when she noticed the white plastic of her terminal on the floor. She remembered the kids grabbing her to send her crowd surfing and knew that's when it was torn off her arm.

She walked over and bent down to pick it up and a wave of nausea hit and she vomited quickly. She knew it was a concussion, but then wondered how she could so clearly diagnose her situation. *Shouldn't I be unable to think straight with a concussion,* she thought to herself as she wiped the spittle from her chin. It was fully half a minute before she realized she hadn't moved, that the terminal still lay on the floor.

She picked it up by the ear buds that were still attached. There was something wrong with it. It felt light to her touch. When she turned it over, she realized the back cover was missing along with the battery. She let out a quick sob. She sank to her knees and tried to look on the floor for the missing battery but the flashing strobes made it difficult to identify anything. She put her hands on the floor, hoping to stumble upon the things she sought. Her palm touched something plastic and sharp and she knew she'd found the back cover.

Munroe watched all this, watched his partner, her hair matted with blood, pawing on the floor for the battery, unable to tell her it was just a few feet away from her, still slightly aglow in his infrared vision.

He'd found his way free of the fenced corridor after the kids fleeing the dance floor had battered it down and opened the door to the outside, carrying him with them in their wake. He'd reentered the gym, rising above the now trampled chain-link fence and had searched frantically for her. He'd been unable to find her until the crowd had thinned enough, then saw her lying on the floor, unconscious until now.

Yamaguchi put the terminal and back cover into a coat pocket and continued searching the floor for the battery, but found nothing except discarded cups and bottles. The song ended and another began, pursuing the playlist of the departed DJ as a heavily sampled version of Amy Grant singing Carole King's "You've Got a Friend" mocked Yamaguchi's plight.

"Give me a fucking break!" she yelled.

Munroe didn't know what fresh pain caused his partner's screaming, all he could see was her mouth forming what could only be obscenities. He'd never seen her like this. She was an animal howling in pain and rage.

In the midst of her scream, Munroe saw her stop and look around.

She had heard something, the banging of a door somewhere. She reached for her gun but it wasn't there. The leather snap of the holster had been torn off during the struggle on the roof or when she hit the ground. *Years of training and you go looking for stupid batteries instead of your gun.*

Munroe realized she'd lost her gun and began searching as well. He quickly found it about 10 feet from her, under a table still upright. *Linda, it's here! For the love of God look over here!* It was incomprehensible that she could not hear his words, which seemed to him the loudest scream he'd ever made.

The sound of a banging door returned again, only this time Yamaguchi thought it was nearer. She looked in the direction of the sound and Munroe followed her gaze. *Someone's coming,* he thought. He sped around the dance floor, looking for some way out, some way to get help for his partner. The trampled chain-link fence blocked the path to the disembodied entrance he had used, and the doors she had entered were to her left, outside her vision. *Just open those damn doors, Linda, and I can get some help. You can get out of here. But she doesn't even know I'm here.*

Her adrenaline and confused state prevented her from thinking she could simply leave the gymnasium. But she did realize she was unarmed and exposed in the middle of the dance floor. She walked to the DJ's stage looking for something to use as a weapon. The bright shiny microphone stand caught her attention in the blink of the strobes. She tried picking it up but realized the heavy disc-shaped base made it too unwieldy to use as a weapon. So she removed the mike and unscrewed the metal rod from the base. She now had a suitably lethal heavy pipe about four and a half feet long.

Go to the outside doors, Munroe screamed.

Instead she went to the swinging doors that led further into the abandoned school. She peeked through a small glass window in the right side door. The interior of the school seemed pitch black because of the flashing lights in the gym. Occasionally the glass reflected the lights and she knew her face was being illuminated as well.

She saw the flicker of flashlights and faintly heard people talking. She ducked her head back from the small window and leaned against the wall.

The rave organizers would be leaving soon, she knew.

They probably feared the fleeing kids might have called 911, but they might think they'd have enough time to clean up any evidence — which might include her.

A voice sounded louder than before, a man saying, "I'll check."

She gripped the rod from the mike stand more tightly, worried that her bloody, sweaty hands would slip. She wiped her palms against her coat just as the right side door swung open. She stepped away to avoid being hit.

A man, white, bald, heavy and around 5'8", walked through the doorway holding his flashlight in front of him. Yamaguchi, blocked by the door, could only see his arm and the flashlight. She stepped forward and brought the club down. Despite her fear, despite her desire to do anything she needed to disable this man, she was still shocked by the sickening feeling transmitted through the mike stand as it slammed into his left arm. The impact made him bend forward slightly. She hadn't overcommitted her swing, so she was able to bring the mike stand back up, catching him under the chin just as he was recovering from bending forward. The impact drove his head back while at the same time his legs flew out from underneath him. She watched in what seemed like slow motion as the strobe lights caught him falling to the floor, flat on his back.

The swinging door had not closed. It was held open by the man's body. She picked up his legs and pulled him into the gym until the door could close. She looked through the door's window to see if anyone was running to the man's aid, but she saw nothing.

She went back to the man and quickly checked his pulse. He was still alive. She searched him for a weapon and found nothing apart from a Swiss Army knife, which she pocketed. On her knees, she searched the area immediately around him as well but didn't find a weapon, but she did notice the beam of light his flashlight sent across the floor. Revealed in its beam she saw the battery. She scrambled toward it and seized it, then took out the terminal and tried to insert the battery and replace the cover, which was cracked and would not remain in place.

Munroe noticed a light playing on the windows of the swinging doors just as Yamaguchi finished inserting the battery. He saw the blue telltale glow of the LCD turn on and then found the field.

Yamaguchi saw the welcome message on the terminal appear. She hoped Munroe was somewhere nearby. She was inserting the ear buds when she heard her partner's voice say, "… GUN IS UNDER THE TABLE TO YOUR LEFT! SOMEONE IS COMING!"

She looked quickly to her left and saw the table 15 feet away. She got to her feet and ran a few steps while behind her she heard the sound of the swinging doors open and hit the head of the man she had disabled. She saw her weapon under the table and lunged the remaining distance, brushing the table legs as she slid between them. Her outstretched hand grabbed the gun. Her momentum carried her under the table as the door opened again, the man behind it shoving aside the man on the floor. The new intruder reached for a weapon after he realized what had blocked the door.

Yamaguchi rolled onto her back. From her spot under the table, she could see the legs and lower body of the man. She raised her head off the floor and held her gun in both hands, pointing down the length of her body at him, and yelled, "Drop your weapon and raise your hands! I'm a police officer and I will fire if you don't raise your hands!"

The man could see no one in the room and the location of the voice was difficult to pinpoint. He put his gun down in front of him and slowly started raising his hands. "Raise your hands and turn around!" she yelled again. He started turning.

She was in an awkward position. It would be difficult to

get out from under the table without making her situation obvious to him. She tried to draw her legs up and get into a crouching position while still keeping her gun on him, but she bumped a table leg and a plastic cup on the edge of the table fell to the floor. It didn't make a loud sound, just a little empty rattle, but enough combined with the scrape of the table leg to draw his attention. He looked over his shoulder and saw the cup spinning on the floor — and Yamaguchi's legs under the table.

The man thought of his chances. He thought she had no shot at him under the table and he was now facing the swinging doors. He decided and leapt at the doors, intending to shoulder his way through.

She yelled, "Stop!" and fired. The sound was deafening under the table. She didn't know if she'd hit her target. In fact, the bullet creased the man's left buttock, and he fell backward.

She was still under the table and she tried to duck walk her way out but bumped her head. The man heard the table scrape and Yamaguchi's curse when she hit her head. He also saw his gun, just a few feet away and reached for it with his hand.

Munroe saw what the man was doing and yelled, "He's going for his gun!"

She rolled to the side, hoping to get out from under the table. She got back into a crouching position and tried to train her gun on him, but she saw two bodies on the floor and was confused.

The man's hand closed on his gun. He brought his arm around and fired blindly over his shoulder at her. She threw herself sideways and saw the man try to stand and turn. Her next shot caught him in the chest and he fell back against the doors.

She stood and kept her gun trained on him as she approached. He certainly looked dead, a dark stain spreading on his light-colored shirt. With her foot, she kicked his gun several feet away. She checked his pulse and felt nothing. A groan from the first man she'd encountered almost knocked her over.

She backed away hurriedly and trained her gun on him. The man groaned again. "Alex, keep a lookout outside the door." He answered her and moved through the doorway kept open by the dead man's body.

She reached for the handcuffs on the back of her belt but the leather case was open and empty. She'd lost them during the scuffle on top of the room. She went back to the DJ's table and grabbed the microphone cable she'd earlier discarded. She came back and hog-tied the groaning man. She didn't know how secure a job she'd done, but he didn't look like much of a threat.

Munroe reported back. "There's no one coming. I'm going to go back down the hallway. How're you doing?"

"Just get me out of here alive, Alex."

"You're doing all the work. I'm going. Keep the field facing the door."

Munroe moved back into the hallway. He realized it must be the central hallway that ran the length of the old school and that the gymnasium/dance floor was at one end. The ceiling was about 12 feet high and in places holes showed through to the floor above. Debris from the holes had rained down onto the main floor. Classrooms opened off the hallway on either side, alternating with rows of lockers. He gave a quick look into each classroom but saw nothing.

Halfway down the hallway he saw a large staircase that led to the second floor. He glanced up and debated whether he should check the upstairs when he noticed a light at the other end of the hallway. He tracked the light to its source, what had been the school's cafeteria. The large room, almost a mirror of the gymnasium, also had large swinging doors, propped open by old school desks taken from a classroom.

Two men flanked the doorway. One had a drawn revolver, and the other was armed with a crowbar. Munroe walked through and saw two more men standing next to a table where a young woman was sitting, facing a laptop. She was Duggan. Also on the table was a box, apparently made of particleboard, about a cubic foot, matching the plans he'd seen online.

From behind him, Munroe noticed that the two men flanking the doorway had entered the main corridor. Munroe raced back and went through the doorway, past the men and down to the other end. He reached the gymnasium doors, still partially held open by the bodies of the two men. But he couldn't feel the terminal's field. He looked for her and saw that she had moved into the hallway and was using a side stairwell as cover. He rushed to her side.

"Linda," he said.

"thought i should move."

"OK, two men, one with a revolver, the other with a crowbar. They're sneaking down the hallway."

"i can see em."

"Drop them when you can."

"yeah."

"Don't need to give them a warning."

"shut up."

Munroe resisted replying. Instead he cautiously peeked around the corner of the stairwell before realizing what he was doing. *Damn, doing it again,* he thought.

He went into the corridor and saw the two men were a little too theatrically using cover. *They've never really done this before,* he thought. *They must be making a racket.*

He went back to his partner's side. *She doesn't need your help, just let her do her job,* he thought to himself, when he noticed the shape on the stairway landing above her partner.

"ABOVE YOU, STAIRWAY," he shouted to her.

She rolled to her side and brought her gun to firing position, grasping it with both hands after dropping the terminal to the floor. The battery immediately jumped out of the case and Munroe felt the field die.

He saw a muzzle flash from the landing and saw his partner's body shudder from the impact of a slug, but she was already firing. He saw her lips move and realized she was again giving a warning even as she was firing. Her gun flashed again and the man on the landing pitched forward down the stairs, finally rolling out into the corridor.

Yamaguchi wasted no time. She got up off the ground, knowing she'd been hit but not caring. She staggered to her feet and stupidly stepped into the corridor, fully in view of the two men. Once she saw them she immediately started firing blind. A muzzle flash caught her attention, however, and she fired at it.

Another shock to her body drove her right shoulder back, but she kept firing. She emptied her magazine, released it and had a new clip ready faster than she ever had in training. But she saw she had no target. The man with the gun was down and the man with the crowbar was running through the doors at the far end of the school.

She ran after him, one foot dragging slightly as she favored that side of her body. She realized it was hard to breathe, but she kept moving. She made it to the end of the corridor and she didn't care about cover and she sure as hell didn't care about shouting a warning.

The cafeteria was empty, however. She scanned the room, tracking her gun to follow her eyes. She saw a card table collapsed on the floor.

She heard the sound of an engine and the flash of headlights coming through double doors that led to the outside. She went through the doors and saw a panel truck and a car leaving the school grounds. The spinning tires of the vehicles were kicking up clouds of snow and dust obscuring the license plates of the vehicles. "Damn it, we should have searched the outside of the building," she said to Munroe, unaware she had dropped the terminal.

She turned to go back inside the school but tripped over the remains of one of the wooden boxes near the doors. She caught herself on the door with her hand and now noticed the pain in her shoulder and that she had left a bloody handprint on the door.

"OK, that's really going to leave a bruise," she said again to Munroe. She looked left and right for him. "Where are you? Oh, that's right, you're dead."

And you'll be dead too if you don't get some help. But if I'm dead, I can finally meet Munroe. Oh yeah, Linda, that's brilliant. Why don't you go to your car and use your terminal to get help? Because I don't remember where I parked it. Just turn right and follow the fence until you find the opening and then you'll find the car. Who said that? It's me, Alex. No it's not because I can't talk to you unless you're dead. I mean unless I'm dead.

She continued her conversation with herself as she stumbled through the opening in the fence and found their car. It took several tries to open the car door but eventually she got inside. She tried the police radio but all she got was static. *Right, we're out of range, I knew that. Phone's busted too. Use Alex's terminal, he won't mind, will you?* She looked for the car terminal and didn't see it. *Right, we're in another car. I knew that.* They'd put the terminal on the passenger seat. When she flipped up the display, however, she realized someone was already using it.

"For God's sake, Alex, I'm dying here and you're on the fucking Internet chatting!" she yelled, just before she passed out.

CHAPTER 17

Munroe checked his partner's breathing and pulse. Although she was unconscious, her vitals appeared good.

He'd accessed a forum maintained by the AfterNet that helped the disembodied contact emergency services. A fellow living cop in St. Louis, who volunteered his time on the forum, promised to relay his message to Weld County 911 and he came back online to update Munroe.

> **steve.hanzon2:** got through to 911. I told them officer down and there rolling. hows ur partner
> **jollycopper:** She's still hanging in there.
> **steve.hanzon2:** so ? r u doing outside ur patch
> **jollycopper:** I know this will sound crazy, but we've got a religious whacko who's trapping the disembodied
> **steve.hanzon2:** ur kidding
> **jollycopper:** Honest. We came out here … hold on

Munroe saw movement from the school, a dark form hugging the side of the building. He glanced at Yamaguchi, saw she was unchanged, and decided he could leave her briefly. But before leaving, he returned to the chat and told Hanzon that he was going to investigate.

He left the car and went to where he'd seen the shape but by now the person was gone. He forced himself up slightly and switched to infrared and saw the shape again, now moving toward a line of cars parked on the street.

Follow or stay with Linda, he thought. He knew he really could do nothing for her. He decided to follow.

He moved as quickly as he could. He was soon close enough to see that he was following a man, who stumbled as he walked and was supporting his left arm with his right. Once beside him, Munroe saw it was the man Yamaguchi had dropped with the mike stand. Apparently he'd freed himself of the microphone cord.

The man got to one of the cars, an older model Chevy Impala with Wyoming plates. He had problems fishing his keys out of his left pocket. He was obviously in one hell of a lot of pain. Munroe guessed that he also had a broken jaw.

Once the car door was open the man leaned against it for support and Munroe used the opportunity to get inside. The man got in and closed the door. Then for an agonizing minute, the man just slumped back into his seat.

No, wake up you bastard. Get going. Start the car. Munroe feared he'd passed out. But eventually he roused himself and started the car, banged it into the car in front and finally backed out onto the street. He drove erratically and two blocks away from the school almost ran off the road when a flashing fire truck and a sheriff's car passed him going the other way.

Thank God, Munroe thought when he saw the emergency vehicles. *Please be all right Linda.*

After leaving Gilcrest, the driver rallied and made it to Interstate 25 without incident. He was now heading southbound, approaching the Denver metro area, driving only 10 miles above the speed limit and no longer weaving. Munroe sat beside him, trying to drink in every detail of the man, or at least every detail on the right side of him. He noted the pierced ear, the scar on his bald skull and his clothing should he need to identify him. He had checked the contents of the car as well, seeing nothing more incriminating than printed directions to the school. In the back seat, he saw a gas station receipt and noted the time, date and location and the last four numbers of the credit card.

Munroe looked up and saw that the driver was leaving the highway at a Northglenn exit and was heading east. They entered an industrial park and as they entered the parking area they passed a black car, a nondescript vehicle like a Ford Taurus, leaving. A car leaving an industrial area at 3 a.m. on New Year's Day seemed suspicious. Munroe rushed to the back seat but couldn't make out the plates.

Munroe's driver parked at the loading dock of one of the small office/warehouses. The man left the car and Munroe tagged close behind.

The dock doors were open and Munroe saw three men unloading a panel truck, possibly the one from the school. One of the men on the dock saw the injured man climbing the stairs to the dock and hurried to meet him. Munroe tried to commit this person to memory and then moved up onto the dock to peer into the warehouse.

He saw that the warehouse held dozens of boxes similar to the one he'd seen in the gymnasium. He entered to get a closer look.

Two more people, a man and a woman, were inside, standing near a desk, and he recognized both from the school. The woman was Duggan and she appeared to be giving directions. She looked away as she noticed Munroe's driver approaching, being helped by the same man who had met them at the stairs.

He took the time to see the room in 360, trying again to capture any details that might help later. He did a quick mental count of the boxes, aided by their being neatly stacked in rows. He did a quick inventory of other items in the room, including pallets of particleboard and power tools for making more cubes. He noted a schedule taped to a wall that corresponded to the dates he saw at the Explorers headquarters. He also saw that the wastebasket next to the desk held a FedEx mailer with a torn shipping label, the words "CENTER FOR" all that remained.

His attention was drawn back to Duggan. She was obviously agitated and was shouting at the men. Munroe wished that he were better at reading lips. He could, however, follow her gestures and she pointed again and again at the desk and at the laptop it held, presumably the same one he saw at the school. Then he noticed that connected to the laptop was a portable AfterNet terminal, a competitive model to Yamaguchi's, apparently in sleep mode.

Why the hell would she need a portable terminal? he wondered. *Does she taunt the people she captures?*

The other men from the dock had joined the discussion, although the injured man was sitting slumped on one of the boxes. The man who helped him was shouting back at Duggan and he started jabbing her in the shoulder with his finger. The last jab staggered her back and she caught the edge of the desk for support. The laptop screen flickered to life and at the same time, the terminal's field popped into being, startling Munroe.

The field felt great, even better when he realized the terminal was set to anonymous access. And on top of that, the laptop was booted into the Linux version of the After-Net OS and the last user was still logged in.

He quickly went to the emergency services forum and thanked God Steve Hanzon was still one of the volunteers on duty.

steve.hanzon2: ?s ur emergency

jollycopper: Steve, it's Alex Munroe, 11578 Sherman Street. Building D. No 34. Send police now.

steve.hanzon2: Alex? ur IDs not confirmed. Give me your partner's badge number.

jollycopper: 5436

steve.hanzon2: got it alex helps on the way

Munroe allowed himself a moment to figuratively breathe when he saw:

> **steve.hanzon2:** alex, no such address. where are u??
> **jollycopper:** in northglenn, north of denver i follweod suspect here
> **steve.hanzon2:** got it

Munroe cursed himself for a fool. The last time he'd talked to Hanzon, he was in Gilcrest.

> **steve.hanzon2:** OK, police on way. ur partner is also OK. at North Colorado Medical Center Give me details ur situation. Ive told them a disembodied officer is on scene. I hope they know how to handle

Munroe summarized his situation as best he could, sending out short snippets, not knowing how long his chat would go unnoticed. He managed to tell Hanzon the number of suspects, gave their descriptions and the descriptions of the vehicles parked outside. Then he noticed that the man who'd been pushing the woman around was looking and pointing at the computer screen.

Munroe had only seconds. The last thing he was able to do before the man smashed the laptop to the ground was to check the name of the user who'd logged in — falstaff.

The men and the woman formed a tableau, all staring at the pieces of the laptop on the ground. They seemed frozen and Munroe stared back at them wondering what else he could do when he saw the red and blue lights of a police car pull up to the dock.

Yamaguchi listened to the sounds of the hospital: the squeaking shoes of the nurses, the incessant ringing of telephones, the PA announcements and the plaintive cry of an old woman saying "nurse." She'd been awake a few minutes, having dozed off and on throughout the day. She'd heard the curtains around her bed open, but she pretended she was asleep.

"Linda, are you awake?" It wasn't the voice she wanted to hear. This was Paul Clemens' deep warm voice, the voice of an experienced bureaucrat. She wanted to hear the flat digitized voice of her partner coming through her ear buds. A voice that changed depending on the terminal or software OS they were using, but a voice she'd recognize nonetheless.

A hand lightly touched her uninjured shoulder and she opened her eyes and said, "I'm awake."

"You're a fuck up, you know that? You and your partner. The shit you have caused," he said, but he said the words softly, gently. Stitches and a dressing had closed her scalp wound, but whoever had cleansed the wound missed a smear of blood on her chin. Her right cheek was puffy, raw and red and a butterfly bandage closed a small cut above her left eye. And her right arm was strapped to her body.

"Where's Alex?"

Clemens sighed. "Talking with the chief and the chief's talking to the Weld County sheriff and the Weld DA. We don't know whether to give you a medal or put you in jail for murder."

"Which one are you here for?" she asked. She tried to sit up but just didn't have the energy. Clemens found the bed controls and elevated the head of the bed. "Neither," he said. "The chief wanted me to come down here and see if you were OK. I'm probably just a couple of minutes ahead of your union lawyer."

"Good, I can't keep pretending to go to sleep on the sheriff's detectives."

"I figured that's what you were doing. I saw them down by the nurse's station and I ducked in here when they weren't looking."

"So what happened? I assume I'm in Greeley."

He laughed quietly. "Yeah. The ambulance brought you here. You weren't just faking with the detectives, were you?"

"I'm a little woozy. They finally gave me something for the pain after they did a CT scan. I guess I broke my collarbone, but that's the worst of it."

"Anyway, they brought you here. Alex followed … well, he jumped in the car of one of the … church gang guys … still not clear what to call these people. He was able to get a message out and Thornton PD picked them up. It took Alex a while to get back to Denver."

"Did anything happen in Denver last night? Were there …"

"Nah, we had some fights, but for once, New Year's Eve was normal. You're in so much trouble now, that's the least of your worries."

"What about the people I … shot?"

"I'll pretend I didn't hear that. One's dead, one's in ICU, the third's serious but OK."

She yawned. The thought of shooting someone was horrible, but she was so tired. "I shot three people?"

"Yeah. The dead one has a record, robbery and aggravated assault."

She yawned again and asked, "What time is it?"

"It's 3:30 and it's New Year's Day, afternoon if you're wondering. Look, you get some rest. When your lawyer gets here, I'll try and stall the deputies till you get a chance to talk." She'd already closed her eyes when she thanked him and was asleep by the time he left.

Munroe arrived at the hospital about 7:30, catching a ride with a patrol officer the chief sent to bring Yamaguchi home. The cop had been on the force fifteen years and apparently thought little of chauffeuring a dead cop. He patiently listened to the chief's instructions, went down to his car, waited an entire minute to allow Munroe to enter, then drove to Greeley. He never once glanced nervously around. *That's a veteran cop,* Munroe thought. *Nothing surprises him.*

The cop, his name was Murphy, had gone to the emergency room and found her sitting up in her bed.

"Hey, Gooch," he said. Munroe, of course, couldn't understand the conversation without her terminal, but he guessed that the look of pain on her face wasn't from her wounds.

"Murphy, right?" she asked. "You come to take me home?"

"Yeah. So what happened? You got shot?"

"Something like that, but the vest took the worst," she said.

"I guess I got Munroe with me."

"Really?" She sat up in bed a little straighter.

"Yeah, the chief said to bring him. I guess he's here. I'm going to the desk, see what I have to do to get you released. Be back in a minute."

Murphy left and Munroe remained beside his partner. She looked better than he'd feared she would, but she still looked pretty bad. He wished he could talk to her. She relaxed in her bed once she'd realized they couldn't communicate. And she had a lot to tell him. She'd had a chance to talk with her union lawyer before she met with the sheriff's detectives. He told her the chief was doing everything he could to make sure she wouldn't be charged in the shootings, at least not today. He remained with her while the detectives took her statement. And the detectives treated her fairly. Everyone, it seemed, was unsure how to treat the incident and no one wanted to commit themselves.

Munroe wanted to tell her of his hours of questioning by Denver, Thornton and Weld County officials. He wanted to tell her of the people arrested at the Thornton warehouse, about the injuries sustained by the kids at the rave during the rush to leave the building and emails he'd already gotten from the Denver papers and TV stations, asking him for interviews. Instead he contented himself by just looking at his partner and seeing she was OK.

Murphy returned after five minutes, followed by a Weld County deputy. "This is her," Murphy told the deputy.

"Officer Yamaguchi?" he asked, despite the identification.

"Yes?"

"Detective Anderson said to bring this to you and to also tell you your car's been towed to the sheriff's office here in Greeley." He then tore open a large manila envelope and took out her ear buds and terminal and put them on her bed. "Can you sign for it?" She shook her head. "I can sign for her," Murphy offered. He and the deputy left her bed.

She picked up her terminal with her left hand and inspected it. The white translucent plastic was cracked and heavily scuffed and marred by bloody fingerprints. A large piece of duct tape kept the battery cover in place and an evidence tag was taped to the front. She turned on the power and saw the display light a little unevenly — one of the LED backlights must have broken — and after a few seconds, she saw the words "User connected."

She put in her ear buds. "Hey partner," Munroe said.

"Hi, Alex. It's good to hear your voice."

Officer Murphy drove them back to Denver, never once complaining about the one-sided conversation he heard the entire way.

CHAPTER 18

"We've interviewed about 200 disembodied people so far, mostly kids, that were abducted," Munroe told the chief. "It's just a start. And now that this story's on the Internet, maybe we'll hear about other abductions from other states."

Thornton police had set up an AfterNet terminal in the warehouse and printed large instruction sheets that asked the freed disembodied to login. Actually the idea for the signs came from Hanzon, the volunteer cop, who worried that once freed the disembodied wouldn't stick around to be interviewed. With Hanzon's coaching, the AfterNet terminal was brought to the warehouse, allowing Munroe and Hanzon a chance to interview the abductees.

Chief Moncrief and Deputy Chief Clemens were paying Munroe a visit at his desk in the detectives' room Tuesday. The chief had appropriated his chair without asking so Munroe was sitting on top of the desk next to his terminal. He was back on duty but without a partner. It didn't matter because most of his time was spent online, processing the statements from the abductees. Detective Rollins was helping him. The missing person's detective was both apologetic that he'd dumped the case on him and also a little jealous that the case proved to be so high profile.

"And thank God a few of them have certified identities," deputy chief Clemens said. "That'll make it a lot easier if the DA can find a way to prosecute them for the abductions."

Moncrief said, "Don't worry about that. I talked with the U.S. Attorney's Office. Apparently there's a presidential executive order that might apply. As much as I hate the feds moving in, it may be for the best, especially if this goes beyond Colorado ..."

"It looks that way," Clemens said. "I just wish something could be done about that group in Colorado Springs."

"I suspect the FBI will be knocking on their door shortly," Moncrief said.

"Linda doesn't think the Explorers had anything to do with this," Munroe told them. "She thinks Duggan went off the deep end after her parents died and the Explorers didn't notice."

Clemens snorted and asked, "What do you think?"

"I think ... I think she could be right. Duggan was kind of an outside contractor for them. She might have been subverting the Explorers resources for her own goals. I did some checking on the guy we interviewed in the Springs, Newell. I talked to his uncle ... he's disembodied. Seems like Newell is on the level."

"What about your missing people? The ones who started this?" Moncrief asked.

"Uh, I've talked to Sgt. Johnson. She's the Fort Carson soldier who disappeared. She says she was taken at the LoDo rave. I haven't heard from Brian Thompson yet." Munroe worried about Thompson. He was certain he and Johnson had been abducted at the same time. He'd already talked to his mother and given her the bad news.

He continued. "I'm guessing some of those kids just ran the second we let them out of the boxes. They're pretty shook up. I've asked a minister I know to help us with counseling."

Moncrief leaned back in Munroe's chair. *Maybe I can chain it to the desk,* Munroe thought. "Good, so we can definitely connect the dots between an official investigation and our decision to ... uh what you did in Gilcrest. So, Alex, we wanted to talk to you about your situation." The chief looked around to see who was nearby. He leaned forward to tap the terminal. "Maybe I should get one of these in my office, at least that little portable thing. Anyway, about your situation … without Linda, it seems pointless to move you to SWAT. So, I think we'll keep you doing what you're doing. Obviously this case will keep you busy for a while. When does Linda think she can come back?"

"Uh, she's got an appointment tomorrow with an orthopedic surgeon. Mary Ferguson's going to take her," Munroe said.

Clemens added, "When I talked with the emergency room doctor, he said it could take up to four months to heal completely." The chief grimaced. "But maybe only a month for the pain to go away. And she might be able to go on light duty in a couple of days," he added.

"Of course, she's right handed and that's the shoulder she broke," Munroe said.

Moncrief smiled weakly. "I don't suppose she's ambidextrous."

"She's never seemed that way to me."

"All right, so we might have her back in a couple of weeks to a month. We're … giving you the intern. What's her name?"

"Marianne," Clemens supplied.

"She'll take you wherever you need. And we think we've got a disembodied officer who can start next week. He's going to work with SWAT, once we can find him a partner. And we realized … I'm sure this had already occurred to you … we realized that we need a link to the disembodied community.

"So you're off the hook. Let's just hope the lawsuits that come from this don't bankrupt the department."

Yamaguchi had just got off the phone with her mother when Munroe called. "Hey, Linda, how you doing?"

"I don't suppose there are any recordings of your voice anywhere?"

"Huh?"

"Never mind. I'm doing fine as long as I keep downing ibuprofen, don't move and don't sneeze. Or laugh."

"Ready to come back to work?"

"Hah! Next question." She was lying on her living room couch, a blanket tossed over her, a hot cup of green tea nearby. The TV was muted and she had a Jane Austen novel spread out on her lap.

"So, we're not moving to SWAT."

"Really? Ow! Sorry, don't spring something like that on a fragile woman. We're not?"

"You're going to be out of commission for a couple of months. So the chief decided we just keep doing what we're doing."

"That's great."

"Yeah. Look I'm going back to work. I've got a lot more statements to process. Just wanted to update you."

"Thanks, Alex." They said their goodbyes.

She got up from the couch and went back to the kitchen to see if there was something to eat. *Maybe Mary can pick up some groceries for me. Food I can eat with one hand.* She decided that a bag of chocolate chips would do. *It's not like I'll be baking cookies any time soon. These could go bad.*

The doorbell rang and she went to answer it. She opened the door and saw a truck pull away. She looked down and found a large vase of flowers on her doorstep. She bent down to pick up the vase but almost dropped it. "Yow!" she cried when her shoulder twinged. She tried again, this time bending her knees completely before picking it up. She carried it into her house and put it on the nearest surface.

It was a pretty arrangement but she didn't appreciate the pain she'd gone through to get it inside. She found an envelope and awkwardly removed the card with her left hand.

"Hope this makes you feel better. Maybe I could stop by? Do you need anything?" It was signed "Bob F."

Wow, how nice, she thought. *Maybe he can bring me groceries.*

— & —

Edwards caught the arm of the man moving the black sphere. "Move it gently," he said in clipped tones. "Move it slowly. Don't bump it or you'll find yourself cleaning the toilets."

"Edwards!" a voice behind him said sharply after the man continued his work, placing the sphere on the trailer attached to the electric cart.

Edwards spun around and found himself staring at Rybold.

"What is ... oh, hello, sir."

"Stop threatening people," Rybold told him. He caught Edwards arm and pulled him aside. In a quieter tone, he said, "You manage people better by encouraging their good behavior instead of rubbing their noses in the bad. And a disgruntled employee is the last thing we need."

"Yes, sir, I'll go apologize," Edwards said nervously.

Rybold clapped his arm around Edwards shoulders. "You don't need to do that either, Stephen. Later on, just say something nice to him. Come on, let's go up to your office."

Rybold led the way up the stairs to Edward's office. He entered and stood against the window overlooking the warehouse full of black spheres. Edwards followed behind and sat on a visitor's chair, not behind his desk. He immediately started tapping a foot. "You're awfully jumpy, Stephen."

"Yes, I … it's this business with the police."

"Nothing to worry about." He said to Edwards. "I already told you. It all worked out in our favor. Any disappearances from now on will be blamed on these religious groups." He turned back to the window and continued watching the admonished worker loading the spheres. He winced as he saw the worker drop one of the spheres onto the trailer.

"Ouch," Humphries said silently to Rybold.

"You're right," Rybold told his avatar. "Get his name later and we'll have Edwards move him to another job."

"Edwards is the bigger problem," Humphries said.

"Yes, Stephen is becoming stressed. I think he has problems at home. It's time I did something about it."

Rybold, still watching the clumsy worker, said over his shoulder to Edwards, "Stephen. I really think you and your wife … Elizabeth … should spend some time together. You like to snowshoe, I think. Why don't the two of you go to the Aspen retreat for a week. On me."

"I'd really like to stay and supervise the new facility," Edwards said. He got up from his chair and stood next to Rybold. "There are another 50 units scheduled for initial assessment and we've got to get these processed units out of here."

"I appreciate the work ethic, Stephen." Rybold turned and looked at him. Edwards wouldn't look at him directly but stared at the gold "AV" pin on his lapel. Edwards looked up and they locked eyes.

"All right. Against my better judgment, you can start the facility. But as soon as the units are in place, you take a week off. There's no need to connect them. You know it won't hurt if they're left idle a while."

Edwards nodded. "Thank you. And you're … a week in the mountains sounds like what I need." His eyes darted to the window. "Clumsy oaf," he said, as the worker banged another sphere onto the trailer.

— & —

Brian floated in deep sleep. He was just a speck in a black void. He was tired but happy, comforted in his dreams by the knowledge that he was in bed with his wife, Karen. A sharp movement disturbed his slumber but his mind converted it into Karen tossing in her sleep. Very quickly he returned to his happy assumptions.

A Quick Guide to the Afterlife

In March 1997, firefighters found hanging from a rope the body of Dr. Antonia Simone, next to the prototype of what would become the AfterNet terminal. On the screen were the words, "What took you guys so long?"

The discovery of the afterlife threw the world into chaos. Even though most religions believed in an afterlife, the reality of an afterlife where each person's intellect or soul exists after death but is completely unable to communicate with the living or even the other dead shook those religions to their core. An afterlife without the reward of heaven or the consequence of hell fundamentally changed the world. Riots ensued, governments fell and the on again/off again India/Pakistan war went nuclear. People killed themselves in droves and the end of the second millennium seemed like the end of civilization.

But civilization didn't end as people slowly began to accept the reality that the living share the world with the dead and that the dead, of course, far outnumber the living. In September 2001, an organization called the AfterNet was created to develop the infrastructure that allowed the disembodied to interact with the living and with each other. Slowly the world learned the rules that govern the afterlife, which include:

Souls exist. That is the unique energy of every creature survives death as a will-o'-the-wisp something, with an almost impossible to measure mass and charge and a volume roughly the size of a beach ball. Since souls do have a physical being, however insubstantial, they cannot pass through solid matter, but they are almost infinitely malleable. A disembodied soul, for instance, can be squashed paper thin, but it is not a pleasurable experience. The disembodied can move from place to place, although it takes practice and concentration, like a baby learning to walk. The faster or higher a disembodied person wishes to go, the more concentration is required.

The disembodied are everywhere. Considering that every person who has ever died leaves behind a soul (and no one knows when in human evolution the soul evolved), the disembodied are everywhere. And as the soul is so insubstantial, any point on the planet can be occupied by an untold number of disembodied persons. It is also speculated that all forms of life have some form of energy that could be called a soul.

The living are unaware of the disembodied. Despite ghost stories, there is no proof that the living are aware of the disembodied. The soul is so insubstantial it can only be recorded by the technology of an AfterNet terminal.

The disembodied are unaware of each other. Until the discovery of the afterlife and the invention of the AfterNet terminal, each disembodied person believed he or she was alone. And being so insubstantial, they could not interact with the living, with the consequence that most disembodied who had died before the invention of the AfterNet terminal have gone insane.

The disembodied cannot hear, taste, smell or feel. A disembodied soul is aware of the entire electromagnetic spectrum and is actually capable of 360-degree vision, but that is the only of the five senses available to them. Until the printed word, the only way the disembodied could learn about the world was by direct observation.

The AfterNet allows the disembodied to communicate with the living and each other, but there are still many obstacles the disembodied face. For instance, it is not easy to manipulate the AfterNet field. The disembodied must imagine their thoughts as letters and words that an After-Net terminal can recognize. The terminal can then project the interface, essentially a web browser, back to the disembodied person at the frequency unique to that person. This allows many disembodied to use a single terminal. In dedicated mode, however, a disembodied person can control a standard web browser that is visible on the display of the terminal, making it possible for the living and the disembodied to see the same thing.

Another obstacle: Every disembodied person exists at an exact frequency, or field fingerprint, which makes it possible to identify that person. Unfortunately, most disembodied cannot prove who they were when alive. This uncertainty, of course, leads many of the disembodied to claim they were Jesus Christ or Napoleon or Elvis when alive.

In fact, it is a crime to claim an identity not your own, but it is a crime difficult to prove. It is also difficult to find a penalty with which to punish the disembodied. International law considers denying access to the AfterNet, which would be the ultimate penalty, a violation of human rights. Of course, in many countries, the disembodied are denied many of the rights the living enjoy, such as the right to vote and own property, all related to the difficulty of proving identity and residence.

Since the discovery of the afterlife, however, the living can use an AfterNet terminal to record their field fingerprint so that they may claim their identity after death.

Although a living person's field can be recorded, most of the living cannot use an AfterNet terminal. It requires extraordinary concentration to imagine the letters and words that an AfterNet terminal can recognize. For some reason, it is easier, although still difficult, for the disembodied to use an AfterNet terminal.